Jack Royce's
Way To The Towers Of Silence

ISBN: 1-884953-03-04
Library of Congress Card Catalog No. 97-60212
Printed in the United States
Technical Communications Services
N. Kansas City, MO

Cover Design: Nancy Del Aguila

Text Design & Layout: Ellen Elfstrom-Perry

Eaton Street Press
524 Eaton Street, #130
Key West, Florida 33040
(305) 293-3050

For Paula, Irene and Gil

Way to the Towers of Silence

It has ever been hard—if not impossible—for laymen to comprehend that performing is a spiritual commitment outside the mundane things of life, that throughout the world acting, dancing, singing, each, has meant much more than just a vocation to be loved, and for which actors stoically suffer privations. *Theatre* is more a state of mind, a secular ideal, a sacred idea, a collective of almost religious involvement unfathomable by the mind, unmeasurable by the yardstick of rationality.

Michel Saint-Denis

Way to the Towers of Silence

PART I

To Ahura Mazda:
> I will sing for you again praises
of great value.

Avesta

Chapter I
Bombay, India
June 8, 1995

It was late in the evening when a young American exited from the Taj Mahal Intercontinental hotel. He was as well-dressed as if he had come from the New York Athletic Club: wool suit, white shirt and striped tie. He looked hot. The youngster was gangly, with a fresh face, and reddish hair. The turbaned hotel doorman had moved away from his post to discourage a legless beggar on a platform with wheels from settling down before the hotel.

The honk of a horn got the attention of the American; he assumed that the vehicle, idling some short distance from the revolving doors of the hotel, was the car he had ordered. The fact that it was old, noisy, and needed repairing hadn't made him suspicious. This was India, a third-world country where most automobiles were the castoffs of the industrial nations.

He was deceived. Two young men took hold of him, easing him into the car. He was puzzled. The four abductors cared not who he might be. He was a for- eigner; they assumed he was a businessman.

In the large old Cadillac, two other young men crouched on the floor behind the driver's seat. Once the American had been settled next to the driver, who had seen to it that he was between the two of them, the car was made to do a screeching U-turn away from the hotel -- leaving black tire marks on the pavement. As the vehicle gathered speed, the two from behind over-powered their captive, injecting him with venom of a cobra, named *ananta* in Hindu mythology.

The American uttered a series of abrupt, breathy cries, his face an agonized contortion, his eyes stared. He had slumped on the seat and his arms and legs flailed uncontrollably. With his body the driver blocked the American's being seen by any passersby. Inside the victim's body the neurotoxins in the cobra venom burned through his bloodstream like napalm, searing his nervous system, shutting down the respiratory system, triggering an hallucinatory tempest in the synapses of the brain.

His breathing becoming shallower; he slipped deeper and deeper into a coma. At first he mumbled, but then his voice weakened and faded to nothing. His pulse started to fall and his chest stopped moving. Paralysis had become complete. Like a rag doll his head lolled to one side. His eyes were half-closed, and his mouth open and slack. The two men secreted him in the trunk of the car. The driver sat behind the wheel, silent and indifferent.

The one asked the other, "Is he dead?"

"No," the other answered. "He'll be in a coma for about 24 hours."

"How do we know he won't die?"

"Sometimes they do die," spoke up the driver.

The American was still unconscious. Before dawn, the inert man's arms had been folded across his chest; his legs were stretched full length and had been tied together at the ankles. A white shroud was then passed all around his body. As was Parsi custom the face of the man, as yet, remained exposed. His body was stiff, and he looked like a corpse.

Americans are assumed erroneously by many around the world to be millionaires, likewise Parsis in India. In truth, Parsis *are* to be found in the upper echelons of business, power and influence far out of proportion to their numbers. The Parsi names Tata and Godrej appear on everything from salt and soap to locks and trucks. The four were unemployed youngsters; two of them were of the Parsi community; two were Christian.

Hours later the abductors strapped the young man down on an iron bier with pieces of white cloth. They knew that most likely it would take a day for the cobra venom to wear off. The face of the man had been covered. As was the Parsi custom the four men, clothed from top to toe in the white garb of pall-bearers, arranged themselves in pairs -- holding a piece of white cloth between them. It was called *paiwand*. They did it more to keep up the pretense, but the two Parsis still believed that it enabled them to withstand pollution emanating from the victim. One carried a small bowl of fire.

The men were in a hurry and the final ritual was rushed. The funeral procession -- oddly lacking priests -- headed down the Old Ridge Road toward the

Hanging Gardens. Dawn was breaking. There were no pedestrians, and only an occasional automobile rushed by.

This June day, most Parsis of Bombay were at the Fire Temples, as is true on March 21, the Zoroastrian New Year. *Muktad* ceremonies were being performed for those who had passed on and

were being commemorated, as they had been observed for centuries in ancient Persia.

Above was a full moon, the bright lunar light enabled them to see the Tower of Silence, the *Dakhma*, toward which they were headed. On the path, almost hidden by dense foliage and undergrowth, birds of prey, glistening black, craned at them expectantly from the vines and treetops. A rustling of scuttling living things made them freeze momentarily.

One cried out, "This bier of iron is cutting into my shoulders."

He was shushed by the elder of the four who then whispered, "Let's get on with it!"

The asphalt part of the path ended in gravel. The weight of what they were carrying caused with each step a scrunch and rasping sound. It grated on their taut nerves as they made their way up the hill to the ramp. As they had been informed to anticipate, four *nasesalars*, the tower corpse bearers, would take charge of the body. They were all in white: white canvas shoes, white gloves, and white skull caps. The *nasesalars* live apart from the Parsi community, viewed as untouchables.

Due to the early hour, the *nasesalars* were

drugged with sleep. They failed to react to the omission of traditional rituals. There had been no *char-chassan dag* rite in which a dog is led around the bier to suppress evil and aid the forces of good. No mourners, not even a few in *duglil* and prayer caps. There were no priests.

The four *nasesalars* were there to take charge of the bier and the corpse. The fact that there had been no procession, no placing of the body on the stone platform beside the gate of the tower, no removing the cover from the face of corpse -- the final ritual *sagid* had been omitted -- caused them to begin to wake up. Then when the four men who had carried the bier up to the tower had failed to turn back, the *nasesalars* became alarmed and protested. The four young men overpowered them and carried the bier and body into the tower. The *nasesalars* lay sprawled and unconscious on the ramp before the gate.

The Towers of Silence are concentric stone walls; with three raked *pavis*, spaces. The Parsis' conviction, stemming from centuries of belief, is that stone and iron are resistant to the pollution of a dead body. The outermost of the three concentric *pavis* are for men, the next for women and the innermost for children. Customarily without touching flesh, the *nasesalars* use pikes with hooks to remove the white shroud, leaving the body, as naked as when born, to be devoured by vultures. When all that remains are dried bones, they are cast into the large circular well which makes up the central core of the *Dakhma*. When rain falls, the bones are washed into the sea.

Though two of the young men were Parsis,

they were ignorant of customs within the gate of the tower. They had not stripped their captive of his shroud. As they started to leave, one of the four turned his head, looking back at the bier which had been rudely dropped on a *parvi*; he sniggered, "No vulture will be put off by a few white rags."

From the trees and from the wall of the tower, the vultures circled, flying in lower and lower. "Vultures! They're coming down on us!" the youngest of the four cried in fear .

"Nothing to fear -- as long as we keep moving," shouted their leader. "But let's get out of here!" They sped out, past the *nasesalars*, leaving the gate ajar.

The young man lying, exposed, forced open his eyes. He had become aware of light through the cloth that covered his face. Suddenly what struck his olfactory sense most forcibly was a rotting smell -- the stench of vultures. A few of the huge birds had alighted within the tower.

Before the cobra venom had taken its full effect, the young American had resisted his kidnappers. He was bruised, and blood had gushed from his nose. Vultures start pecking where there's already blood. Their sight may be poor, but vultures have an acute sense of smell.

The man struggled against his bonds and had succeeded in freeing one hand. He ripped the cloth from his face. To his horror he saw a vulture with wings spread, hovering over him.

Before he could do anything other than register the fact that a vulture was intent on making a meal of him, the vulture swooped down, landed on his chest, and quickly plucked out an eye. The man let forth long, agonized screams of pain, while simultaneously striking the bird with his one free hand.   The vulture flapped his wings furiously, squawking in protest at the blows, but it did not back down from its prey. Two other vultures joined in the attack.

The Tower attendants came to.   The foreigner's cries attracted their attention. They rushed to the tower where the young man lay. With their staves, they drove off the vultures and dragged the bleeding body to the gate. There was no hope now for the victim, for the vultures had been too savage and voracious. They had been known to pick clean the bones of a corpse in twenty minutes.

The senior attendant looked to the other one and said, "Call the police. We'll lay the body outside on the road. It was not a Parsi. A white foreigner has been murdered. The Towers of Silence have been defiled!"

June 10, 1995
New York City

Paul Drake didn't think he would be in danger when he'd responded to the invitation to go out to India as an American writer, a delegate to an International Writer's Conference. He was an optimist.

Janis had made a phone call to Paul Drake. She blurted out, "Damon Rupert has disappeared! As you know, he had been first choice, and he went early. My sister Mary Lou, with Search Group, Inc., in Washington, D.C. told me Damon Rupert's parents have hired their agency to investigate their son's disappearance."

"Had he arrived?" asked Paul.

"No question of that. He had registered at the Taj Mahal Intercontinental Hotel. His luggage was in his hotel room, unpacked!

"Paul, you're to go! Come pick up your British Air ticket. It's Business Class," said Janis all in a rush.

June 10, 1995
Washington, D.C.

Mary Lou Peacock, a secretary of Search Group, Inc., Washington, D.C., had telephoned Bert Appleton before the crack of dawn.

"Bert, something is afoot here. I'm sure it's good and exciting. It may be the result of my cousin Janis having leaked something to me."

"Can't a guy get his rest?" barked a sleepy Bert Appleton. "I'm not in Tokyo. You can't say you don't know how god-damned early it is!"

His angry voice positively dripped icicles and would have stopped most people in their tracks. Mary Lou, however, was made of sterner stuff.

"God-damn it, Mary Lou! Are you listening to me?" Bert's voice drilled into her brain, interrupting her lapse into fantasy. "What in the Sam-hell do you want at this hour?"

"Forgive me, Bert," she said, quickly and reluctantly pulling herself back from fantasy into the present. "I'm an early riser, and I think -- for you -- there's a wonderful trip in store."

"Gee, thanks! Now I *am* awake."

"They want us to locate their estranged son, Damon, a young writer who had been picked as a delegate to the International Writer's Seminar in Bombay, India."

Mary Lou took a deep breath and began to speak very fast, "The publisher who had sent him to the conference telephoned his parents that he had arrived June 8th in Bombay, had checked into a hotel, but was reported as missing. You," she paused dramatically, "are to find him."

We are prepared to kill our own relatives
Out of greed for the pleasure of a kingdom.
Bhagavad Gita

Chapter II
Later
June 8, 1995
Bombay, India

The four abductors were two Parsi youths, Rustom and Nusswan, and two apostate Indian Christians, Arun and Varun. The latter had been brutal with cats, loved killing rats. For that they had the praise of all the people living at Sodawalla Baag. Their mother Julia had ignored what neighbor woman Mehroo had told her about their stoning cats. If she didn't have those two cats, reflected their mother, she'd not have given it a second thought.

Now the two Christians were upset by their experience of the past night. Arun kept dwelling on how the young fellow had reacted when he had shot the cobra venom into him. He'd thrashed about. He's going to die, he had feared, and I did it. It all happened so fast.

Rustom asserted himself, as he had done all along. He denied caring; he kept saying to all of them, "Just think of the money. What you can do with it." Arun suspected he was saying it as much for himself as for them.

Rustom jabbed Arun viciously with his elbow. "Snap out of it. We're out of there. It's all over. Get the car started." Arun did as he was ordered. He feared Rustom, who was much bigger than he was.

Rustom was given to punctuate an order with, "I mean *now*; <u>or</u>, I'll beat the shit out of you." He never cursed in Hindi; he liked to think of himself as being a Sikh. He had had fantasies about the Sikh soldier who had shot Indira Gandhi, once head of the country.

They went for a joyride. At Chowpatty Beach, they waded. It felt cooler with their feet in the water. No one of them suggested that they swim. That close to Bombay city, the water was polluted.

The elder Bulsara fellow shouted and pointed across the water, "*Are, bapre!* It's beginning to dawn. See how red the horizon? They all stopped the horseplay of splashing each other and stared.

Silently they gathered their clothes from the sandy beach and made it to where Arun had parked the car. Before the old Cadillac ignited, Arun impatiently slammed down the gas pedal. The car flooded. He got abuse from all, and they sat there fuming. But, in five minutes they were off.

As the jalopy pulled up before their Baag, they saw Peter Findley sitting on the worn steps.

Nusswan jumped from the car, even before it had come to a full stop. He was the younger Bulsara youth -- naive and trusting.

Peter looked up and saw the car and one of them jumping out. What a muck-up this has been.

Damn! But, I had better ease into what I have to tell them, he thought. There would be hell to pay if I were to have them quit on me.

"I've been waiting for you. How did it go?

"What's it like over there, The Towers of Silence? I've never seen them. Couldn't. They're beyond the Hanging Gardens. I hear entangled vines surround the place."

Nusswan's non-sequitur response was, "Great to see you, Peter. Now we're back..." Before he had finished what he wanted to say, older brother Rustom pushed him aside. Rustom was feeling cocky.

"As they say in American films, `It was a piece of cake.'"

Findley was shaking his head non-committally, "And the Towers of Silence? They're towers? You've seen them. Well?"

"Bet you're here to give us the rupees!" spoke up Nusswan excitedly.

Peter Findley waived his hand, "We'll come to that in a moment. All too dark? You saw little? Well, the two of you are Parsis, you've been there before -- with your mother, right?"

Rustom hemmed and hawed, but then figured, what the hell, "They're circular; the walls are about, I guess, ten feet or more high. The foundation, brick, but the walls are of stone. Iron and stone are not polluted by a dead body. A ramp leads up to the gate, above which is an opening. There's a gate. All around are palms and trees. Usually on the wall are perched vultures, and small birds that scavenge. Not much...."

His brother had been nudging him, "This time

we saw what was inside; a well -- big around and about ten or more feet deep. Looking down into the well, I saw two barred doors facing each other. See, Rustom, you were forgetting that." Nusswan was breathless from getting all that out fast. Before Rustom could respond to his younger brother's criticism, he added, "We didn't know how to get down into the well and through the doors, so we left the guy we grabbed in front of the hotel right there beside the well. We beat it." The other three nodded their heads in agreement.

There was a scowl on Findley's face. Rustom sized up the situation; something was wrong. "Let's have it, Peter," he said.

Findley gestured that they follow him into the back area. He was phrasing in his head what he would say to the four of them. I don't want to lose them. I'll shift the buck, he resolved without voicing it. They'll get the bad news at the meeting later today.

They had arrived. The place was dim and fetid. The four crowded Findley, and he backed away from them several paces.

"I don't have the money for you. I can tell you that all did not go well..."

"What!" came from the four youths like rapid fire from an assault weapon.

The Britisher actually welcomed the interruption. How to explain, he had to ask himself. Well, here goes.

❖

Earlier
June 2, 1995
Bombay, India

A meeting had been arranged for Peter Findley to enlist four youths. He had fierce resistance to carrying out the rendezvous with the Bulsara brothers and others, but he had been blackmailed into doing it. Findley was involved in smuggling gold concealed in pieces of sculpture that were then shipped out to Hong Kong. He cleverly covered the metal with marble chips and dust mixed with plastic. These inferior pieces hacked out by him had escaped the scrutiny of Customs in both ports.

This had been going on for months, despite the fact that in Hong Kong Customs officers were so thorough he had observed them opening huge tins of canned fruit and running their hands around inside. Airplane passengers returning home to Hong Kong protested, but to no avail. Pails of soiled diapers received the same digging by Custom's women's hands, sans gloves! Peter Findley had become very sanguine about his outwitting these -- in his opinion -- minions of bureaucracy.

On a recent trip to Hong Kong, Peter had been approached by the `China White' gang to smuggle cocaine and heroine into the United States and Europe -- using his method. He'd been wined and dined, but after a troubled night with no sleep, Peter declined the invitation to be a partner with the Chinese in their operation.

They threatened him, but Peter remained adamant. Gold harms no one, he thought. It's the persons and what they do *with* and *for* gold that is destructive. Drugs enslave. They're out-and-out evil. So, he told the `China White' mafia that he wanted no part of their trafficking in drugs.

In the lane some distance from the Sodawalla Baag, Peter was of a mind to turn around and leave. I have been blackmailed, and I'm little more than an indentured slave having to do the bidding of another. He procrastinated and fumed aloud, "Drinking has got me into this fix. Talk is cheap? No, it is deadly."

He recalled the dreadful moment when he'd been pinned down to agree to do as the blackmailer de-manded. (He had scowled and wanted to say `no,' but he realized he was captive.)  He had nodded his head and between clinched teeth had said `yes' scarcely above a whisper.

He was asked, "Are you telling me it is `yes'?"

He nodded again, which now seemed to satisfy the *daaken* who had wrung from him his acquiescence.

As he looked at his watch and saw that he was late, an old expression came to him: `Touch pitch and you are blackened.' Then he had a sardonic laugh, he had cronies in crime who had told him where to go to enlist four young men. A rendezvous -- for a price -- had been effected for Peter at the Sodawalla Baag, there to meet the Bulsara brothers Rustom and Nusswan.

It had not been a year since the death of Mehroo's husband, a lawyer, father to Rustom and

Nusswan. It irritated her sons that much of her time was spent in grieving, ever since the funeral and the four days spent mourning in a bungalow as is the custom at the Towers of Silence.

"It's too much! Momaiji's grief," Rustom often said to his younger brother. Their mother insisted that the two men accompany her twice a week to the Fire Temple, inside which she found perfect calm and peace. Sometimes Mehroo went more often, staying for all fire rituals performed each day by the priests, and that exasperated the two sons. But, they were dutiful. However, the two grumbled when they were out of earshot of their mother.

Before the inner sanctuary, dark and mysterious on each visit she would offer a sandalwood stick, placing it in the silver tray at the door of the sanctum sanctorum restricted to the priests who tended the sacred fire burning in a large vessel.

The mother's devotion to the memory of her husband, who had been held in high esteem, had not gone unnoticed. Parsis are on the whole not poor, as they are one of the richest business classes in Bombay. However, a widow with two sons drifted among those who are poor. As is their custom, the Parsi communities charitable groups gave support to her. She was not to go hungry, and always to have a home. Mehroo held the purse strings tightly, but preoccupied with mourning, she did not manage at all well.

Rustom, the older and the more assertive of the two, would whisper to his mother, "We have little enough money for food." In exasperation he would mutter, "Here at the temple: the price of sandalwood!

How could you use the money given to us for food to buy sandalwood? We starve, momaiji."

"Hush!" she would say as she would reverently smear their throats and foreheads with sandalwood ash from the tray, held out to her by the priest. As she did so, she'd murmur, "Your father! For shame. It's for the memory of your father." This was her stock rebuke.

When *Dustoor* Framjisha, all in white, of the Fire Temple appeared, once they had entered, Mehroo would rush to hug the priest. This excess of emotion annoyed the sons. The *Dustoor* became weary of her frequent visits and her effusive embraces. Murmuring condolences, he would forcibly extricate himself. The visits kept the sons from their games of cricket.

The moment Mehroo Bulsara felt the priest backing away from her, she would forcibly lead her sons, as if they were wee children, to the lintel, where by custom all Parsi bowed; she would push their heads down for ritual obeisance. Each time, Rustom and Nusswan were impatient to leave. Usually unaware of their departures, Mehroo momaiji would linger on, savoring her grief.

Peter Findley made his way to the compound where the brothers lived, on the top floor rear with their widowed mother, Mehroo.

When the four young men assembled in front of him, their eyes were cast downward, their feet scuffing the dirt.

"*Aree*!" said Rustom, the leader of the group, as he lifted his gaze to stare at Findley. "What is it you want -- of us?"

"First, I need two more fellows," said Peter, staring hard at them. Rustom turned to Nusswan, telling him to get the two others. "We need a place that's private," said Findley. "Well?" he snarled back.

With a backward toss of his head Rustom silently indicated they go in back.

The Sodawalla Baag had two wings, three stories high, which enclosed a small yard. Each evening after the meals had been consumed, from upper floors, garbage rained down into the area. As Peter followed the young men into the area, he thought, what stinking
filth! Their sweeper too lazy to get rid of it properly. A gathering place for vermin.

Cats and kittens slowly crept back into the area. They had been wary, for boys often made games of throwing stones at them. What rats had remained, the large toms chased from the heaps of refuse.

They were joined by Dara and Firdosh Lal, who dwelt with their parents on the floor below the Bulsaras. Findley decided to get to the point speedily. "There's money in the offing for you -- more than you're likely to have seen." He waited for reactions. They're cool customers, he decided.

"Your lack of interest indicates to me that you Parsi lads either have indulgent parents, or you're related to Sahib Tata, owner of Air India." Peter let his gaze linger briefly on each of them, giving his words dramatic pause to sink in. "I haven't got all day," he said sarcastically. "Money is of little interest to you, eh? Well, if this is true for all of you, then I don't have to waste any more time standing in this stinking yard." He grimaced in disgust. "All it lacks is shit."

He turned, and without a backward glance began to leave. He hadn't taken more than a step or two before a voice came from behind.

"Wait!"

Peter halted his steps, pausing briefly before turning to face the young men. Feeling he was well on the way to having them, Peter asked, "All four of you are Parsis?" They nodded affirmation, but without much enthusiasm.

Findley was quick to pick up on that. "You are not to abduct persons of your faith. Only foreigners."

I nearly have them, Peter thought. Just one more turn of the screw.

"Are you prepared to do what is dangerous?" he questioned. "Even if it is contrary to the teaching of the Fire Temples?"

Firdosh and Dara turned away and left.

Rustom sent his brother Nusswan to fetch two other fellows to make up the four. Peter asked, "How do you know them? What are they? Parsis? They'll be like those other two."

"No," snarled Rustom, dragging out the 'no'.

He was irritated that what he was to set up was being questioned. "Here in the Baag is a Christian family. It's said they've been Christians for three generations. Maybe 'yes', maybe 'no'. I figured it out; they don't want to be thought *shudra* who've converted to Christianity."

"*Shudras?* I'm confused," said Findley.

"You know the lowest caste, outcasts: sweepers, tanners..."

"Gotcha," interrupted Peter. "I thought this was a Parsi dwelling place--Sodawalla Baag. How come they're here?"

"Ask 'em," said Rustom. "Here they come."

Nusswan shoved the two up to face Peter Findley, who at once asked, "Did he tell you why we may need you two?" He pointed at Nusswan. They remained silent, looking frightened.

"Relax! Come on, there's money in this," He forced a smile he did not feel. He waited. Sensing he needed to change tack, "You smoke? Here, take the pack. They're American cigarettes." He held out the Camel cigarettes, first to Rustom, who refused, shaking his head.

"Parsis never smoke. It's a defilement of fire." He turned sharply to his brother, knocking down his hand. He cursed, "*Melya.* You know better!"

This brought a laugh from the two Christians. Now more relaxed, each took a cigarette.

"Take the pack. My pleasure!" said Peter, as he forced the package into the hands of the one closest to him. "Let's be friends. Tell me something about yourselves. Rustom tells me you live here."

"We grew up here. When we had just arrived from Goa, an old Parsi couple sub-let a room in the Baag to my parents. When the couple died, our parents took over the whole flat. Momaiji sees to it that the rent is paid promptly. No one has complained."

"You're of Bombay?" asked Peter.

"We know Rustom and Nusswan; we're in the same school, St. Thomas. A lot of the students are Parsis -- like them. We're taught in English. Our parents are converts to Catholicism, it was natural that they would send us to St. Thomas School. Knowing English is important. But, we *think* of ourselves as Hindu."

" If we had the money, we'd make our way to America -- New York. There's a Hindu temple now on Long Island. We have relatives there; they have news stands -- two of them on Fifty-seventh Street."

The other one, finding his courage, interjected, "We're from Goa. Our grandparents were born there -- that's when it was Portuguese. We were little when we left, but we remember it."

"It's clean. Goa. Not like this dirty Bombay. We could swim at the beaches in Goa. Not like here," added the first one to have spoken.

"Look, I gotta know your names. What *are* they? Christian? Hindu?" asked Peter.

The older one spoke up, "My Christian name -- a Saint's name -- is Peter; his is Joseph."

Before he could go on, Findley interposed, "Peter. That's my name. Well, we'll get on..."

"Not if you use those names! They're for

school. Our parents. We've picked *Indian* names,"
interrupted Peter. Pointing at his brother he said,
"Call him Varun. And I'm Arun."

"But, not giving full attention, Peter said,
"Hmmm, Goa. I've yet to go there. A place, I'm told,
it's easy to get whatever you want. Do you follow
me?"

He drew a blank; the two just stared at him.
They were too young and naive to grasp that Peter had
heard that there was a lot of trafficking in drugs in
Goa.

"A lot of tourists go there," Varun said. "In
the cathedral, they can see St. Thomas. He's now a
mummy. You should go."

"Yeah, yeah, a great idea. But, I've got us off
the track," was Peter's response. At once he went over
what he had told to Rustom and to Nusswan.

When he asked if they wanted money, he saw
that they were eager for rupees. Immediately Arun
spoke up, "We have no jobs. The Hindus are
suspicious of our telling them that we're Christians."

Varun said, "If a Hindu knows I'm Christian,
he won't accept a glass of water from me -- a
Christian."

"All Hindus?" questions Findley.

The older one answered, "Orthodox Hindus.
I took a drink of water at the home of a Hindu
classmate. The mother snatched the cup -- it was of
metal -- and held it over the fire to purify it. Do you
wonder we're without jobs here in Bombay?"

"We told you," added Varun almost shouting,
"we're going back to being Hindus. And it's money we
need -- and want."

"But," said Arun, "the Parsis take care of their own. We're among the thousands unemployed," point-ing to Nusswan and Rustom.

"It wouldn't be so bad," added Varun, "but St. Thomas School is expensive. The money my father earns as a shoemaker goes there. Momaiji cleans apartments here, but it is hardly enough to feed the four of us."

"I keep telling both of them: 'Skip the school!' We know enough English. We'll get by -- unless we die of starvation," said Arun.

"All that gets us is a cuffing -- and no supper!" added Varun with bitterness in his voice.

"Our parents nag at us to go out and get a job." Varun spread his hands wide, in a pleading gesture, "'Where?' I ask them." He nudged Arun. "It's like a broken record. Momaiji says -- God, I can hear her now -- 'We can't afford to have you lie around the house in idleness.'"

"What I wouldn't give to have money, enough to paper the walls of our miserable apartment," Varun said somewhat wistfully.

Peter Findley was not taken aback by the ability these two had in expressing themselves. That's some vocabulary, too, he reflected. Well, the Parsis as well as Christians do send their children to St. Thomas Catholic school. The church, I'm told, makes no direct effort to convert. Smart.

He turned to Rustom and Nusswan. "What about you two?" He knew their father was dead.

"We have to know more -- a lot more," said Rustom.

"We're hungry all the time," Nusswan whined. "There isn't much I wouldn't do for a lot of money." Nusswan looked at his elder brother, Rustom, "I could tell Momaiji, `No more Fire Temple!'"

Rustom stepped in front of Nusswan, but before he could say anything negative, Findley said, "Money, it is. And not for just one time." He held up his hand to keep their full attention. "There will be a leader who gives the orders. You're not to know or try to find out who it is. That's to be understood. Orders and payment will come to you at a designated place."

"Where?" interrupted Rustom.

"Yes, where?" echoed the others.

"That I can't say. In fact, I don't know. You'll be told exactly what to do -- not by me, but by the person who is to pay you," said Peter, who now had the good feeling that he was very near to getting the four he needed.

"As I told your classmates here, what you're to do is dangerous. But, no taking risks. If you do, no money...for any of you. So...?"

As had the others earlier, they swaggered and shook their shoulders and filled out their chests. "What exactly do we do?" asked Arun.

"I know little, but it's abduction -- of foreigners. They're to be young, and you four look strong." He stuck out his head and stared at them. "Ya' still with me?"

The four quite spontaneously went into a huddle. Findley waited. Their talk, which overlapped, grew loud. Peter was growing impatient. He was dying to get back to his guest house for a drink.

"Come on," he shouted. "I can't stand here all day and all night. Make up your minds! A 'yes' or a 'no'! Which is it? What are you, pussycats?"

The taunt of cowardice did it. Rustom broke from the group, saying, "It's a deal. Now what?"

Their entire demeanor changed instantly. Peter knew he had pushed the right button. He watched them as they laughed and swaggered, poking each other to show bravado.

"That's all, for now." Peter said. "I, too, take orders from the leader, and at this moment do not know much more than you. Tomorrow evening, I'll be able to give you more details," said Findley. "And," he added tantalizingly, "tell you when!"

He turned and hurriedly made his way to the opening by which they had come into the yard. An animal shriek caused him to turn sharply. What he saw made him shudder. The light of day was failing, but there was enough for him to perceive that Arun had grabbed one of the tomcats. It continued to cry and wail. Varun had already grabbed a young cat scarcely more than a kitten. They were hooting and hollering, egging each other on. With a swift movement Rustom had kicked off the head of the tomcat. Without hesitation, he grabbed with both hands the head of the cat held by Varun and wrung it off.

Peter blinked to remove the cruel and sadistic scene from the retina of his eyes, but then he smiled. I needn't have worried about what these four are going to be asked to do. Cruelty feeds and grows from acts of violence.

Just as fire is covered by smoke and
A mirror is obscured by dust . . .
Knowledge is hidden by selfish desire.
Bhagavad Gita

Chapter III

After his meeting with the four young men, Findley rushed back to the cheap guest house in which he'd taken a room. He'd told the manager of the Bombay guest house that he'd probably need the room for two or three nights. Findley's hunch was that it would take more than one meeting to talk these rebellious youngsters into committing crimes that would be dangerous for them. There was one thing he hadn't been able to do so far. Try as he might, he just couldn't figure out what motivated the instigator to do this, or exactly what crimes were to be committed. His questions had been greeted with stony silence.

Findley opened the door of his room, intent on only one thing: a drink. He'd practically run the last few steps to his room, impatient to have it.

The door swung inward. "Jeez," he muttered as a wave of heat hit him. "This place is like a fucking oven!"

He crossed the room in three great strides, intent on opening the window. "Ahhh," he sighed, "that's better." The breeze that immediately began coming in was hot, but any movement of air was better than nothing.

He shook his head and angrily muttered, "I could have sworn I'd left that window open so this wouldn't happen. Damn *naukar*, or *naukarani* must have closed it. What the hell were they doing in here anyway?" He added, sarcastically, "Left a mint on the pillow? Not likely, here." Even to a liverish Peter Findley, the question was pointless.

When he turned from the window he saw there was a message on his bed. At first he found it hard to read; the hand that had written it was firm, but the style of penmanship was strange. "Continental," he said aloud. "French or German."

He carried the note over to the small writing desk and let it lie there. He picked up the single glass provided by the guest house, and into it he poured a third of the fifth of Johnny Walker scotch. That brand of whisky was Findley's one extravagance. He cursed prohibition in India each time he stared at an empty fifth.

The scent reached his nostrils a microsecond before the glass reached his lips. His mind wandered. "That blackmailer," he muttered, followed by a second gulp of scotch. He ran his hand through his hair. "I'm no Samson, but..."

He had frequently told himself, "It's no problem, my drinking. I'm handling it." Falser words were never spoken, as the families of every drunk well knew. His feelings of guilt had led him to stash the empties in a closet in his house.

"It was never the bloody houseboy to open that closet! No, it was that siren who opened it, and a cascade of bottles hit her."

The more Peter drank, the more he talked to himself. "No one's business, really."

Peter finished the drink. He poured a second glass, picked up the message and strolled to the window to read it, wanting to feel the gusts of hot air, hoping futilely it would evaporate the sweat dribbling down from his arm pits. He removed his shirt.

"It's so hot here. Too hot to rush to do anything. A guy could have a stroke, if he wasn't careful!"

Peter deciphered the message on the scrap of paper as he sipped his drink. The words on the paper began to sink in. "Jesus H. Christ!" he shouted. "I'm supposed to pick up the four shits in a cab and take them to Dharavi, that stinking ghetto!"

The walls were thin, and a neighbor in a room to the left of his room banged on the wall and shouted curses in Hindi. Cowed, Findley kept his murderous thoughts to himself.

"Thank God all I do have to do is get them to a shop across from that old tumbled down Catholic church," he muttered through clenched teeth.

Next Day
June 3, 1995

The two Christians, Arun and Varun, were waiting for him, sitting on a stoop that sagged from the tread of hundreds of tenants over the years.

Management never failed to collect the rent, but cast no eyes on any part of the building that needed repair or replacement.

Findley stared at them in consternation. "Where are the other two?"

"You must mean Rustom and Nusswan?"

"Look, don't get smart with me. You know as well I do that the meeting is an important one. You also know that the meeting was to be with the four of you. You got that? Four," spit out Findley. Drinking inflamed his liver and it took very little to make him wrathful.

As if on cue, Rustom and Nusswan Bulsara stepped out from the shadows of the darkened hallway. They smirked. "You need us -- four of us?" was Rustom's rhetorical question. "Are we to feed the vultures? Four to carry the dead to the Towers of Silence!"

Peter didn't know any more than they did about what the leader would be asking them to do. Once they had met the instigator, they'd be told as much as they were supposed to know. Theirs is not to reason why, thought Peter. He did know that the clever Rustom was on a fishing expedition to find out what was expected and would no doubt keep at it.

Rustom opened his mouth, but before he could utter another word, Peter pointed at him, snapping orders at him. "Get me a taxi. A beat-up car will do. I'm to take you four to meet the leader. Leave you there."

He brushed his hands with a couple of swipes, a gesture to reassure himself that once he'd delivered them that would be the end of it.

The teeming streets of the Bombay slums were crowded with people and rickshaws and packs of naked children competing with pigs and goats and rats to forage through piles of stinking garbage that clogged the narrow lanes.

They had parked the ancient, noisy American car a couple of blocks north of the market. They walked then through an odoriferous arcade, where stalls spilled out into the surrounding streets. They were accustomed to this clamorous labyrinth. Rusted corrugated iron sheets above the stalls did provide shade from the sun, but they increased the heat below to almost intolerable intensity.

Peter and the four walked the short distance to a small shop. Before they entered, the sculptor told them that this is where they would pick up instructions and their payment in rupees. The four studied the place; they didn't want to lose the memory of where it was. The money meant too much to them.

Peter Findley nudged Rustom as leader of the four to move on into the shop. It was dark in the interior, and they paused to let their eyes adjust to the gloom. They heard a harsh rasping voice tell them to pass through the door there at the rear. (They would in time hear often that voice and very soon see to whom it belonged; he would be passing them the rupees. He was fat and sweated copiously. The sour odor of his body permeated the shop, crowded to overflow with merchandise.) More familiar with the place, Findley moved them along.

There was a single lighted bulb hanging by a cord from the ceiling. In the dim light they made out a figure seated on the floor. He had a yellow turban on his head. His face, not fully covered by a grizzled beard, was deeply lined. His eyes were closed as if he were meditating or deeply concentrating.

Out of the shadows stepped a person in the habit of a monk. The cowl was pulled far forward, concealing the face.

The four fellows were familiar with the garb of a holy man, they weren't intimidated nor did they feel fear. Even the presence of the swami made them also want to snicker. In Crawford Market they had seen repeatedly a man with a pipe and a basket which contained a cobra or two. They rarely watched. This was for tourists, they thought.

The atmosphere and smell of the dingy and suffocatingly hot place was getting to them. Rustom spoke to the other three, who were getting restless. "Cool it," he whispered. (He'd saved money from his school lunches to go to American movies. His addiction. When he could get away with it, he'd sit through two or more screenings -- memorizing the American lingo, especially the slang expressions of gangster characters.)

The person in the garb of a monk remained silent, but pointed so they would fix their attention on the swami. They obeyed, and they were hardly aware that the personage was standing behind them. The swami, like a guru, sat meditating. A servant in a kurta dhoti appeared. He remained silent until the turbaned figure with a light tip of his head informed the servant that the burlap bag he carried was now to be put in place before him.

The sound of a chant manifested itself. The four leaned in closer. "It's he," whispered Nusswan -- although there seemed no noticeable movement of the swami's lips.

"The one word I make out is 'Ananta,' came from Varun. "Hindus refer to the cobra by that name." As if on cue, a sleek cobra slid out onto the floor. The chanter now picked up from behind him a flute-like instrument. A high-pitched monotonous sound pealed softly from the pipe and it mesmerized the snake. As if in slow motion, the swami placed the musical instrument on his lap. With no break in motion, he reached forward and slid his hand up the length of the cobra until he was behind the bulge of the head.

Likewise were the young men hypnotized. They did not breathe, so as not to break the spell. Confident that the master had full control of the beast, the servant came forward out of the shadows and held in readiness a small round disk of glass. A nod from the turbaned head was sufficient communication for the servant to kneel and press the glass between the now extended fangs of the cobra. The hissing of the angered snake seemed loud in the airless small room. A milky viscous glob issued from each fang, making a smear on the glass object.

Quickly, the lithe servant rose, as might a dancer, and withdrew into the shadows. As tension had built at the sight before them, the boys had involuntarily closed their eyes. When they re-opened them, both the swami and the bag with the cobra were no longer before them. His exit had been silent.

The servant reappeared. The monk moved to meet him. A small package was thrust into the hands of the monk. Rustom noticed that the monk was wearing gloves. He asked himself. Why would anyone wear gloves? In this unbearable heat!

The monk spoke very softly, "You know where to come, the shop, to be paid? When you've completed the mission -- successfully." The four nodded that they understood.

"I'm told your schooling is in English. Here is a list of what you're to do. Here is cobra venom. My instructions tell you what to do with it. Remember, only

male foreigners and they're to be taken to the *Dakhma*. You understand?"

Rustom spoke for the group, "It's a piece of cake." That Americanism was greeted in silence. The waiting was painful. Then a gloved hand dismissed them.

They were relieved and happy to get out into the sun. To breathe. They said little to each other until they had reached the car.

"Now what do we do?" asked Nusswan. His echo was Varun, "What do we do?"

"We'll park over by Chowpatty Beach, study the instructions. Then, I say: we act. The sooner the better."

They shrugged, accepting Rustom's mandate. In truth, the three of them were scared.

Mehroo Bulsara, the mother of Rustom and Nusswan, sat -- as was her wont -- in the small apartment there in the tenement. Sitting in one of the two chairs with seats she shook her head as she looked at the battered sofa. Ever since the death of her husband they had been poverty stricken. She managed to pay the rent regularly, but her efforts to get the management of Sodawalla Baag to provide a simple thing like paint were fruitless. The apartment was badly in need of paint, among other things.

How I would like to get a new dining table and a new set of china. Several of the dishes are chipped and many of the cups are cracked, she thought. They say it's unhealthful to drink from a cup that's cracked.

Her thoughts turned toward her two sons. She had been downstairs to the front to call them, but they were nowhere in sight. She'd told them over and over and over again not to go into that filthy back yard. A neighbor had told her that they were often back there stoning the cats. She had wanted them to accompany her to the Fire Temple; it had been three days since her last visit.

When they grimaced at her request that they accompany her to the Fire Temple, she was prone to say, "Need I remind you that you are so fortunate to have been born Parsi? We live here in India, and we're grateful -- as Parsis -- to have found refuge long ago in the city of Bombay. Reflect on what it is like to have been born Hindu."

For Hindus, caste is like a timeless chain. She wanted to impress upon them what it was to be a *Chamaar*, an untouchable in village society. "*Chamaars*, the caste of tanning and leather working. They live in sections downwind from the Brahmins and land owners. They have to be aware of an invisible line of caste that they can never cross."

The mother would drone on to deaf ears. "Walking on the upper caste side of the street, an untouchable was likely to be stoned. How fortunate you are to go to a temple. Were an untouchable to go within hearing range of a Hindu temple while prayers were in progress, molten lead might be poured into his ears."

Nusswan spoke up, "We've never heard of that happening to the Hindus living over there in the gully." The mother promptly boxed his ears, for she considered his speaking up and what he had said as being insolent.

"You attend school, you two. If untouchable children draw too close to the village school, they are chased away and even sometimes punished."

Rustom ventured to put in his two cents, "The St. Thomas Catholic school we go to keeps us poor."

The mother would throw her hands in the air and wonder what was she to do with these sons of hers. She bemoaned the fact that her husband was dead. When the ambulance brought him home from his office after his fatal heart attack, she had to remind the driver that Parsis do not permit their dead to be embalmed. In retrospect, she took some comfort from the fact that Rustom had taken charge of funeral arrangements. He tended the oil lamp at the head of his father's bed where he had been laid out. This freed her to wash and iron her white sari and to make sure they had an ample supply of incense and sandalwood in the house. Both sons were a comfort to her during the full four days of death ceremonies in a bungalow at the Towers of Silence.

Mehroo realized that she was now sitting in darkness, and she rose to turn on a light. Just then her sons entered the apartment.

The thought of big money had made them feel cocky. "Momaiji, when do we eat?" spoke Rustom.

Without turning, their mother said, "I've been waiting for you to accompany me to the Fire Temple. It's been three days."

Anger took over, and Rustom spoke loudly to his mother's back, "Will this mourning never end? Your husband has been dead and digested for more than a year now." He knew that he was being shockingly irreverent. It accounted for his failing to refer to the dead one as his father.

Their mother began to cry, and she turned slowly, and as she gazed at them, she said, "Would you have me go to the Towers of Silence and let the vultures eat me up? Would that make you happy?"

The two hung their heads and feeling ashamed they urged their mother to go with them to the Fire Temple.

India is made up of communities Hindu, Jain, Sikh, Parsi, as well as Christian. The second largest is Muslim. India has its Jews, though hardly more than 20,000. There is an acceptance of diversity as a way of life. In view of the density of population, it comes as no surprise that tension from time to time exists and results in conflict. Emperor Akbar, who ruled at the time of Elizabeth I of England, truly believed in peaceful co-existence. He had a Muslim, a Christian, and a Parsi wife! He is a metaphor for India's uniqueness.

Every act is done with complete
awareness.
> *Bhagavad Gita*

Chapter IV
June 3, 1995
Bombay, India

Bombay has a style of its own -- heavy and dignified. Recently, modern buildings have sprung up. It has become a Mecca where many -- even from the small villages -- come in hopes of making their fortune. It is strangely attractive, combining Indian domes and minarets and scrollwork with Victorian ornament. Romanesque and Gothic arches surmount doorways. These are the buildings that have heaviness and solidity. But like other cities of the world, India's Bombay is undergoing change.

Malabar Hill

Kursi and Alina Mehta were neighbors -- on the same floor -- to the Paranjoti's, Kamala and Narendra. Alina had been feeling the pre-monsoon heat; she lay on a *charpoy*. Her husband Kursi entered the apartment quietly, so as not to disturb her. Alina brightened and greeted her husband, "I've invited our neighbors, the Paranjoti's, to dinner this evening."

"Some special reason?" he asked.

"I was out on our terrace this morning, scolding our houseboy for not having adequately watered the plants. I wasn't eavesdropping..."

Kursi cocked his left eyebrow. He thought, I take Alina with a grain of salt, always. "Yes...?" he made of the `s' a sibilant sound which evoked from her one of those looks that could kill.

"It's long overdue, our entertaining the Paranjoti's. What I learned was that Kamala has invited to Bombay a classmate from long ago -- with her husband. He's a police inspector."

"Who?" said Kursi nervously, now paying attention. He traveled on business and often slipped dutiable articles past customs.

"Josephine Utsumi's husband. If only you'd listen. They're Japanese." I've always wanted to visit Japan. I must see to it that we cultivate them, was the thought that Alina did not share with her husband.

Kursi Mehta was short and pudgy. What people reacted to first when introduced to him was his knobby hands. He was that rare person -- contented. His smiles came easily to him, making his face seem more attractive than it actually was. As a child he had had small-pox and his face had the pox mark scars.

PART II

Those who take wisdom as their highest
goal . . . attain wisdom quickly and enter
into perfect peace.

Bhagavad Gita

Chapter V
June 3, 1995
Tokyo, Japan

At the end of the day Inspector Utsumi arrived home to be greeted, as was the custom, by his wife Josie and the maid. Both knelt. Over the arm of the maid lay a neatly folded, fresh cotton yukata kimono. His wife held slippers; the inspector preferred them to flip-flopping zoris.

Once inside the traditional wing of their comfortable Tokyo home, Josie looked at her husband, saying, "*Shujin*, either you're very tired this evening, or ..." she raised one delicately arched eyebrow, "is it possible you're ill?"

The inspector sighed. "I find it difficult to admit, but...all these senseless murders. I find myself thinking back to that young man. With so much for him to look forward to...his committing *seppaku* on the roof of the kabuki theatre, and then being beheaded. Ah, but that *yakuza* Haruki! I have no particular feeling about his being shot. He was a scoundrel!"

Josie eased him toward the bath. She planned

to join him, for she knew that a good hot bath in their capacious tub would be helpful in relaxing him, maybe cheering him up. Large windows gave the bather a spectacular view of their traditional garden: small trees, arrangements of stones, and just a few flowering plants. Her husband always found gazing out on the garden restful and quieting to his spirit.

Earlier she had nodded to the maid, and in a soft voice said, "Have a bottle of sake at the dinner table this evening. You know the kind that the inspector likes."

Once they were immersed in the very hot water, having first laved themselves with wooden buckets of hot water to condition their skin to the heat of the water in the tub, Josie ventured to say, "I have had good news."

"And what might that be?" asked Utsumi of his wife.

"I received a letter from my dear friend, Kamala Paranjoti. We were together in the Swiss school I've so often reminisced about with you."

The only response she got was a humming, by way of acknowledgement, as the inspector continued to pour hot water over his head.

Josie was not put off by her husband's taciturnity. She said, "You may recall my referring to her as Kamala Jamnadas. Before she was married.

"This job of yours -- a police inspector -- is not easy on you. Your days are consumed by all the evil people bring upon one another. Bodies, blood, weapons ...having to tell someone a loved one has been brutalized...it is much weight to carry on your shoulders, *shujin*." The inspector's eyes gave Josie sad, silent affirmation of her words.

"These crimes of late -- have taken their toll," she sighed, "on both of us. Never before had I been forced by circumstance to be not only a witness to one of these crimes, but a participant in the investigation."

"You very much solved it," interrupted Utsumi. "There in the *onnagata's* Kabuki dressing room."

Josie smiled, "Solving crimes is not only taxing for you physically, but, I suspect, is painful mentally."

Utsumi waved his hand in the water of the large bath, as if to dismiss what his wife had just said.

"You won't convince me otherwise," asserted the inspector's wife. "I may have a solution. We need a vacation -- a trip."

The inspector groaned and rolled his eyes heavenward at the very mention of the word `vacation.' The last one had ended in a disaster when they'd discovered two bodies in an antique store in Kyoto. He wasn't sure he wanted to take on another trip.

That rumble of his indicated to Josie a need for a quick change of words. "Perhaps vacation was not exactly the word I had in mind --"

"*So desu-ne?*" he muttered wryly.

"-- but rather what in the states they call a sabbatical," Josie finished smoothly, ignoring his somewhat sarcastic `*so desu-ne.'*

"You recall the letters I've been reading to you from Yoriko?"

Hearing Josie read daughter Yoriko's letters

to him while he relaxed was often a high spot in his day. In this letter, she asked when the family -- her mother's family -- had become Christian.

"As you know, my family has been Christian for many centuries, even before sixteen hundred. I wrote her as much as I know."

Utsumi spoke up, "Write her that we Japanese are accepting of different religious beliefs. Many Japanese are Christian as well as Shinto and Buddhist.

"At first Christians were permitted to continue to practice their religion. But, the Shogun came to fear internal dissention and another war. Then began the massacre of thousands of Japanese Christians. Religious bigotry was not a motive."

As always, Josie was filled with admiration for her husband's learning. She nodded agreement and continued as if she had not been interrupted, "My family was fortunate. They went underground and survived. Married to you, I am most sympathetic with the Buddhist faith. Much of it has rubbed off on me."

"Where is this leading to?" asked a puzzled Utsumi.

"If we were to accept the Paranjoti's invitation, did I mention that she's married to the mayor of Bombay? At any rate, you would have an opportunity to visit sites where the Gautama Buddha preached. That, I'm sure, would be like a balm to your spirit."

Seemingly there was no response, but in fact the inspector was deep in thought.

"Husband, it's been so long since I've seen one of my school friends...I do look forward to a visit with

Kamala. Meeting her family." Josie gave a quick sidelong glance at her husband, attempting to gauge his reaction to her request to see a friend. His silence weighed on her. But then his facial expression suggested much. She smiled inwardly; he was considering her wish.

The inspector was as much in love with his *okusan* as the day the Shinto priest had made them man and wife -- which had been more important to him than the brisk civil ceremony which had preceded.

Josie was the name by which his wife was known to him and to her friends. As the daughter of an ambassador, Josephine had, since early childhood, grown up in both England and France. She was westernized, but upon her return to Japan she had come to a full realization that for most occasions she needed to suppress her western ways and be a Japanese housewife.

As for the inspector, growing up in the home of his parents he had heard endless talk of the war...of the occupation by the Americans. He'd come to know that his stature and build stemmed from the vitamins his parents had given him, in addition to the new, healthier diet that had been taken up by his parents, as it had been by many Japanese -- an adaptation to the *gaijin* conquerors.

From an early time he was ambivalent about *gaijin* -- foreigners. Hearing of his nation's defeat was a wound that had never completely healed. As a Japanese, he had felt diminished. But mingled with this bitter feeling was also an intense admiration for that freedom to act that he had observed in *gaijin*.

Thus his encounter years ago with Josie was apocalyptic.

Despite Josie's assumed demeanor as a Japanese young woman, he -- as a sensitive man -- picked up that there was something very different and tantalizing about her. For him it was love at first sight. Small wonder, too, for she was beautiful.

As the courtship progressed, each of the two families searched backgrounds. Utsumi's grand-parents were suspicious of the Owada family. Josie's western ways alarmed them. Might she be an *ainoko*? The child of a mating of a Japanese and a Caucasian? they worried. All sighed with relief when the marriage intermediary revealed to them that, like the recent Premier of Japan, the Owadas were accounted aristocrats.

Hmmm, Utsumi reflected. He tried to see himself in India. More and more the idea of getting away from Tokyo -- his job -- began to appeal to him.

Let's see, a sabbatical is...what? Ah, yes, I remember. Josie explained the word to me when it came up in a letter of our daughter's. One of her favorite professors was to be away for a year -- a sabbatical.

No, he thought, I'll not ask for a year's leave. But I'll take the bull by the horns (that expression of Josie's) and go over young Commander Okubo's head. He'd claim I would be missing too much work. He was Japanese and a yard wide, so it rankled him to be ordered -- at times imperiously -- by Commander Okubo, his junior in age.

The inspector was goal centered. Utsumi's job, while challenging and demanding, was also rewarding. Catching a criminal and seeing him brought to justice always gave him a great deal of satisfaction.

His thoughts ran on...visiting sites where the Buddha achieved enlightenment and spoke to his disciples...I like the idea.

"*Ha-chan*, I'll think about this, I promise."

The corners of his mouth curved upwards slightly, "You always come up with these, I confess, startling, but in the end, very good ideas. I am weary; not physically weary, but soul weary. What's the western word for that?"

Josie said, "Yes, there is an English word. Depression." She thought, that's very descriptive of what my husband is experiencing.

I know him so well, ran her thoughts. I think I have an agreement that we accept the invitation to visit the Paranjoti's. India!

The Following Morning

Kneeling at the low table for breakfast, Josie ate her western food -- by choice -- and the inspector had his customary rice and pickles and green tea.

"*Ha-chan*, you tempt me," said Utsumi softly.

"I, tempt you? *Shujin*!" replied Josie concealing a smile. She suspected what was coming.

"India," answered he meditatively.

This morning Inspector Utsumi's hair was brushed back from his high forehead. He was that rare Japanese who wore glasses. While contact lenses had made western cartoons of bespectacled Japanese less than an ingratiating memory for most, Utsumi could not wear them. His eyes were too sensitive to permit contacts.

The inspector had finished eating, and at the corner of his mouth hung a lighted cigarette. The smoke curled up to the ceiling and ashes fell, landing on his clothing. Josie was not only cultured, but fastidious. Long ago she had sagely given up trying to cure her husband of his addiction. She knew there was no chance of his quitting smoking. Among Tokyo's policemen Utsumi's omnipresent cigarette was a trademark for the inspector.

Once again Josie brushed the ashes off the front of his cotton *yukata* with one hand while handing the breakfast plates to the attending maid.

"India," repeated the inspector.

Before Josie could respond, he went on, "What has guided me in the twenty or more years as a policeman, has been the Middle Way."

"The Middle Way?" Josie said in an encouraging way.

The inspector, like many Japanese men, verbalized little of his innermost feelings.

Without meeting her gaze, he went on, "The Middle Way is enlightenment, leading to clear vision, wisdom. It leads to peace, insight..." His face was a mask of seriousness as he turned to face his wife.

"That is what has made me love you all of these many years, *shujin*," said Josie as she lightly brushed his cheek with a kiss. During the long, comfortable silence such as is possible only after years of marriage and companionship, Josie paused to reflect on her husband.

As a young man, Utsumi had been handsome. He had a high forehead, large eyes, and attractive, well-shaped, full lips. Photographs showed that even as a youngster his full eyebrows seemed to beetle.

It's small wonder that I was attracted to him, she thought. It never even crossed my mind to think about the great differences in status between our families.

The talk of the older members of his family about the war, the defeat, and the occupation by the Americans had at last been dismissed from Utsumi's mind. As an omnivorous reader of books -- a preponderance of them foreign in Japanese translation -- he had early on developed a view that people were much the same underneath. The family's pride in having had as an ancestor one of the Forty-seven Ronin had instilled in him a keen sense that law was to be respected.

Utsumi had done well in school. Parental pressure saw to that, but he had failed to be accepted by either of the two prestigious universities. An uncle had suggested that he try his luck at police work. Utsumi acted upon the advice and never looked back. At once he found he liked the camaraderie of men working together for law and order. He rose in the ranks to inspector, and seniority in Japan counts -- usually.

At age fifty, his good looks had altered to make him serious and formidable. He wore his long hair brushed back with no part, often hanging over his jacket collar. His wife had to remind him to go to the barber.

As Josie had commented to their daughter Yoriko, "Your father never seems to be without a cigarette jutting between his lips."

A young recruit to the police force had quipped, "He's learned to smoke while he sleeps."

He had adjusted, more or less, to Commander Okubo's western ways. He had married Josie, who sometimes seemed to him an exotic person from the west.

Josie was first to break the silence. "Tell me more, *shujin*. It is the Buddha, yes?"

"Tradition would have it that Gautama Buddha had come to Benares -- I looked it up in our atlas. Today, it is called by the ancient name of Varanasi...rather a journey from Bombay -- that is where your friend Kamala and her husband the mayor live? Bombay?"

"Yes," replied Josie, suppressing her mounting excitement. "Dear Kamala. We were so close. Both of us were lonely at first at that school in Switzerland. We missed our families."

Utsumi nodded thoughtfully. "We think nothing of a trip to Kyoto or Osaka," he rambled on. "We could fly to India. I'm told its trains are slow compared to ours, but it would please me to sit there in the park where the Buddha preached the sermon of the Middle Way. I forget what else he enunciated there..."

With some fear of disappointment in her heart, Josie looked directly at him, asking, "You are telling me we *are* going to India?"

Inspector Utsumi Tatsuo nodded his head, leaving no doubt in his wife's mind that his answer was a firm `yes'.

Josie was tall for a Japanese, and she was handsome, pleasantly plump. She walked erect, and `poise' was the word that came readily to mind of her many friends. She looked stunning in kimonos of which she had many.

She was thinking, For my arrival in Bombay I will wear an Yves Saint Laurent serge suit. Having inherited a considerable fortune, Josie indulged herself in French originals.

As she began to look through her wardrobe she murmured, "It's been a long time since I've been out of Japan. To India it will be!" She knew that India was a country where the most-used second language spoken by most in India is English. I miss English, she thought, more than French. Although we did study French at the boarding school, and German, I wonder if my dear friend Kamala has kept up with her French? When I return to Tokyo, Yvonne, the wife of the French ambassador, will be interested to know if there's an opportunity for people to speak French in India. She, too, had been a classmate of Kamala Jamnadas in Switzerland.

At once Josie's mind was awhirl with thoughts of what both of them would need to pack for such a hot country as India. However, she did love shopping.

The department stores, she speculated, will

have summer things still? Ah, there may be sales! I'll just have to see.

Oh, there will be so many things to bring to Japan from such a fascinating country, ran her thoughts. We lived abroad so many years that I forgot that we Japanese always have to bring something -- even something very small -- to all the servants and to all the relatives.

Josie was an optimistic person, ever of a positive frame of mind. The big thing was that she and the inspector were to go to India; that country, she knew, would be so very different.

Competing with no one,
They are alike in success and failure
And content with whatever comes to them.
Bhagavad Gita

Chapter VI
June 10, 1995
New York City

Paul Drake perused his ticket and was delighted he would have a few hours and a night in London before he continued on with Air India. He was to enter this sub-continent at the city of Bombay. Here were to be a series of meetings and seminars.

Paul's invitation to substitute for Damon had been quite unexpected. He knew that he had been in the running to go to the seminar. Janis Peacock, secretary to the publisher of Contemporary Novels had let it slip on a date with him. Once he had the invitation, Paul accepted with avidity. All expenses paid, he thought. Who would refuse?

Damon probably did something stupid, Paul thought. So like him. Paul was in a dither now that he knew that he was to go to India. India is a country of multiple languages, customs, and taboos, he reminded himself. What a multiplicity of people.

This fascinated him as a writer. His desire to visit India had been stimulated by reading Rohinton

Mistry's *A Fine Balance.* He'd read it in manuscript when it had come to the publisher for whom he worked.

Paul's boss congratulated him, "India is different. There'll be cultural shock!"

"What better experience for a novelist," was Paul's rejoinder.

"Pack for very hot weather. You'll be arriving before the monsoon. Pack very light-weight summer clothes," said the boss as he slapped Paul on the shoulder. "Will you join me for a drink downstairs in the pub?"

"Speaking of packing," said Paul, "I have little time myself to pack before that flight. Thanks anyway."

At the airport he called Janis. "I'll send you a postcard from Bombay," he said, and he hung up rather abruptly. They had called his flight.

The United States had given great aid over the years to India as a loan. Since the country had blocked rupees, billions of Indian currency had been piling up in India. An Indo-U.S. writer's seminar was a way for the State Department to make use of some of the money due the United States and its taxpayers. In the city of Bombay there would be a week-long series of meetings.

June 10, 1995
Washington, D.C.

Search Group, Inc. had its discrete head office just off DuPont Circle, in the nation's capital. Bert Appleton took the elevator down from his sublet apartment. He hadn't wanted to buy, for since his dismissal from the Tokyo office, he feared that -- like his friend Fred of the C.I.A. -- he, too, might go from having been praised to ending up in the agency's `Siberia'. What made him anxious was that rumor, gossip, hearsay and innuendo could ruin a promising career.

The rental agent had said to him, "The owner is an odd fellow -- never know what he's up to. World Bank. Traveling all the time."

Bert took the elevator down. Suppressing his disquietude over Janis' early telephone call, he exited from the apartment building at 2420 Virginia Street. The weather was cool and crisp; he decided to walk. He hit a brisk stride. In his military days, Bert had been a Green Beret. He missed his green beret. It would be quite out of place in Washington, he thought. But, I cut a figure when that beret was tipped jauntily above my left eye. It did get attention.

His thoughts rambled on. I don't mind D.C.. Its heat and humidity in summer is rather like Vietnam. Ugh! Vietnam. Now there's stinking heat!

A head-hunting office had sought Appleton out for Search Group, Incorporated. The pay was most attractive, plus most expenses. When the front office proposed to him that he'd immediately be going to Japan, he had at first protested. But he was deeply pleased to be away from the States for a stretch. It still smarted that he'd been fired by the *Washington Post*. Besides, he liked Asians.

Bert's superior one day asked him why he often came to the office unshaved -- a two-day growth of beard. "Unkempt! Why don't you shave, Appleton?"

Bert's answer was simple. "It keeps the women off."

Bert was tall. He looked six feet four inches, but, in reality, he was six feet two inches. The look of exaggerated height came from the manner in which he carried himself. His ramrod straightness suggested that he'd swallowed a swagger stick or an umbrella, for his squared shoulders never seemed to relax. One knew at once that he'd gone to military academies -- and that he had taken to them with enthusiasm.

On an assignment in Paris, his mistress asked him, "*Cheri*, what means `unkempt?' I hear Mme. Concierge say to English neighbor, `*Regardez* that homme! *Oui?* Unkempt, *non*?'"

"Speak French or English, please," shouted Bert from the tiny bathroom. "I don't understand your mixed-salad -- some English, some French."

She walked to the bathroom door. "We say in French: *Tu as l'air d'ace de pique.* I translate: You have look of Ace of Spades."

Hmmm, he thought while shaving, blackhead. If I had time, I'd take care of that: squeeze it, the little bastard. Damn! I'm out of alcohol.

Our jaunty soldier had an Achilles heel -- vanity about his appearance. Since high school days he knew he had looks. `Handsome,' his parents would murmur, thinking it was behind his back.

During Bert's brief stay in Washington, D.C., he had returned to his Korean tailor, trained by an Italian. He gave excellent tailoring, but it took some persuasion to get the man to do two suits -- one silk and one white linen -- in forty-eight hours. Towering over the little man, he talked him into doing the two suits.

Bert had tried to clothe his lanky frame with suits off the rack of a department store; none suited him. While in the military, he had seen to it that his uniforms were tailored, feeling that this added not only to his comfort, but to his look of authority.

Outfits are costing me more this time, thought Bert, but perhaps I can slip in some of the dollars on my cost of living allowance. Everybody does it.

Bert liked striding up New Hampshire Avenue; it took him past the campus of George Washington University. Well, thought Bert, those young ladies must have early morning classes. What attractive things they are. Oops! I should refer to these babes as women. Always. Even in my thoughts. That is `politically correct.' As the Japanese would say, *Zamamiro!* -- kiss my ass, you left-wingers!

As he strode by Watergate, he asked himself, "I wonder how people feel about staying in the

Watergate Hotel? Anyone with the surname of Mitchell must get a laugh from the desk clerks. This is where they caught up with John W. Mitchell, Attorney General."

Bert sometimes talked aloud to himself on walks. On occasion it prompted people to turn around and look at him as if he were odd or strange.

He reminisced. My father had just landed in Johannesburg, and there in South Africa were the papers with the headline `Nixon Resigns.' It made dad's day, so he told me.

Bert arrived just as the office was primed to get into the action of the day. He had decided he would not get there early. His boss had been a psychoanalyst before becoming one of the partners of the agency. "He'll make some crack about my being anxious -- `You know what being before time means!'" muttered Bert to himself. "If late, I'm hostile. I can't win with him." He checked his watch. On time; so I'm conforming!"

In Mary Lou's eyes, Bert Appleton was a hero, a romantic figure of cinematic proportions -- like John Wayne in *The Green Berets*, or even Sylvester Stallone as the brooding Vietnam veteran hero Rambo. She couldn't resist hearing his deep, sexy, masculine voice over the phone. Even when he cussed her out. She'd spent endless hours fantasizing about him. Did he snore? She visualized his face on the pillow next to hers, heard him murmur words of love. His voice whispering her name over and over, Mary Lou, Mary Lou --

Mary Lou restrained herself with some

difficulty. She would have liked nothing better than to rush up to Bert and throw her arms around him. She was petite and her head would have rested just above his belly-button. She was too intelligent to be a figure of fun amidst her co-workers.

I'll be strong, she had long ago said to herself. I'll let him come to me. Ultimately, he will, I hope.

Bert had interrupted her train of thought by saying to her, "Here I had planned to have a few days of rest and relaxation -- on company time. You woke me up while it was still dark out, Mary Lou. Now tell me. What's so important?"

Her eyes darted back and forth quickly, looking at those nearby to see if they might be eavesdropping. She grabbed him by the arm. "C'mon. Let's go to my office. Office! That's laughable."

Mary Lou's office was a small, glass-partitioned cubicle. Others might be able to see us, she thought, but they won't be able to hear us.

"Oh, Bert," she took a deep breath to calm herself. "I think you should be seated for what I have to tell you."

He pulled up a chair close to the side of her desk. "So...?" he prompted.

Mary Lou leaned forward, bringing her face closer to Bert's. "India!" she said in an excited whisper, as if this single word would make everything clear.

Bert held up his hand in a `hold-it-for-a-minute' gesture. "Suppose we start at the beginning, okay? I'm all ears, Mary Lou. What's the scoop?" He leaned in just a bit, and with a lower tone of voice, flirtatiously said, "C'mon, babe, give!"

Mary Lou almost squealed with pleasure. She loved it when he called her babe.

"The Ruperts are here in D.C. They're oil-rich Texans. That's what's going around the office, anyway."

"I've heard of them," said a puzzled and impatient Bert. "Humble Oil -- but the rumor is that they're anything but humble." Bert was a little piqued that his joke had not gotten a rise out of Mary Lou. "Okay, so who's after whom?" he prompted.

Mary Lou reached into the upright metal paper/file sorter on her desk and quickly plucked a single piece of paper from one of its sections. She placed it on the desk and slid it towards Bert.

"This," she indicated with a nod towards the paper, "is a letter from the front office." When he hesitated, she said, "Go ahead, Bert, read it."

A quick look told him much. He was to leave that night. There would be a brief stopover in Paris. He frowned. Not London for a briefing on India. Damn! Our London office, with a British staff, is best equipped to tell me the do's and don'ts of India.

"You see? India."

"What?" He once again held up his hand, signaling her to stop... or at least slow down a bit. "That's the assignment?"

"Just like I said. The stopover is Paris and is for you to confer with Interpol."

"I can see the rationale of that, Janis. Interpol is at Saint Cloud. It's not possible to have a bad meal in France." With a grimace Bert added, "I sure am full of corny phrases this morning. Must be the hour, Janis.

"I know this much. India will be hot. So, it'll remind me of 'Nam -- but, no land-mines. A plus, in my book."

He began to visualize India. Beautiful young women in saris. Held up by magic, it always seemed to him.

"The Paris office says that Interpol was moved," said Janis. "You're to go to Lyons," she said, pronouncing it as if it were `Lions!'

Bert winced, and couldn't resist bedeviling Janis, "You'll be telling me I'm to go to a Lyons Tea-Shop? There's none in Paris. I doubt there's is one left in London." He was ever the one to rib Mary Lou.

"`Lions,' France!" Seeing his innocent expression, she laughed. "Oh, Bert, you scamp! You pronounce it. Where the head office of Interpol is now."

"From what I've heard of their comprehensive computers, I'm certain Interpol can fax to me all they have that I may need. What did the Rupert's tell us about their son -- the missing American? What did you say his given name was?"

"Damon," replied Mary Lou. "Unusual."

"Yeah! But I've barely unpacked yet!" Bert moaned as he pulled himself up to his full six-foot-two inch height. He stared off into space for several moments, mentally assessing the situation.

"Okay. Right. Fine," he verbally concluded the mental discussion he seemed to be having with himself. He brought his eyes back to Mary Lou's face.

"Is the water cooler still down the hall?"

Mary Lou was keenly disappointed that he

was leaving her. She had hoped he'd stay -- for a time, at least -- and chat for a while. But, it was obvious he wanted to be elsewhere. She just nodded a `yes' and sadly watched him go.

Bert took his time getting to the Watergate Hotel, where he was to have his meeting with the Ruperts of Houston, Texas. Bert needed the walk to take in all that had just been dumped in his lap the last hour. The thought, `Now India!' repeated over and over in his mind, like a needle sticking on a flawed record.

His mind wandered. He recalled the night he'd been the guest of a gay senator. They ate in the French restaurant Jean Louis in the Watergate Hotel, lower level. The Montana congressman was almost as tall as Michael Crichton, who is six-foot-nine inches. No closet was big enough to accommodate this congressman. The food was the best, he decided, in Washington, D.C.. What impressed him about the young legislator was that he sent the white wine -- a French label -- back three times, saying, "There's still a taste of cork." That man has balls, had been Bert's appraisal.   Soon after, Bert had tried to get a reservation at this swank French eatery. He wanted to impress Janis. It was fully booked! One has to be a congressman, I see, thought Bert -- straight or gay.

The Watergate Hotel manager came out from behind the reservations counter. He stepped boldly in front of Appleton.

"The Ruperts," he said breathlessly.

Pretending not to know to whom the hotel employee was referring, Bert said, "The name is Appleton. Bert Appleton."

The manager stood there looking stunned. "They're waiting. You *are* Mr. Appleton? A meeting with Mr. and Mrs. Rupert? Yes?"

Bert felt sorry for the flustered young fellow. "Traffic. And, some cab drivers in this town seem never to have heard of Watergate. Would you believe it?"

At this juncture in this charade, Madame Rupert rushed up to them.

"Search Group? Appleton?" flustered the woman with an accent, overlaid with nasality, that probably carried up the elevator shaft.

A few paces behind her was a tall gentleman wearing a ten-gallon hat; there were leather pads at each elbow, and he sported a studded belt big enough to hold down a horse's saddle, if needed. His gaze was of a man not comfortable, but bored.

"At this hour, the bar is empty," said the manager. "Perhaps you'd be more at ease transacting your business in there," said he as he spread wide his arms to maneuver them out of the small lobby.

Now `Ma' Rupert acknowledged the manager's presence. She worked her mouth, savoring, tasting something sour. Before speaking, she swallowed.

"Of course. Come Charles," she prolonged the vowel in her husband's name. "After you, Mr. Appleton."

Once seated in the gloom of the empty bar, she extracted from her empty purse -- large as a reticule -- a dainty handkerchief. Bert could see no tears, but mother Rupert mimed brushing away tears.

"We quarreled with our son Damon before he left for that writer's seminar in India," she stated flatly.

Rupert Père was taciturn. He still gave Bert his profile which caused him to sit in the booth in an awkward position.

Mrs. Rupert -- Bert had learned that her name was Mame -- jabbed her husband with her elbow.

As if thinking long and hard about it, Mr. Rupert said, as if talking to the far wall, "Spare no expense."

Mame Rupert gave a sob. "We've been so opposed to his wanting to be a writer. Everyone we know in Texas has long given up reading. Everything is TV now. Disgusting."

Bert thought, That's a non-sequitur. Texas. I heard that long ago there was a musical on Broadway with a song: *I'm tired of Texas*. Half the audience of backers got up and left.

"Mr. Appleton," cooed Damon's mother, "you will find him? He's our only son. We have daughters, but Will -- my husband -- always wanted a boy."

Bert had been wool-gathering. He snapped to, and nodded affirmatively, vigorously. "Janis, in our office, has given me all of the relevant information which she took down from you earlier today. Respecting your son Damon -- to coin a phrase -- `I'll leave no stone unturned.'"

The two Ruperts laughed, as if Bert had said something arrestingly novel and newly minted.

As Bert made it back to his apartment on Virginia Avenue, he shook his head to clear his thoughts. Has Damon used the seminar to take off? That's my guess. He may be as wacky as those two.

Cultivate vigor, patience, will, purity;
Avoid malice and pride.
Bhagavad Gita

Chapter VII
June 3, 1995
London, England

Paul's British friend, Norris Brown of Pan Asia Travel Agency, had always proved to be an exceptional friend. Whenever Paul arrived at Heathrow, Norris Brown had sent a limousine to pick him us as soon as he had passed through customs.

I'm so glad I have a stop-over, reflected Paul as he moved easily through customs inspection. It'll mean a bit of an adjustment to time-lag -- which will be so great once I've hit India. They've arranged for me to stay at the Savoy, he gloated. I'm told it's on the Strand. Several of London's theatres are right there.

Paul arrived early. As if he had extra sensory perception, Norris was there waiting for him; he had learned by chance that Paul had changed to a Concorde flight.

While standing in line for checking in for a business class flight on British Airways, a uniformed, bearded representative of the airline had come up to Paul.

"Would you like to go Concorde?"

Paul was puzzled, and replied, "But, I've already checked my luggage."

"I'll take care of that," said the Englishman with that characteristic rising inflection.

"I'm so pleased. The man ahead of you turned me down."

Paul laughed at the thought that anyone would turn down taking an upgrade flight...on the Concorde! Paul was very pleased. On a Business Class ticket I'm going Concorde!

At the Savoy, Paul showered and took a nap before Norris Brown came by to pick him up for a night on the town.

"We'll have a look-see at my club," said Norris, as he looked admiringly at the new suit Paul was struggling to get into. "It's a membership club -- near the Comedy Theatre. Not far from Leicester Square, where there's that bust of Shakespeare."

"I'm not a member, how will I get in?" asked Paul.

"You'll see."

"What is this club?"

"Oh, it's a young man's club. You'd call them yuppies. It's noisy; men with their dates sing around the piano."

"You spoke of it as a young man's club?"

"These days everything is co-educational, as I hear it is now in the United States."

That little ol' passport USA did the trick. At Norris's prompting, at the top of the stairs, in a flash Paul was made a member -- an overseas member. It cost only a pound, which when translated into US currency, was only abut a dollar-sixty.

"Be sure to order a double or triple gin," advised Norris. "What pubs and clubs consider a shot hardly wets the bottom of a glass. VAT makes things expensive."

"VAT? What's that?"

"Value Added Tax, a kind of sales tax."

The club was convivial. Paul spent much of his time perusing the log, as huge as an atlas. It was a `baedeker' of private clubs and bars around the world.  On the cover it read, `Add where your dreams have been fulfilled.'

Norris was hailed by many, "Hi, Brown. What'll you have? Your friend?" Very hospitable were the fellows in the club.

"Tell me again where you're headed for," asked Norris.

"It's India. Bombay. A writer's conference," replied Paul. He went on to talk about his eagerness to get to India for the first time in his life. Out of the corner of Norris' eye he noticed that a dark raven-haired women with startlingly large blue eyes and pale skin had edged close to them. He was close enough to detect the hair was a wig. And she was wearing a gold lame gown, here! Must be a tart, or an actress, he mused.

What's this? he asked himself. Could it be Paul's reference to India? He was puzzled and felt strangely anxious for his friend.

As the woman became aware of his glance, she drifted away from the bar where Paul and Norris were sitting.

Now Paul began to feel strangely uncomfortable. No reason, he thought, but he said to Norris, "I'm beginning to feel jet-lag. I need sleep -- before the next time change." Norris was understanding.

"Damn! It's past midnight. I've missed my train." (He referred to the train, which shut down at midnight.)

"Well, back at the Savoy there are twin beds," said Paul.

"I'll take your offer. Peckham is too far to walk and too expensive by cab," said Norris.

Peck-him? What an improbable place to live, thought Paul. The name...I've never heard of it. Then he felt that he was being uncharitable about where his friend lived and that name was improbable to him as an American.

Hotels are very accommodating to travel agency personnel; besides, the Savoy was too fine a hotel to question who accompanies whom.

After hurried ablutions -- the hour was late -- Paul donned his pajamas and stepped into the bed nearest the window. Only a sliver of light from the bath -- where he'd left it on -- made a streak across the rich oriental carpet. The first night in a strange abode always made him feel a bit disoriented. I need Ariadne's thread of light to get me to the bathroom, he rationalized. It may be only 8 p.m., my time, New York, but here in London its 1:00 a.m. Paul was fast drifting off to sleep.

Next morning, the two of them had room service. The breakfast at the Savoy impressed Paul:

Georgian silver, exquisite china; no department-store cutlery on the table that had been wheeled in.

"Let me give you the address of the Sabavalas of Bombay. Their daughter's a delight -- and of an important Parsi family.

Lyons, France

Bert would have liked to have had a few days in London -- a customary break when traveling to India, he'd been told. But, the office was impatient for him to get to France, to Interpol's headquarters. He looked at the memo which had been thrust into his hand along with farewells when he left the office of Search Group, Inc. There he read:

Members of Interpol number one hundred and fifty-eight nations. The basic important function of Interpol -- an acronym fashioned from *International Police* -- is to coordinate, internationally, police activity. In its long history, Interpol has had great success in locating persons suffering from amnesia as well as in tracking down fugitive criminals.

"Get what news there may be on Damon Rupert," said Bert's boss, "from the horse's mouth: Interpol headquarters. If the young man has turned hippie and is running away, Interpol may have a recent hotel or motel listing."

"Gotcha," said Bert as he swung out of the office. He left a note with his superintendent, packed hurriedly, thinking he'd be gone just a few days.

Next morning he was at Charles de Gaulle Airport. Bert had dozed over the Atlantic and was feeling cramped and sleepy. He was tempted to look up his former mistress in Paris, but as he rode down on the escalator to claim his baggage he said to himself, "I'd better get to Bombay...but quick!" But why fly to Lyons, he thought. I've had my troubles with domestic Air France. No seat assignments! I'll take France's bullet train T.G.V. to Lyons.

Interpol had as yet nothing on Rupert, except that he had registered at the Taj Mahal Intercontinental. At first Bert had fumed, but he could be of a philosophical turn of mind. There is the other side of the coin, reflected Appleton, Lyons is famous for its restaurants. Ah, yes, I'll take a taxi to Paul Bocuse's -- just outside of the city. On my expense account it will show up as costing a pretty penny, but it serves the Ruperts right for sending me on what may be a wild goose chase.

Be self-controlled, sincere, truthful
loving, and full of the desire to serve.
Bhagavad Gita

Chapter VIII
June 10, 1995
Bombay, India

Kamala and her husband had been to Santa
Cruz airport early in the morning to bring the Utsumis
to their home on Malabar Hill -- only to discover that the
Air India plane had been delayed due to an unscheduled
stop in Rangoon, Burma. "There is always unnecessary
tension between countries neighboring Burma," groused
the mayor. He was exasperated at the wasted trip to the
airport; he had a taxing day ahead, and Kamala had not
been feeling well. She had insisted, however, on going.
"It's just an upset stomach. Nothing. I must go." Is she
pregnant? thought her husband.

Later that morning Kamala had agreed with her
husband that now their Premier car and chauffeur go to
the airport to pick up Josie and the inspector. The
chauffeur had a sign made by Kamala ready to hold up
with the name Utsumi, but it proved unnecessary, for
they were the only Japanese passing out from
Immigration that morning.

It was high noon when the inspector and Josie
arrived at the terrace apartment. The sun was high in the

sky and it was hot and humid. The inspector's face shone from perspiration. He paused to take from his coat pocket a large linen handkerchief to dab away the beads of sweat. An elevator took them to the top floor, and there in the foyer at the open door were Kamala and her husband. All smiles.

Alina had staged it so that she would be just leaving the Mehta apartment. She achieved her carefully plotted goal. Kamala introduced her to Josie and the inspector. As she had played Shakespeare's Juliet in the ball scene, Alina was shy and demure. She made her exit via the elevator.

Once over the threshold the Utsumis spontaneously started a low bow before their hosts. As is the custom in India, the Paranjotis raised their two hands, palms pressed together to their chests; the mayor, knowing that the Japanese bowed, added a bow. Utsumi and the mayor cracked heads. Josie and Kamala burst out laughing -- like the teenagers they once were in that Swiss school.

Josie thought at once, How useful is the English expression: `the ice is broken;' now we can relax.

"How pleased I am that you have come!" said Kamala as she placed her arm around Josie, who returned the gesture. For the moment Japanese reticence was in abeyance. She touched Kamala's lips with her index finger as if placing a kiss there.

Escorted by their hosts they were ushered into a large living room furnished with elegant rattan and cane chairs and sofas piled high with deep pillows in contrasting color. The inspector didn't mind his coat, because there was air-conditioning; the marble flooring added to the effect of a cool room. He suppressed a sigh of relief. Josie was fascinated by how different were the appointments of the apartment from their Tokyo home. In this country ever warm, I see that the chairs and divan are of woven reeds and rushes, low and close to the floor, she thought as they found seats. Josie had an interest in decor; she had seen to the furnishing of the western part of their Tokyo home. Our deep sofas and lounge chairs would not do here.

Josie looked a good ten years younger than her fifty-odd years. She had a clear complexion, but at this moment she was conscious of her shiny face, due to the heat of noon-day Bombay. From her purse she took a handkerchief and discreetly removed perspiration.

She had brought one silk kimono, in which she knew she looked stunning. The others were of fine cotton, for she had anticipated the humid, hot weather in India before the monsoon rains.

For the long flight from Tokyo, she had chosen to wear a white gabardine jacket and skirt. It appeared simple, but it was a Cardin original. (She dismissed any guilty feeling with the reflection that it was one of her few indulgences.)

In a third-world country, is it possible, the inspector thought, for the Mayor of Bombay to live like this? Before he could comment to Josie, Kamala embraced her friend.

Ever a thoughtful host, Kamala quickly escorted the Utsumi's to the guest room that they were to occupy. There was a large Kashmiri rug with green tendrils encompassing bright blue birds and yellow and pink flowers. The large bed was close to the floor, which pleased the inspector.

"We differ from Japan, traditionally, in that we do not sleep on the floor, but our beds, chairs and tables are low. In such a hot, humid climate, it is cool near the floor. In fact, for that reason, most of our countrymen prefer to sit on the floor rather than on chairs."

"That does not seem strange to us," laughed Josie, in response to Kamala's comments about the height of the furniture. "My grandparents spent most of their waking hours on tatami, sitting and sleeping."

"Since 1947, independence, there's been a big change in the way in which we dress," said Kamala. "Narendra's having been educated at Cambridge, he always dressed formerly and very smartly in London suits. Saville Row. Jermyn Street for shirts and ties."

"As mayor, is Paranjoti-san expected to dress as we've seen him...?" asked the inspector.

Kamala answered, "Despite our speaking English most of the time, men in government and education wear Indian dress -- those tight, white jodhpurs and a knee-length fitted coat buttoned high up to the neck. When my husband's away from the office, he chooses to change into white clothes of hand-spun cotton. I hope you'll not take amiss our casualness here at home."

Josie embraced her dear friend. "I greet *shujin* each evening with a cotton *yukata* and slippers. He's so eager to get out of his uniform and to relax.

"India, dear Kamala, and Japan may be so many miles distant, but, you see, in homely things..."

"We're much the same!" added Kamala. "Our two older children are with my parents. They are so happy to be with my parents, from time to time, in the country.

"My step-daughter Indira has returned from a trip to New Delhi. You'll meet her at dinner."

"Paranjoti-san's daughter by a previous marriage?" asked Utsumi, who had quietly listened to the conversation between his wife and their hostess, Kamala.

"I feel for her. She is resisting an arranged marriage by her maternal grandparents. She's unhappy because she is dark complexioned.

"She has said oh so often, `I wish I could be taken for Italian or Spanish. Not Indian.'" Kamala shrugged.

Josie was shocked, and decided the better part of wisdom was to say nothing.

"You've met our neighbor Alina Mehta. She looks magnificent whether she is in a sari or in an evening dress. She and her husband will dine with us, as well," interposed Kamala, sensitive to Josie's discomfort.

"We dine late. It's cooler..." said Kamala to her guests. Before she could explain further, a bare-footed, *dhoti*-clad servant entered quietly, speaking Hindi to the mistress.

"We're to have tea. Please join me when you are ready," explained Kamala.

Later on the Terrace

"I feel so at home here," said Josie, taking Kamala's hand and pressing it.

"I'm so pleased," said Kamala, smiling at Josie. "Ours has been a lasting friendship." She paused. "But, as we've sat here over tea, I've had the feeling that something is on your mind. Josie?"

Josie's spontaneous reply was, "*Honto, desu.*"

Kamala laughed, "Oh, Josie! Will you ever live it down? That! In Japanese `it's true.' And what you've just said *is* true." They toasted each other with their cups of tea.

"Not a breath of air. It will be hot through the night. We do not have air-conditioning throughout the apartment. Much of the year we depend on fans. We think cool," said Kamala, looking at her friend Josie. "Are you terribly uncomfortable? In the guest room?"

Josie reached out her hand to Kamala, "We have terribly hot and humid weather in Tokyo in July and August. It was like our Tokyo weather when *Shujin* was in New York last August -- so he told me," said the inspector's wife, to reassure her dearest of friends.

"We're always told that the monsoon comes to Bombay by the 10th of June. That's today. It has not drenched Trivandrum in the south of India. We'd have heard. The southwest, Kerala, is panting for it."

Josie let a wrinkle appear on her forehead, "Yes,

it is the 10th of June. Our arrival." She paused a moment, and asked, "You would know if the monsoon had arrived?"

"You'll know, with a certainty, Josie, when the monsoon is upon us. It pours down rain in torrents. You'll think it will never stop. Streets will be flooded," responded Kamala.

"Is it sometimes very late? asked Josie.

"There have been parts of India in the North...A year without the monsoon. I don't like to think about it," sighed Kamala.

"It must be dreadful!" said Josie.

"It is. Famine. The suspense..." said the mayor's wife, closing her eyes.

The two of them sat quietly for some moments. Josie realized it was time to change the drift of their conversation.

"I'm curious about your neighbors, the Mehtas -- Alina Mehta. When I met her -- she was wearing a sari -- I knew that she was not Indian because of her beautiful long blonde hair."

"Indian! Blonde! By no means. But she does wear the sari skillfully. For someone who is not from India, she certainly wears them with flair," responded Kamala. "Unlike us Indians, she does have to use safety pins!" Kamala laughed while divulging this little secret. "Alina discovered that all that we wear in India is with the thought of the climate. A sari gives greater freedom of movement -- it is relatively loose. We feel cooler, even when we're not cool.

"Alina has been in India a long time. She's Polish. An actress. Her maiden name was Crezmar."

"Ah, Polish," commented Josie.

"She came to India from Poland," Kamala reflected. "*Actually*, from London."

"She speaks English very well, and without an accent, but I detected a melody pattern different from what I have been hearing here in Bombay," added Josie.

"I forget when she and her husband Kursi first became our neighbors -- just down the hall. She was far from aloof. Almost at once she took to barging into our apartment. She has spent a good deal of time with us socially. Her husband travels a lot. His business is a travel agency. She seems to have a chip on her shoulder where men are concerned. I bided my time, and eventually, she told me her story," said Kamala.

"I thought communism in Poland had legislated greater equality for women," said Josie.

"Oh, they lay bricks and sweep the streets as women do -- as I've seen them in Moscow," said Kamala, smiling.

Both women laughed. Kamala, as an educated woman working for women's rights in India, did not see in laying bricks and street sweeping the liberation of women.

"Alina thinks she did not fare well under communism," added Kamala. "She had a whirlwind of success, however, as an actress. One leading role after another."

"That can bring in its wake envy of the other actors in the company," said Josie.

Kamala went on, "Warsaw has forty theatres. Just imagine! One of the smaller capitols of Europe."

"Yes, Warsaw is not a large city -- compared to

London, Rome, or Paris. It has forty theatres.? How interesting," interjected Josie. "What prompted her to leave her country?"

"Alina had been married to a doctor. Both had been guilty of open criticism of the Polish government, the Soviet Union. As punishment, her husband was separated from her. He was sent to a small village to practice medicine."

"That would be hard," said Josie, "if she deeply loved her husband."

"To speak frankly," said the mayor's wife as she leaned in closer to Josie, "I think Alina missed the money her husband made as a specialist -- in Warsaw."

"And now she's Mrs. Mehta. Married to a Parsi, you said."

To know when to act and when to refrain
From action, what is right action and what
Is wrong . . .
>   *Bhagavad Gita*

Chapter IX
June 10, 1995
Early Evening

Josie and the inspector had awakened from their rest. It was dark. A barefoot servant was at the door. He spoke directly to the inspector.

"*Sahib*, dinner is served. Please to come."

For her friend Josie, Kamala had donned much of her jewels. A band of diamonds lay in the part of her hair. An emerald graced the left side of her nose, and there was a tiny red paste *thikka* mark of a married woman in the middle of her forehead. Like the band of jewels above in the part of her hair, her earrings were diamonds. Obviously, the mayor -- much in love with Kamala -- indulged her in costly presents. The gold-edged blue sari of Benares silk suited her.

A servant had spoken quietly to Kamala Paranjoti. She turned to her guests and gestured in the direction of the dining room.

Turning to the inspector, Narendra Paranjoti said, "Our custom is to have meat at lunch. The doctor has told Kamala that she lacked protein in her diet. However, our evening meals are traditional Indian meals.

"We're to have pilau with peas, browned onions and raisins, and almonds." Then she added, "There will also be *narigl ka bhat*, coconut rice."

Kamala's family had cotton mills north of Bombay. Husband and wife both came from that area. The mayor's family had income from chemical works. Questions and answers flew back and forth between the couples as to how their flight had been, were they hungry?

Once the amenities had been disposed of, Mayor Narendra Paranjoti looked squarely at the inspector and said, "We've heard a lot about you and your cases in Japan. Your wife Josie is very proud of you, as I daresay you know." The inspector stammered and blushed. He always found it difficult to deal with compliments. He did recognize, however, that it was not false flattery.

Kamala said to Josie, "Your husband is speaking very fluent English! From your letters, I thought it might be difficult for us to communicate with him. It's no problem at all, I see."

The mayor broke in and said, "Oh, I've also heard how the inspector was invited -- and did go -- to spend some days at Quantico, the FBI's national center for the analysis of violent crimes."

The mayor's rapid fire questions had prompted Josie to reply, "The American investigative agency known as the FBI, for the analysis of crime, has created an investigative support unit."

She did the talking now, because she knew that her husband would have had painful difficulty in dealing with so many polysyllabic words.

"The success of the men in the unit's profiling murders had led to requests throughout the USA," Josie went on, "for this unit of the FBI to assist local police in focusing their investigations, to help them catch serial killers. Newspapers around the world began writing about the investigative support unit. It had become news.

"The innovator, Hagmaier-san works in the FBI's Behavioral Science unit. In the FBI's efforts to solve some of the world's most violent crimes, he and his colleagues try to comprehend the incomprehensible. The key, they feel, is to see through a killer's eyes."

"Were the police of Europe ever invited by this unit of the FBI to participate in their seminars for solving crime?" asked the mayor.

"Yes," answered Josie, looking to the inspector.

"Several," spoke up Utsumi. "French, German, English."

"Last year the suicide of the American on the roof of the kabuki theatre had been reported by all of the international wire services, and my husband's role in unmasking the man who had cross-dressed and strangled his victims."

Utsumi would have had difficulty in expressing all that Josie had said in English, but he had followed her last remark and was embarrassed. He waved his hand to get his wife to desist boasting about him.

"Yes?" said Kamala. "Josie, you were about to tell us more? Do go on."

Thus encouraged, Josie went on despite her husband's flushed face. "My husband was invited to attend Technical School, a special two week police course in New York. Sponsored by the FBI."

"FBI? What agency is...?" asked Kamala.

"FBI is an acronym for Federal Bureau of Investigation.   What they had sponsored was a homicide school for two weeks," replied Josie. "It was largely for detectives of the New York City police department. Seven foreigners had been invited to be in the group. My husband was the one Japanese to come to New York for the school."

"*Honto desu,*" said the inspector, interrupting with Japanese. He thought better of it and added, "It's true."

"Oh, that phrase! It brings back memories for me, Narendra, of our school days in Switzerland," chimed in Kamala. She turned to Josie, "Josie was ever using it, Josie. The French students teased you about it. Remember?"

The inspector impatiently wagging his head, interrupted with, "Most informative; privilege of being taken under wing for instruction by Investigative Support Unit. We...a cheerful group. Some from abroad; most from police forces USA." All had been spoken in English, but then he turned to his wife, who recognized at once that he wished her to answer further questions.

Kamala said, "How did you acquire your English, if I may ask, inspector?"

Josie smiled. "Most think we Japanese are always formal. That is not the case," she said. "I know that *shujin* would be honored if you would call him by his given name, Tatsuo."

The mayor laughed, "If I'll not give offense, I think `inspector' would be easier for me. Foreign names are difficult for me, as our Indian names may be difficult for you." All laughed appreciatively.

The inspector wiped his eyes; the laughter had brought tears to his eyes. He said, "I went to intensive course in English at language school, Tokyo. I suffer. One student, me; one teacher. Oh, they change teachers. One teacher not able all day to talk -- teach -- face to face. Eight o'clock morning, to six o'clock night."

"There were five minute breaks after each hour *shujin*, yes?" said Josie.

"*Hai, hai.* Saturday morning at school also," responded the inspector.

Josie nudged her husband as she said, "Let me tell them about the really strange experience you had during the second week of this school. You know, we went to a small *Gaimusho* party -- that's our Foreign office. That evening it was all Japanese."

The inspector grimaced at the recall of that evening. "*Ha-chan,* tell."

"My husband knew the people at this gathering were all speaking Japanese, but the curious psychological phenomenon was that he was hearing them in English."

"That's something for psychologists, right Mr. Mayor?" asked Utsumi.

The mayor nodded vigorously to convey his amazement.

"Were there simultaneous interpreters for the foreigners? As at the United Nations in New York?"

"Yes, but all had to speak some English and understand English, of course," replied Josie.

"*Shujin* -- sorry, that's Japanese for husband -- went to two weeks intensive immersion in English at Tokyo's international language school. As they say, a language school as a business has to succeed with its pupils."

The mayor had reasons for his questions that night. Three more foreigners have been kidnapped. First it was the Joint Commissioner of the Crime Branch that had come to the mayor expressing his concern over these disappearances and serial killings. Why have all these killings ended up at the Towers of Silence, questioned the Joint Commissioner of the Crime Branch?

The mayor knew that it was a delicate matter to take that up with the powerful Parsi community as they might react to it as an accusation.

Despite the smoldering heat -- which had increased it seemed to all -- because of the failure of the monsoon to arrive, the Governor of Maharashtra came to Bombay. In his limousine he had loosened his tie and removed his shoes. On these trips he preferred to wear a European suit. The air-conditioning had failed midway on the trip. He got some small comfort out of cursing in English; his chauffeur, who was Muslim, only spoke Urdu. Like the Sikhs, Muslims are good drivers, thought the governor.

On his last trip to the States, every cab driver he had in New York city was a Sikh. They had abandoned the turban, but the surname Singh, posted in the taxi, confirmed for him that the driver was a Sikh.

He forcibly expressed his concern to the mayor regarding these deaths of foreigners. He cited the fact that the American Ambassador, the French Ambassador, both, had come all the way from New Delhi to call on him.

"The ambassadors have gone to Bombay's city morgue and have been shocked by the state of the bodies. The mayor is under pressure as well from the Rupert family back in the United States. Where might Damon Rupert be? is asking the mayor.

The mayor told his wife Kamala that he was hoping to get Inspector Utsumi -- unofficially -- to help the police force of Bombay solve these crimes that were putting him under a lot of pressure.

That evening a depressed mayor said right out, "Inspector, would you help? We have had these serial killings of foreigners."

"Worst homicides I solve; killings -- without motive," said the inspector.

"Homicides, called stranger murders, have been committed by killers who don't know their victims," elucidated the mayor. "Random killings for the pleasure of killing," he shook his head. "We've had nothing to go on. Nowhere to start."

He turned to the inspector and Josie, "Do you think there's a chance we'll catch him? Or, them? The city of Bombay has twenty-three thousand officers on a day-to-day basis. It would seem ample to me -- with your help."

"I tell you *ha-chan*," said Utsumi. "You are a much better detective than Commander Okubo." He grinned. "Maybe you should be boss."

"Oh, *shujin*," said Josie, knowing her husband was teasing her, but was serious.

He raised his hand to cut off her modest denial. "I want be of help to Indian host, Paranjoti-san. I did..." he hesitated, "well in FBI seminar, New York City. My thought now my English too little."

"I understand what's troublesome for you," said Josie. "It's the Indian melody pattern when our hosts speak English. Had I not spent those early years in England with my parents, I, too, would be lost -- much of the time."

"*Hai, hai, wakarimasu,*" said the inspector. "I tell mayor and commissioner ...more..." He lapsed into Japanese.

"My husband says it's more than he can manage. "I think," she said, " He may have a method, handle, for solving what is happening -- these serial killings."

The inspector's brow was furrowed. "A handle? *Wakarimasen.* I don't understand," said the inspector. "English expression? *Ha-chan?*"

Josie laughed. "They do creep into my Japanese. Do excuse me, *shujin*. I have an idea -- and a plan. I'd rather not speak of it just now, for it may come to nothing."

The inspector clapped his hands together softly. "You have plan."

Once again he turned to his wife, speaking to her in Japanese.

Josie translated, "Together we have plan. We'll do as the FBI does, suggests my husband. We'll try to make a profile, such as is taught, of the serial killer based on the scene of the crime. I'll be in the background, however. In fact, out of view of the ones you talk with. As *Shujin* says, I have a command of the English language."

"It is agreed, *ha-chan*?" the inspector broke in, in English.

Without saying a further word they reached agreement; the four of them were in the study of the mayor's spacious apartment.

Josie brushed the inspector's cheek with a light kiss. This was her way of informing the inspector that she was in accord with his plan.

By devotion to one's own particular duty
Everyone can attain perfection.

Bhagavad Gita

Chapter X
June 10, 1995
Later That night

Alina was sitting in the dark, smoking, on the terrace neighboring to that of the Paranjoti's. She was a mixture of frustrated intelligence and warped, distorted emotion.

"I'm feeling lonely," Alina called over. "I'm bored! This Bombay. All they talk about is the monsoon."

Josie arose and looked across to the Mehta terrace. "Last year. Did the monsoon come as expected? June 10th?"

Alina lighted a cigarette, inhaled deeply, "It was late. All the talk didn't bring it any sooner." Alina expelled the tobacco smoke, making a circle through which she poked her finger. "That's for the monsoon."

Alina regarded Josie admiringly. "May I join you, Mrs. Utsumi?"

"By all means, Mrs. Mehta..."

"Please, call me Alina -- just Alina."

"Very well," replied Josie, "if you agree to call me Josie. Yes?"

Josie heard no reply, for Alina had left her terrace. Little time elapsed before the actress arrived on the terrace to join Josie Utsumi.

Alina had reacted to Josie's speaking English fluently.

With a bluntness that would have jarred most Asians, Alina said, "I'm curious how a Japanese can speak English with no accent."

Josie reacted as a Japanese, but she had become enured to the probing questions from Americans and some Europeans.

"My father was an Ambassador for Japan. My formative years were in England and France -- and Switzerland.

Do you wish that I elaborate?" asked Josie. She hoped she was not being sarcastic.

She ignored Utsumi-san's caustic question, saying "How is it possible for someone Japanese to have the name Josie? Is that for Josephine?"

Adjusting now to Alina's questions, Josie answered, "Upon my return with my parents to Japan, most relatives and friends asked *why* I had the un-Japanese name of Josephine."

"So...?" pressed on Alina.

"During my father's years in Paris as Japanese ambassador to France, my mother joined the French in their fascination and idolatry of Napoleon. She took me often as a small child to the Louvre Museum. Although it bored me and made me impatient, she made a ritual of standing there before David's enormous painting of the coronation of Josephine."

Alina nodded gravely.

"It's no great mystery, you see now, that my mother named her only daughter Josephine. The nickname Josie, from childhood, has stuck. All my intimate friends, and my husband, are accustomed to using it."

"Ah, so you grew up abroad. The child of an ambassador, first to England, then to France. I envy your fluency in French," said Alina, who now felt on closer terms with the inspector's wife.

"Your accent is British. I like it so very much. We ran a risk during those communist years of listening to BBC broadcasts beamed to us," inserted Alina.

"That was most daring and courageous. Mrs. Mehta, Alina, you speak of accents. Yours seems to my ear to be American?" That her English was very good, was implied by Josie in all seriousness.

"Kamala Paranjoti told me that you had in Poland a woman who taught you English. Now you are bi-lingual in English and Polish. What a wonderful thing that is."

"Cecylia Zagorski -- I thought of her as `my governess' -- was born and spent her early years in the United States." Alina detected a slight lifting of Josie's eyebrows. "Oh, the vanity of us theatre people. I should stop this referring to Cecylia Zagorski as a governess. As you undoubtedly suspect, a governess is hardly something that would have existed in communist Poland."

She could almost be Asian, thought Josie. She picked up the slightest reaction -- slightest cue. Ah, that's it, she is an actress. I'm told that's a key to great acting. Acting is more reacting than acting.

"Shall I tell you how it is that I am bi-lingual?" queried Alina.

Josie nodded that she was interested and eager to listen.

"Cecylia's parents had been able to make it out of a refugee camp in Germany -- after World War II. There is a very large Polish community in Chicago, where they settled.

"The church -- the Catholic church -- had helped them make contact with cousins over there, and they were the ones that felt that blood was thicker than water."

"Ah, that expression... thicker than water.' I wonder...do we have something like that in Japanese?" said Josie as much to herself as to Alina.

Alina reacted to this, thinking, Josie after all wasn't very interested. How irritating.

Alina did as she would do on stage; she made a grandiloquent gesture over the tea service and projected rather loudly, "Père Zagorski may have rather detested," she bit out the word, "communism in Poland, but he was active in a neighborhood club committed to socialism."

"Another of life's ironies," interposed the inspector's wife.

"It was more than irony," said Alina somewhat tartly. "He lost his job teaching. He'd been a successful engineer in Warsaw." Before a comment could be made, Alina swept on. "It was a witch hunt, and it had not ended with the death of that senator..."

"McCarthy, I think, was the senator. Yes?" asked Josie, wishing to communicate that she was interested.

"I was about to say: McCarthy," said Alina with a touch of tartness in her voice. "To make a long story short -- how I do of late clutter up my lines with banal idioms. Well, very soon after their return to Warsaw, our families met. The Zagorski's had trouble getting their food coupons. My mother proposed that we share our food from the country in return for their daughter Cecylia teaching me English."

"You had more food than you required?" asked Josie.

"Oh, indeed," replied Alina, warmed by memories of her happy childhood.

"Mother was of a large family. Her brother had remained on the land. My father's being a lawyer and needed by the courts of Warsaw was fortuitous; he had government contacts. As things worsened in Poland under the heel of the Soviet Union, father saw to it that needed parts for farm machines went to mother's relatives."

Alina became pensive.

"Do go on, Alina," said Josie.

"My mother withdrew more and more into herself. Cecylia replaced her, becoming more than my mother.

"I'll never forget the day Cecylia told me she was to marry. My world ended."

Alina had closed her eyes, and she trembled. Josie experienced a flush of sympathy for Alina. She took one of Alina's hands in hers, and squeezed it gently.

Moments passed. Josie broke the silence, "I venture that you found in acting solace, excitement even. When we're young, time does seem to heal."

"Men!" said Alina in a hoarse voice -- much to herself. "I'll always hate the man who married her and took her away from me. They went to Cracow, and I never saw her again."

Josie was taken aback by the intensity with which Alina had uttered, "Men!"

With scarcely a pause, Alina let escape from her a quite theatrical peal of laughter.

"Oh, theatre! I pity all who have not fallen under the spell of incarnation. Yes, that's what it is: taking on the passions of all the myriad characters that live in the pages of the text of a play."

"The inspector and I are more than fans of the kabuki theatre of Japan. For the kabuki actors, theatre is akin to a religion. Their living -- almost totally -- is backstage."

Alina was gazing off from the terrace to the bay -- looking as if she were dreaming.

"I must, I must, must return to the stage. Here in Bombay."

"You are dedicated to your work," said Josie.

"Yes, yes, yes," said Alina without looking at her newly found friend. "I have my own goals. Nothing will stop me from achieving that one single goal."

Josie noted that Alina had ripped apart the dainty lace-edged handkerchief she held in her hand.

Alina had blue eyes which were enhanced by long, dark eyelashes. Her skin was white and opalescent. Her hands were among her best features-- long tapering fingers. She eschewed nail polish. When she chose to wear a sari, which was often, she revealed a taut physique. She seemed taller than she actually was. She moved gracefully. It was possible to see that on stage she would project an illusion of very great beauty.

Her voice was low and melodic. She spoke English with great precision, caressing each word.

"English is a treasure of a tongue," said Alina, speaking softly but with her stage voice.

"My Cecylia spoke to me only in English. Yes, she was more like a mother to me. Now that years have passed I think of her as more important to me than my mother."

There was no response from Josie.

"Polish," said Alina, "is, of course, my language. We Polish actors are not different from our French confrères," said Alina. "We love the nuance of our Slavic language. To feel the words in our mouth is a sensual pleasure."

Alina once again took center stage, "My husband met with an accident. It was fatal, and it was never fully explained to me what caused his death."

"You are now, of course, Mrs. Mehta," said Josie.

"My husband, Kursi, was in Poland arranging for Polish groups to visit India. Over the years Poland -- like the Soviet Union -- sent groups to non-communist countries. He, a travel representative, and I, an actress, met. But that was all."

"How do you find India?" asked Josie.

"*O cholera*, these arranged marriages in India..."

Before Alina could continue, Kamala joined them. After the mayor's wife had observed this innately aloof actress wincing in dismay from those she took to be clods around her, she reflected. *It is then Alina who makes me feel I am touched by ice.* She spoke up, "Ours was a love marriage, Narendra's and mine, but I can see and understand the tradition of arranged marriages. It can be a good thing."

"Never," said Alina, and turned away.

Kamala chose not to react to Alina's disdain and rudeness.

"Even modern-thinking Indian couples have their birth stars plotted before they tie the knot. I'm old-fashioned, I guess, but I think the right birth dates -- an exchange of horoscopes -- is wise before the marriage takes place." She paused. "My step-daughter Indira rejects all that."

Josie was quietly taking it all in. She felt she was not qualified to assess aspects of an entirely different culture. Acceptance, of course, of Kamala's views was easier for her. They had spent so many happy hours together as teenage girls. Although she was Asian, there was much about India she had to work at to be empathetic.

Alina was an enigma. But doubtless Josie resolved to accept Alina as a challenge. She did want to know her better -- if that were possible.

"There are English language theaters in Bombay," said Alina, changing the subject as she turned to Josie. "I've set as a goal that one of the companies produce a play of my heart's desire."

Kamala was called to the nursery by the *ayah*.

Further conversation on the terrace enabled Josie to learn more about Alina.

"I was a leading actress at the National Theatre in Warsaw," Alina revealed. "My husband -- an M.D. -- had run afoul of the communists in Warsaw, and the government had sent him to practice as a physician in a village; so, we were separated. A short time afterwards, he disappeared. I got an annulment to our marriage."

"So Kamala told me. Did you give up acting?" asked Josie.

"No. I managed a move to the *Teatr Wspolczesny* -- the Contemporary Theatre. It had been doing English, French, Swiss plays -- even a few American plays. Thus, I hoped that theatre would do the play that I've wanted to act in ever since I was on the stage."

"Did you succeed eventually?" asked Josie.

"I became disappointed with the Contemporary Theatre. It's director, Erwin Axer, told me, `I prefer to do recent plays.'

"I was frustrated, and I became aware that the shadow of communist disapproval hovered over my head. I became depressed. My mood became darker than it has ever been in my lifetime."

"It was not easy to leave Poland? That's what I have been led to believe," stated Josie.

"Fortune smiled on me. I was able to go with a theatre troupe made up of actors from several of Warsaw's theatres to perform in London. I learned that Roger Lobb of the Royal National Theatre earlier had worried about defections when a young troupe of Soviet actors played there. None did, so management relaxed.

"I defected."

"What, if I may ask, prompted you to come to

Bombay -- to India?" asked Josie.

"Earlier, Kursi, whom I had met in Warsaw, happened to be in London on travel business. He had seen a National Theater poster in his hotel lobby. He reacted, Polish actors in London!

"He bought a ticket. At the performance he saw my name in the program. He came back stage to see me," elaborated Alina. "I knew he was attracted to me, and I seized the moment.

"Kursi enabled me to leave London and to come to Bombay -- my refuge from communism."

The demonic do things they should avoid and
Avoid the things they should do.
Bhagavad Gita

Chapter XI

A young Frenchman, Jules Viaud, stood at the
entrance to the Fariyas Hotel, one of the cheapest
Bombay hotels, but only just. His boss had that
typically frugal Frenchman's attitude towards travel
expenses. A small crowd poured out from the lobby
and jostled him. He was out of sorts. Although his
arrival via Air France had been on time, his travel by
taxi from the Sehar International Airport as part of the
Santa Cruz local airport had been impeded by heavy
traffic.

The driver kept insisting that the hotel was
full. He said, "*Sahib*, I take you to Ambassador Hotel.
Most modern."

M. Viaud was insistent that he be taken to the
Fariyas Hotel. Bombay's hotels, he knew -- as did the
company for which he worked -- are India's most
expensive. At last the taxi pulled up in front of
the hotel, he stared in disbelief at the meter. He was
calculating what it was costing him in francs.

Have I been cheated? he wondered.

Viaud was slight and young looking, despite
his sedentary work in the office of Lysée Import-
Export firm's head office, Paris. He felt stiff from the

long flight. Monsieur Viaud had been in Bombay two years before. After having registered and deposited his luggage in the room assigned to him, he decided to walk the block and a half north to Arthur Bunder Road. Turning right into Mereweather Road, he knew he'd get to the Taj Mahal Intercontinental Hotel and to the monument: the Gateway of India, Bombay's principal landmark.

The Frenchman had read in his travel book that it had been built after the visit of King George V, in 1911. He saw in it resemblance to Paris' Arc de Triomphe. He had an interest in architecture and noted in the description that it was of a Muslim style of the 16th century. He'd been motivated to go there because he'd also read that it was a popular Bombay meeting place in the evenings.

There is bound to be a breeze there off the water, he speculated. Maybe I'll meet someone here who would welcome dining with me. Not all young women are behind locked doors today, in a modern city like Bombay.

Already he could tell that there was more air stirring where the ferries set off for Elephanta Island. Shaking his head, he thought, I am headed in the right direction to see that sand-colored monument, the Gateway of India.

Then he noticed a black limousine drawn up by the curb. But there were other cars about, so he didn't bother to think anything of it. It was not until he was threading his way through the crowded area that he noticed the car seemed to be following him. He could hear it whining along in low gear just behind him and see the yellow glare of its headlights. At the corner of Adams street -- rather than continuing on -- the Frenchman turned left, walking down the other side of the street.

The driver probably had missed his way, Viaud reassured himself. He reached Bhushan Marg. He stepped into the road to make up his mind as to whether to go to the right or to the left. He was confused. A fraction of a second later the car accelerated violently. Jerking around quickly, he saw it swing over towards him. The headlights grew suddenly larger, blinding him. He shouted and tried to jump clear, but the car hit him.

He felt a terrible pain shoot through his legs up to his waist. He lay still, as he was dimly aware that he was lying across the edge of the sidewalk. He tried to raise himself. Then the pain surged up to his chest, and there was a thin, high singing noise in his head. He was losing consciousness, and that noise was his last conscious perception.

The Contessa car had stopped several yards farther on. Rustom got out of the seat next to the driver, walked back, and bending down roughly pushed back one of the injured man's eyelids. He returned to the car.

"Dead?" asked the driver.

Rustom risked a small smile, and said, "No! We want no part of taking a live one to the Towers of Silence this time."

"I'll go back and make certain," shouted Nusswan, as he shifted the gears into reverse. It was late and the side street was for the moment without crowds of pedestrians. The car moved back to the corner. It jerked forward. The wheels bumped twice and came to rest close to the building.

When Rustom returned to the car, he was wiping his hands on his *dhoti*.

"Now?" whispered Varun; he and Arun began to sweat with anxiety.

"*Acha*, dead," Rustom whispered back as he climbed into the seat beside his brother, the driver, and slammed the door. The tires screeched as the car shot forward; it was headed toward Old Ridge Road. Within an hour it would be dawn. The dead man lay in the trunk of the car.

It was twenty minutes before a waiter, leaving the Taj Mahal Intercontinental Hotel and making his way to his home, came upon a pool of blood in the gutter. He paused to study it. He looked in both directions. No one. He walked on.

Every action, every activity is
Surrounded by defects as a fire is
Surrounded by smoke.
                              Bhagavad Gita

Chapter XII
June 14, 1995
Karachi, Pakistan

First Class on Air India was befitting an Indian Mogul. Saris may be hell for the uninitiated to put on and keep on the left shoulder, thought Paul, but they do make a trim Indian stewardess seem the ultimate in femininity. The attentiveness on this flight is just right.

Following lunch he started to nod. Unobtrusively, the stewardess pulled out the leg and foot rest -- all the while slipping a cozy pillow behind his neck.

Thus the flight seemed a short trip -- until the plane thudded down in, of all places, Karachi, Pakistan. "We're making an unscheduled stop at Karachi Airport," came the announcement over the plane's loudspeaker.

"Will it be long,," Paul asked the stewardess. "Will I have time to see something? I've never been in Pakistan before." The stewardess smiled at his naive remark, 'I've never been in Pakistan.'

"It's been requested that passengers not leave the plane." Then she bent low to whisper in Paul's ear.

"There's ever tension between the two countries, India -- my country -- and Pakistan."

Paul thought about that. Religious difference. What had once been one country, ran his thoughts, now is two countries.   Moreover, there was Bangladesh far to the east, a Muslim country. What a world we live in! Will some measure of sanity ever take hold?

Two men in uniform boarded the plane. "A mere formality," came the announcement. "Officers will request to see your air tickets and passports. As captain, I apologize for the delay and any inconvenience." The announcement seemed unusually loud in the quiet cabin.

Paul overheard a stout woman with flaming red hair say loudly, "I think we should all protest. We were not to set foot in this country. How they treat the Hindus..."

"Shhhh! There has been excess on both sides -- India and Pakistan," whispered her male companion. He had a British accent, and his mumbled speech made him sound as if he had just come from the dentist. `Frozen lips,' I'd call him, thought Paul.

Paul extended to one of the Pakistani soldiers his air ticket and passport. The two of them stood close to him. They smelled of sweat and leather. Were it not for the moustaches, he thought they'd look exactly like Hindus. Well, my air ticket seems of no interest to them.

But, as Paul reached for his passport, the soldier holding it stepped away. He was very intent on studying -- memorizing it seemed -- Paul's photograph in the passport and the entrance and departure stampings of European countries he'd backpacked through the previous summer.

What is all this, Paul thought? It gives me an unpleasant feeling.

The youngest of the two soldiers studied his face a couple of times more, checking it against the passport photo.

I'm unhappy about that photo, thought Paul. But then, is anyone ever pleased with a passport photo?

Balancing the passport in the palm of his hand, the soldier quite rudely tossed it into Paul's lap.

These Pakistanis are not very welcoming, Paul thought. "Did the soldier think I was on some list?" he asked the flight attendant.

"No," she whispered.. "One of the soldiers lived in India before Independence. I recognized him. We were such good neighbors. I'll find out more."

The plane took off; at once, champagne was offered to each. In economy, stewardesses assured all that there was no charge for the champagne.

"We want you to overlook this unexpected delay," the steward said as he placed on Paul's table a gift parcel of chocolates, and moved on.

The stewardess returned and whispered to Paul, "Interpol's message to Karachi's NCB was to look for a European woman -- perhaps disguised. Her profile is that she's able to pass even as a man."

Paul said to the stewardess, "I see your name-tag on your blouse. If I were to send you a book of verse I've written in care of Air India, would you get it?"

The stewardess smiled. "Yes," she said. "Poetry. Oh, I love romantic novels. American women have such freedom in your country. We have less in India."

She looked over her shoulder. She seemed poised to say more, but she thought better of it. The male head steward gestured to her to move along.

Paul was never to know what she might have told him.

Bombay, India

The distance to Bombay was covered in a very short time. They landed, and the `buckle your seat belt' sign went off. Up by the cabin, each who had attended them so efficiently were lined up, thanking the pas-sengers.

"We hope to see you soon on an Air India flight," said the head steward. The three sari-clad damsels smiled shyly at the passengers as each passed as if in a receiving line. Paul paused to thank his flight attendant personally.

He concealed his surprise when he felt pressed into his hand a minuscule scrap of paper. He nodded and thanked her.

Once in the airport, Paul could hardly wait to find the men's room. He secreted himself in a cubicle so as to read that unexpected note.

In the dim light, he squinted at the word. The letters were very small, and in an unfamiliar style of writing. His head jerked back as he made the word `beware,' then there was a telephone number. It was not the air-conditioning at the airport that made him shiver as he thought of the disappearance of poor Damon Rupert.

Paul emerged from the men's room and headed to collect his suitcases. Lalit Gupta, one of the conference hosts, was there to greet and assist him.

"Mr. Drake, what a pleasure to welcome you to India. It seems such a short time since we met in Boston. I thank you again for the interview. Our journal was so pleased with what I wrote."

"The pleasure was mine," Paul responded.

Paul was thankful that he would be taken by car to the Taj Mahal Hotel Intercontinental. Customs and Immigration formalities had been brief, and shortly they sped away from the airport.

Mr. Gupta said to Paul, "Tomorrow after you've had your breakfast, the reception desk can direct you to the bureau where you need to go through certain immigration formalities."

"May foreigners drink?" asked Paul.

"You may do so. You no longer have to get a permit in Bombay. We do have prohibition in parts of India," replied Mr. Gupta. "It is due to our great poverty. Many of the poor spend their pay on alcoholic beverages."

From the car, Paul looked out over the flat swampy lands extending in both directions from the paved highway. It was still early morning. He shook himself with disbelief as he saw whole families crouched by rivulets. At no distance from each other -- and with no privacy -- they were defecating. Not far off there were hovels crowded together. Paul now realized fully that he was in a poor country with more than 800 million people. Over-populated. He was deeply moved by the plight of the people. He closed his eyes to blot out what had distressed him. He knew that there was little he could do about it. The Ford Foundation had tried to be helpful.

That there was no comment from Mr. Gupta, seeing his embarrassment at this aspect of India, puzzled Paul. Is he so enured to seeing countless abject poor, that he no longer reacts? Mr. Gupta seems not to be moved at all.

The word *karma* flashed like a bulletin across the retina of Paul's eyes. He had read that Hindus have a deep conviction that the life one is living at this time and in this space had been preordained by the individual's *karma*. It's all part of the belief in transmigration: sins of omission, or sins of commission, account for one's good fortune or for one's bad fortune.

It behooves each, I suppose, thought Paul, that belief in *karma* motivates one to be a better person -- to have good fortune in the next reincarnation.

"You are tired?" said his host. "You would be wise to rest your eyes. It is such a long and tiring drive into the city."

As is characteristic of the peoples of densely populated Asia, Mr. Gupta was sensitive, and he had his own thoughts. Indians are not callous or indifferent to what you, Mr. Drake, are reacting to, he thought. What each of us experiences is tied to what we did in an earlier life. The goal is by good deeds to achieve in the next life a better place. I wonder if he knows about *karma*?

These ruminations brought a lull in the conversation as they drove along in the car, frequently stalemated by heavy traffic.

Paul had read in a travel book for India that taxi drivers are prone to tell newly arriving tourists that the hotel of their choice is full. They suggest another hotel. It's bound to be an expensive hotel, and they pick up a commission for bringing in a guest. `The fact of the case is that they haven't a clue whether a hotel is full or not," read the text. "No taxi driver checks the hotels for occupancy levels. If the tourist wants to go to a specific hotel, he must insist that the taxi driver take him there.

How pleased and relieved was Paul that he had been met and taken by Mr. Gupta to his hotel, who broke the silence with, "The Taj Mahal Intercontinental Hotel overlooks the Apollo Bunder. Launches run from here across to Elephanta Island, which is close to the gateway of India. You will want to pay a visit, as will the seminar group, to Elephanta Island. The sculptured heads of Shiva are accounted among the great works of art of India -- and of the world as well."

Making conversation, Paul asked, "What make of car is this?"

His host replied, "It is a Contessa, made by the Hindustan Motor Company. Some find it uncomfortable. I hope it suits you?"

"I'm most grateful to be met and driven to the hotel. It's a splendid car, as far as I can tell," said Paul.

Having left Santa Cruz's International Airport far behind, they encountered Bombay traffic: cars, trucks, buses, rickshaws, motorbikes all thronged in three traffic lanes. There was swerving, breaking, and a bedlam of honking; each vehicle was fighting for a piece of the road. A policeman vainly tried to control the anarchy.

The chaos continued all the way to the hotel.

Paul had remarked on the flawless blue of the sky. His host responded, "There's still no sign of the rains of the monsoon. All of us long for the relief that it brings. Everything will be different then, and the air will be fresher, lighter. You'll see, all will be cheered and refreshed by the rain."

Bert Appleton was headed for the Taj Mahal Intercontinental, having a confirmed reservation. The driver had met his match. Bert knew what tricks Bombay cab drivers were up to. The drive in from the international airport was spent in silence. The driver sulked. Bert had insisted he turn on his meter.

"Not working," said the driver.

"Very well. We'll report it right now to this policeman over there," said Bert.

"I forget. It fixed. I turn on meter," said the driver. Off they went.

My Tokyo friends, Inspector Utsumi and Josie! I'll be damned! That was a real surprise, thought Bert. We meet here in India.

Bombay traffic slowed the cab to a pace in which both a lazy rabbit and an eager turtle would have reached the city before them. They lurched and stalled as they forced their way to the commercial capital of India.

Bert whiled away the time a, reminiscing. My having shot that *yakuza* youth upon the roof of the kabuki theater was my undoing; possessing firearms in the `Land of the Rising Sun'. I'd have liked to have seen the inspector stare down his commander on my firearms violation.

Yeah, what made me a *persona non grata* among the `nips', remembered Bert ruefully, was my off-the-record chat with that asshole Dick Shepherd. Cultural Officer of the American Embassy! Ha! Everyone around the embassy knew that he was CIA. How dumb of me to tell him that Takashiro Hideoki collected stolen masterpieces: Van Goghs, Monets, Degas. Takashiro, CEO of Sakura Entertainment Enterprises was powerful. Law and order in Japan was a fiction -- for him.

He slapped his forehead in recollection. I knew that! Too bad the inspector's talk with Gaimusho's Kitamura had been futile. I was on my way -- up! No, Kitamura had said bluntly -- I was told -- "For a Japanese to buy stolen goods from abroad makes a bad image for Japan. Search Group, Incorporated has twenty-four hours to remove Bert Appleton-san from Japan."

Ah! sighed Bert, that farewell meeting, and the inspector had to give me the bad news. There was bad with good. He had telephoned me that *okusan* Josie and he wanted to see me. They had made a reservation at a very special restaurant.

"It small. Seven people. Chef *ichi-ban*, number one. I not order. Chef need two days to think. Then remarkable meal for us."

Bert remembered his reply, "It sounds good, but I'm to be out of Tokyo. You told me. No chance for me to stay on for two more days."

That Inspector Utsumi -- a fox. "I have idea. I arrest you, Bert-san." How he chuckled. Bert had screamed into the phone, "What! I'm to be arrested? For what?"

"Bert-san, you no understand. I arrest you. You leave after -- *tabun* -- forty-eight hours."

By god, Utsumi was ever the clever one. "Okay, arrest me. But no handcuffs!"

"*Kekko-desu*."

Bert laughed until tears came to his eyes. That exceptional meal in a tiny restaurant. Josie was bursting with the news. They were going to India.

Now *we* are in India! Me and the two of them -- at the same time. What a coincidence; we've run into each other, in of all places, Bombay's airport.

They suggest my meeting their host, the mayor of Bombay.   I hope that'll make my investigation a helluva lot easier -- a greased track to the Bombay police.

"Whee! What luck," he shouted. The driver jumped.

He who is free from selfish attachments,
He who has mastered himself and his passions,
Attains the supreme perfections of freedom.
                                        Bhagavad Gita

Chapter XIII
June 15, 1995

The morning following Paul Drake's arrival, he was feeling light-headed and irritable from jet lag. He wondered if a Scotch on-the-rocks would lighten his mood.

Damn, he cursed inwardly, I have yet to register. Where is that slip of paper on which Mr. Gupta wrote out the directions to the office for businessmen and non-tourists?

Paul found it tucked into the shirt he'd had on upon arrival.

"What's this? It's wet. The ink is blurred," he exclaimed. He smelled it.

Sweat! What is it they say in 19th century novels: Ladies glow, gentlemen perspire, horses sweat. This has an equine smell. India has turned me into a horse! Such were his reflections, and he laughed at his silly meandering thoughts.

He was able to decipher what Mr. Gupta had written; the Taj doorman -- topped off with a turban -- summoned a taxi from those waiting in rank. Paul had no altercation this time with the driver, for the driver had received directions in staccato bursts of Hindi from the doorman.

At the government office Paul joined a queue and waited. There was no air-conditioning, so it was stuffy and hot. He began fanning himself with his passport. The clerk called him up to the counter.

"This is the place to register? That is what I need to do -- am required to do, as you would say" said Paul, smiling.

The clerk frowned, thinking Paul was being sarcastic.

"You're a tourist? Tourists don't need to come here."

The clerk took Paul's passport. "What's this? An entry visa?" questioned the clerk as he was flipping through the passport, and the visa stamp had caught his eye. "You are here on business?"

"No," answered Paul. "I'm here as a member of an International Writers Seminar. Your consulate back in the states told me to apply for a visa to cover that."

The clerked slapped the passport against his forehead in exasperation. "More rupees from you; more work for me. You see this line?"

Not waiting for a response from Paul, the clerk continued. "Next time, come as a tourist. No one will be the wiser; no one really cares. Spare yourself the expense and the time. Independence didn't free us from red tape..." On and on he unburdened himself with a lecture.

The line of applicants waited in bovine patience. Silent.

At last the clerk dropped on the counter a sepia-colored sheet of paper. "Sign here. Pay your rupees at the cashier." He fixed his eye on Paul Drake, "They don't cash travelers checks."

Paul did as told, and fled the office. Fortunately, the cab had waited.

Norris telephoned Zarina Sabavala. Not only did he make the connection to Bombay without much delay, but he found her at home. He hadn't bothered to check what the time difference was between London and India, and had awakened her. Fortunately, she was delighted to hear from her friend Norris and did not reprove him.

"Zarina!" Norris exclaimed. "How are you today?"

"I'm just fine, Norris. And it's night, not day."

He looked down at his watch and did a few quick mental calculations. "Oh, my gosh, I'm so sorry," he said when he realized the time in India.

"Don't worry about it. I'm always happy to speak with you. What's up? Is there something I can do for you, or are you just calling to say hello?"

"Well, actually," he said a bit hesitatingly, "there is something."

"That's fine, Norris, what is it."

"A good friend of mine, an American named Paul Drake, will be arriving shortly in Bombay. He's going to be a participant in an International Writers Seminar here."

Before he could say more, Zarina cut in, laughingly, "And you'd like me to play tour-guide to this American friend? Well, I will. I so miss New York. The four years I spent in America at Barnard College were the best years of my life, so far. I'd love the chance to help your American friend."

"Thanks so much, Zarina. I thought if you could help him get oriented to the city a bit, he might get on better."

"I'm sorry, Norris, but what did you say his name was?"

"Paul Drake," he replied at once.

"Wait. Let me go get a pen and paper so that I can write this down. Hold on, okay?" She put the phone down and hurried to find writing materials.

Norris, meanwhile, was feeling very pleased that all was going so simply -- getting the two of them together. He was thinking, too, that were he to have to pay for this call...Well, he didn't want to go on talking much longer. He heard her returning to the phone. The phone began to crackle and hiss.

"Norris?" Zarina shouted. "Are you still there?"

"Yes."

"It sounds as though our connection is beginning to go. Better give me his name and hotel -- fast."

"Paul will be at the Taj Mahal -- not the old one -- but the Taj Continental. Just leave a note for him at reception. Paul knows your name, but he'll need to know how best to contact you. Okay?"

Norris faintly heard her saying, `I will...' The

connection was severed. "Damn! So like a long distance call to that part of the world. Oh, well, it saved me money."

Paul was really feeling the heat. His hair stuck to this scalp, and his shirt was soaked through. He sped past the reception desk, walking briskly to the bank of elevators. All I want is to get to my room and change, he thought. But first, he thought, a tub full to the brim of nice, cold water.

Just as he was stripping off his clothes, he noticed the flashing red light on his bedside phone. "Who could be calling me here?" he muttered.

"Oh, wait, of course! I know who it is. It must be Mr. Gupta." It wasn't.

"Mr. Drake," came a disembodied voice, "this is the reception desk. There is a message for you. We will deliver it to you at once -- if it is of no inconvenience to you."

"Please do," was Paul's reply. Someone from the front desk must have already been on the way, because there was an immediate knock on the door. Forgetting that he was standing there naked, he went to the door and was about to open it.

"Just a moment!" he cried in panic, suddenly remembering his state of undress. What to do? he thought, his eyes raking the room for something to cover up with. He settled for the nearest object to hand, a large pillow from the nearby easy chair which he picked up hurriedly. Holding the over-sized throw pillow in front of him, he opened the door a crack and grabbed the envelope off the tray, before hastily closing the door.

"Now I've done it," he muttered. "I didn't give him a tip. Word will spread fast about that, you can bet. My name will be mud around this hotel. I'll have to try and find out who brought it up to me...so that I can -- Oh, shit!"

He simultaneously dropped the pillow on the floor and tossed the unopened letter on the bed, then rushed into the bathroom, where the huge, oversized British-type tub was about to overflow. "Oh, my god," he exclaimed, surveying the tub. "It must be gallons and gallons full. What a mess that would have made if it had slopped onto the floor."

Paul slid into the water, mindless of the goosebumps its temperature induced. "Now this feels good," he said, punctuating each word with enthusiasm. Fully immersed at last, and just as he was beginning to relax, it struck him that he'd not opened or read the letter. Curiosity being one of his failings, he jumped out of the tub -- nearly slipping and falling spread-eagle on the marble floor.

Paul was twenty-seven years old, lean and tanned; he had straight blonde hair which he had let grow long. As of now, he kept it pulled back in a ponytail which was presently dripping water all over the floor as he headed straight for his bed, and the envelope he'd tossed there.

Once he'd torn open the envelope and had read the short note he said, "Not Mr Gupta, after all. It's from Norris Brown's friend."   He dressed hurriedly, bent on telephoning Zarina Sabavala as soon as possible.

Fully dressed, he headed for the phone. It suddenly struck him that it was mighty silly of him to have dressed to make a phone call. "I needn't have dressed to telephone her from the privacy of my room." He laughed. "I could have done it at once, stark naked. She'd never know the difference. Now I may have missed her." He hadn't.

The call was brief, as Zarina was on her way out the door when the phone rang. A meeting was arranged for that evening. "We'll meet in the downstairs of your hotel," had proposed Zarina. "Hotel reception -- I'll arrange it -- can point us out to each other. I'll be seated in the lobby."

Later that evening Zarina arrived at the hotel, and as promised, arranged for someone to see that she and Paul did not miss each other. The clerk at Reception came out from behind the desk and ushered Zarina to a chair. The Sabavala name was well known, and one to be reckoned with.

Covertly he studied her as she waited, poised and calm. She wore the lavender, gold trimmed sari with elan. She preferred pastel colors. Although pastels were not seemingly easy to come upon; the fine cotton sari she now wore had been found on one of her shopping trips to the market place. The color had been vegetable dye, and she knew that they would not fade.

She was somewhat dark-complexioned, and one who did not know that she was a Parsi would assume that she was Hindu. She was not tall of stature. Dark brown eyes added to her beauty -- like lustrous pools. She seemed to look out on the world as if she were amused.

The clerk sighed and returned to his duties, leaving Zarina to wait alone. She did not have to wait long.

Paul was prompt. He exited the elevator and headed straight for the Reception desk. The clerk pointed. Paul turned...and promptly thanked whatever gods that be for the fact that he was leaning against the Reception desk. She's astonishingly beautiful, was his immediate thought.   He was momentarily speechless.

Regaining his tongue, he muttered, "Thanks," before heading towards the beauty before him.

"Zarina?" he stammered. "Zarina Sabavala?"

And then she smiled.

He'd thought her stunning just moments before, but when she smiled, it was like the sun coming up at dawn -- beautiful beyond words.

"Yes, I'm Zarina Sabavala," she said, immediately put him at ease by taking his arm and walking him toward the hotel's revolving doors. Zarina found Paul handsome. Her one reservation, so far -- which she'd keep to herself -- was his hair. Attractive as she found blonde hair, it was long. Oh, I understand it's now the fashion, she mused, but....

She found the thought of an evening with such a handsome American exciting, but masked her excitement by taking charge. "I suggest we go to eat in Nabob Corner, in the hotel Nataraj."

"Where is it?" Paul found his tongue long enough to ask.

She stopped just short of the revolving door and turned to face him. Her intention had been to answer his question about the restaurant, but when their eyes met she forgot what she was going to say. They just stood there like two wax figures.

Paul suddenly snapped to, and with a sweeping gesture indicated that Zarina precede him through the door. He leaned forward, intending to push on the door. Unfortunately for Paul, the turbaned doorman had beat him to it; one of the revolving door's fins knocked him in and up against Zarina.

As accidents will, it broke the tension between them. "I'm so sorry," said Paul, who had joined Zarina in laughing.

"Think nothing of it. It's another form of introduction," she managed between peals of laughter. The door forcibly ejected them out; they almost bumped into the doorman.

Once more serene, Zarina said, "To answer your question -- if you remember it -- the restaurant and hotel are on Marine Drive. Not far. The food, I'm told, is excellent and there's a sitar player."

"Wow!" shouted Paul with enthusiasm. "Now I know I'm in India!" He couldn't resist taking a leap in the air, bringing his heels together a foot above the pavement. He was exuberant as they waited for their taxi to pull up.

Once in the back seat of the auto, Paul was in for a surprise: Zarina took a package of Pall Mall cigarettes from her purse -- offering one to Paul. He declined with a nod of his head. He had never smoked; nor had his parents.

"I needed that!" she said after inhaling deeply. "I smoke an occasional cigarette. I got the habit at Barnard College. All my friends smoked," Zarina said. "I know what you may be thinking. Parsis don't smoke; it's a desecration of fire. I do get twinges of guilty feelings."

Paul's reply was, "I knew from Norris that you were Parsi, but why is fire important to Parsis?"

"Fire in our temples is sacred, symbolic of divinity," said Zarina as she put out the cigarette.

Nothing that Zarina might do was to disenchant Paul Drake. The evening went swimmingly for both of them.

Soon she introduced him to the Mehta's -- Alina and Kursi. This, in turn, led to his meeting Mayor Paranjoti and Kamala, and their guests Inspector Utsumi and Josie Utsumi.

> He who fills his lamp with water
> Will not dispel the darkness,
> And he who tries to light
> A fire with rotten wood
> Will fail.
> *The Gospel of Buddha*

Chapter XIV
June 18, 1995

Josie faced a dilemma after her rest during the heat of the day. What to wear that evening. Should I wear a kimono? she wondered. If it just weren't so hot!

She decided to cleanse her face thoroughly, knowing that removing the excess perspiration and oils from her skin would help to refresh her even more than her rest. Josie smeared a thick, deep-cleansing facial mask on first, muttering to herself, "The monsoon is late. Eight days late! Will it come soon?"

Then she caught sight of herself in the mirror, and couldn't help but laugh at the reflected image. She not only sounded strange to herself -- uncharacteristically grumpy -- but she looked funny, too. Her face was presently covered in a green facial goo. The green face did it -- snapped her back to her usual humorous and unflappable self.

It's just that everywhere I go, she thought, someone mentions that the monsoon is late, and will it come soon? Ah, well, she sighed. I wonder about that myself. Josie returned to the closet in her room, her face still tingling from the recent cleansing, a not unpleasant sensation.

Now to the problem at hand, she thought. What to wear this evening. A kimono? *Iie*, a kimono's too confining, reaching down below the ankles.

Kamala entered, having knocked. Josie could not help but notice how cool she looked in her sari.

"How do you do it, Kamala?"

"Do what, my friend?"

"Look so cool on such a hot day!"

"The proper clothing helps."

"Yes," said Josie, returning to look at her closet space contents. "I was just trying to figure what would be coolest to wear this evening. My conclusion is that I own nothing suitable for this pre-monsoon heat."

"Which is precisely why I am here." said Kamala with a smile. "I thought you might wish to go shopping. Perhaps to find a sari?" Earlier, Josie had expressed a desire to buy some saris and was enthusiastic about the idea.

"It sounds like great fun, but you will have to teach me how to wear them," said Josie.

"Oh, you'll get the hang of it very quickly, I'm certain. It does take practice. They don't stay put, much as we would like them to. You'll notice how I seem to be repeatedly adjusting the sari."

"A reflex action of which you're unaware, I dare say," commented Josie. "Like our slipping out of zoris -- changing them for different parts of the house."

"Hmmm," murmured Kamala. She rang for a servant. A woman appeared, and she spoke to her in Hindi.

"I asked that several of my saris be brought. Let me start to teach you. Then you may better be able to decide, Josie, if you want to shop for saris -- to wear them."

Josie beamed. A new experience, she thought.

"When you wear a kimono, what undergarments do you wear?"

Josie opened her suitcase. A simple hand gesture gave Kamala unspoken permission to examine the contents. With no hesitation whatsoever she immediately extracted a simple skirt and blouse.

Once Josie had put on her underskirt and blouse, Kamala picked up a green silk sari, trimmed with a band of gold. Josie watched as Kamala shook open the yards of material. The breeze from a nearby fan caught the folds of the green silk garment, which for a moment caused it to linger like gossamer in the air before drifting gently to the floor. She moved in close to Josie and picked up one end of the sari, tucked it into the waistband of Josie's skirt, made the pleats and then with a flick of her wrist, inverted the pleats and tucked them into the waistband.

As she draped the *palu* -- the end of her sari -- across Josie's breast and pinned it into place with one of her broaches, Josie said, "I can't believe how quickly you did that!"

Kamala just smiled. She mimed that Josie turn, for she wanted to check to make sure that the back of the sari had not risen up with the pinning of the *palu.*

Kamala was pleased with how the sari looked on Josie and nodded her approval. "It looks very good on you. The green and gold go well with your skin and hair coloring." She waved her hand toward the mirror in the corner. "Go. See for yourself how beautiful you look."

Josie glided gracefully toward the large, free-standing, oval mirror, turning this way and that to get a good view from all directions. "Oooh!" she sighed breathlessly, pleased with her appearance. "I will most definitely want to buy saris! A lot of them." She smiled happily as she once again gazed at her reflection.

Kamala preferred to shop for saris at the stalls that lined the markets. She enjoyed friendly bargaining, while sitting on a small bench, relishing the feel and the beauty of the silk saris tossed one after another by the merchant before her on a white sheet.

It may have been a custom once in Japan, ran Kamala's thoughts, but I know in the big cities and in department stores in Tokyo prices are fixed. I don't want Josie to be upset. Seeing her as a tourist, the sales people would raise the price.

Kamala liked to drive her own car, but for taking Josie and her step-daughter Indira shopping, she had her husband's car and driver. They slowly made their way through Bombay's heavy traffic.

"So many cars, like Tokyo," commented Josie. "In Tokyo I don't like the underground -- except in off hours, I *do* use it. It gets me there quickly."

Kamala's step-daughter Indira had asked to go with them. "I need a change of saris. Mine have become ragged at the edges," said Indira.

Fortunately, she was slim, because she had squeezed in between Kamala and Josie. As was often Indira's habit, she was silent, staring into space as they inched their way among the competing automobiles.

Sacred cows had begun to munch some vegetable greens that had fallen in the middle of the road from a truck. It was twenty minutes before the cows moved on. Drivers accepted such blockage of a highway and waited until the sacred animals move on.

At the shop Indira began to remove saris from shelves, shrugging off the attentions of the clerk.

In another part of the store Josie and Kamala were offered a cola soft drink or tea by a young boy. The clerk gave the orders and shooed him away.

He greeted the mayor's wife with a *'Namaste,'* hands pressed together close to his breast. He bowed slightly.

"May I help you? What, may I ask, do you require?"

Kamala made a token *namaskar*, a spontaneous reaction from years of having done it. Josie followed suit -- though it felt strange to her. She never remembered returning a bow to a clerk in a Tokyo department store.

Indira, with a pile of saris at her feet on the floor, called over to Kamala, "Momaiji, just look at this, and this, and this!" She held up one sari after another. Tearfully, she cried, "They make me look so dark. Positively black."

The clerk had returned, and Indira said to him disdainfully, "Take them away!"

Josie was very pleased with the saris she had purchased, and she chose to stay on and do more shopping in the area. Kamala took a taxi, so that the driver and car could bring Josie and Indira back to the apartment when they were prepared to leave the area.

After the fruitless visit to the shop with Kamala and Josie, Indira was silent on the way home. She turned to Josie as if to say something, but changed her mind. For a Japanese, thought Indira, she seems very modern. No accent in her English. Were I to hear her talking without seeing her, I'd think she was English.

Josie asked, "Indira-san, is there something you wished to say to me? I'm `all ears,' as the Americans are prone to say."

"No, Josie Aunty," responded Indira. "I've forgotten what it was. Probably something banal." She turned to look out the car window.

A man weighted down with a huge bundle on his head, wheeling a cart, had been jostled by pedestrians. The bundle from his head lay in the road. The chauffeur braked at once. A crowd gathered. Cars and bicycles began to honk angrily.

Why doesn't the chauffeur help the poor old man? thought Josie. No doubt it's this caste thing. I'll never understand...!

"Why doesn't our car push it out of our path? If he were my driver, I'd tell him," spat out Indira. She'd been cross all day, and this triggered her need to vent some anger.

Josie was shocked. She dearly wanted to tell

this spoiled child, `The inspector would have been out there to help, even if someone told him that it was a *burakumin*,' but she held her tongue.

A policeman stepped out of the staring crowd. Quickly sizing up the situation, he ordered two nearby beggars to load up the old man, then proceeded to sort out the traffic jam. The Paranjoti car moved along speedily to Malabar Hill.

Indira, recalling her manners, opened the apartment. "Josie Aunty, I hope you have a good rest."

"Thank you, Indira-san. Too bad you didn't find a sari you liked," said Josie. She went at once to her room

Indira stood there before the elevators, immobilized by her feelings. She was in a quandary.

Alina stepped out of the elevator. Seeing Indira in the hall, she turned on the charm. "*Moi Bozie,* what a hot and humid day!" she exclaimed, fanning her face with one hand. "You agree, Indira?"

Her dramatics were totally lost on Indira.

"We're used to it," said Indira. "That's why we never fear invaders. The heat always finishes them off."

"Do you mean me, a poor Pole?" sighed Alina. Then she laughed. "Indira, dear, would you help me with this key?" Alina was too vain to wear her glasses, except in the privacy of her own bedroom.

"Hmmm? I'm sorry, Mrs. Mehta. You were speaking to me?"

"Yes, I was, but you seemed in another world. Day-dreaming, no doubt, as all young girls are prone to do, yes?"

"What was it you wanted?" Indira replied, ignoring Alina's probing.

"I was asking for help with this key."

"Key?"

A lesser woman might have been put off by Indira's brief response -- not so Alina. She fumbled with the key. "Will the monsoon never come?"

Indira seemed to be in some sort of a trance. Alina gently steered her to the door of her apartment, placing the key in Indira's hand. The door swung open, a bare-footed servant stood within the opening. "What we both need is a large glass of lemonade," she said. "And I'll not accept `no' for an answer." Indira smiled faintly.

As Alina pulled the blinds against the late afternoon sun, she expostulated under her breath, "That houseboy! He never follows orders. I'll speak again to Kursi about this. My husband is too soft with the servants."

The houseboy did have a large jar of lemonade in the refrigerator. Alina tasted it. Not bad, she thought. A dollop of vodka will make it just what Indira needs. A pick-me-up for me as well.

Deep shadows in the darkened room, air-conditioned, invited relaxation.

As the two sat there, Alina appraised the young Indian girl. She has a shapely figure any woman would envy, me included. Deliciously long black eyelashes. What a pity! she thought. Such beauty wasted. So right for the stage. But she lacks the temperament. No brio!

Indira became conscious of the gaze fixed

upon her. It did not disconcert her, rather having lost her mother at an early age, she liked the admiring glances and attention of women.

"My cook is such a prattler. She keeps saying she can't understand why you're not married. Of course, she's locked in the culture -- India. She thinks your father should have picked a groom for you at thirteen at least." This was all fiction. Alina was trying to find out if Indira were betrothed.

"Oh, Alina! You're European. Maybe you'll understand. I've wanted to talk with someone for so long."

"What is it, Indira? I will help in any way I can...if you will let me?"

"I feel so trapped. There's been no change here in India. Fathers, family...they rule our lives!" Indira exclaimed, throwing her hands up in a gesture of despair. "Was your marriage in Poland an arranged one?" The words seemed to gush forth as if they had been pent up for a long time.

Figuratively, Alina took center stage. She moved closer, taking both of Indira's hands in her own. "Tell me," she said in a commanding voice. "Everything. Leave nothing out." She evoked in her voice cello tones, closing her eyes dramatically.

"There isn't much to tell. Daddyji is the mayor. It is politics that gets his attention -- and Kamala." Before Alina could respond, Indira rushed on, "Don't misunderstand me, I love Kamala. She's my best friend -- perhaps my only friend."

"Now that we're sharing feelings, I hope you'll think of me as a friend," said Alina. "In the country -- of Poland -- marriages are still likely to be arranged.

To join farms. It can be as simple as that. Country men can be such louts. Poor girls." She paused to keep the attention of her audience.

"I was very young. The doctor was very ardent. I'd gone on the stage at an early age. Two professionals made the decision to marry. We liked each other -- I suppose you could say we loved each other."

"How wonderful such freedom seems to me."

"So," said Alina raising her brows. She looked Indira up and down, pausing briefly at her arms and feet. "I don't see any chains on you. Is there someone you fancy?"

"I'm not sure," said Indira, blushing a bit. "There is a young man I came to know while I was in school in England..."

"An Englishman!" Alina said teasingly.

"No, no," said Indira. "He's from Bombay. In fact he's here in Bombay now. He's Parsi. I slip out from time to time to meet him; we have tea or walk on the beach. If my grandparents knew!" She shuddered, not wanting to think about what would happen if his parents -- her grandparents -- ever found out.

"India. I could say `Asia'! A young woman -- unattended -- in the company of a male."

"Men have it all their way!" Alina added with a fierce intensity.

"The Paranjoti family is very powerful. Very rich. It's difficult for Daddyji to stand up to them. You see..." said Indira.

Alina's misanthropy swept over her. "Your young man's being a Parsi -- I'm convinced -- would

not upset your step-mother or your father. Right?
They've been educated abroad. They are modern,
emancipated, I'd say," said Alina.

"As you know -- silly of me to even say it --
my husband is a Parsi. Might we not find -- soon -- an
opportunity to introduce -- sub rosa -- your Parsi
young man at one of your father and mother's dinner
parties?"

Indira burst into tears. "I'd be so grateful,
Alina Aunty." This was the first time she'd linked the
Aunty appellation after Alina's name.

Alina nodded. "Fine, then. Leave everything
to me. In fact, I'm eager to meet your young man.

"This lemonade is too tame. Let's have
cocktails. What do you say?" Alina kissed Indira on
both cheeks as lightly as if done by butterfly wings.

Kamala arrived home. A servant had let
down the bamboo shutters, so that the sun was shut
out and the room became dim and cool. On the floor
lay grass mats -- she rested for a moment on a chaise
lounge beside which was a low table. The house-boy
had brought her an iced tea.

Some flowers would be the right touch,
calculated Kamala. I'll send a servant to buy some;
and a place setting for the dinner table as well. She
crossed to a cabinet and picked up a fine wood carving
of Lord Shiva.

"How gentle and smiling were the Balinese
craftsmen where I bought this statue of Shiva,"
murmured Kamala. "How different seemed Hinduism
in Bali."

        Mayor Paranjoti had taken the inspector to the Bank of Tokyo, which was not far from the town hall. Later he took Bert and the inspector to the David Sassoon Library at 152 Mahatma Gandhi Road.

        "This was founded in 1847. Sad that it's now in a street of dingy shops," said the mayor. Then turning to Bert, he said, "If your investigation involves research, this may prove to be of some help to you."

        Paul Drake and Zarina Sabavala, as dinner guests, arrived. The Mehtas walked in without having knocked or rung the bell. The inspector ushered in Bert Appleton.

        Josie asked Kursi Mehta about the Parsi community.

        "The Parsi leaders early on advised the community that they not alienate their Hindu hosts, admitting into their ranks caste Hindus," said Mr. Mehta.

        "The Christians have had their troubles for having accepted lower caste Hindus into their community," said the mayor.

        Kursi Mehta was asked by Paul Drake to tell them more about Parsis, as practicing Zoroastrians.

        "Ours is an ancient religion of the Aryans, and the prophet Zoroaster is said to have lived in 7000 B.C. What is little understood by non-Parsis -- even here in India -- is the *Dakhma-nashini* mode of disposal of our dead, " Kursi began. "The belief has persisted for centuries untold that the dead body is polluting spiritually as well as physically. In the scripture, burial and cremation are both considered wrong actions; the one polluting of the earth and the other polluting fire.

"You told us on another occasion of the importance of fire in the temples," commented Kamala.

"The Towers of Silence. The fact that we can't go near them has made me curious. What happens there?" asked Paul. "I choose to think it is not morbid. I'm a writer, and I want to know as much as I can about -- everything."

Kursi nodded his head indicating that he understood. "The area is entangled in vines; not even Parsis, unless they are dead, are welcome at the burial towers. The body is placed by special bearers in a circular well-shaped structure. You know about the vultures. Guides never fail to point them out flying and circling high above the area. Well, the vultures and the sun destroy the dead body.

Paul either had not noticed Zarina's gesture that he desist from asking still more about burial customs, or he ignored her wish that she wanted him to change the subject.

"What about the bones? Are they gathered up?"

"No," replied Kursi. "The limestone contributes to the decomposition of the larger bones, and whatever bones are left over are washed away by the rains of the monsoon.

"I am not repelled by this Parsi practice. We are convinced that we've found an admirable solution. That you may not agree does not trouble me." Kursi Mehta smiled, turned, and left the room.

The path of action is better than renunciation.
Bhagavad Gita

Chapter XV
June 19, 1995

One morning Alina, unannounced, slipped out on the terrace. She had seen Josie from her terrace. After a rather curt acknowledgement that it was a good morning, Alina asked Josie, "Are there cases of AIDS in Japan?"

The question, having been put so bluntly and out of left field, as it were, shocked the inspector's wife. I am Japanese, she thought; such a question would have come after some conversations leading up to it.

Alina greeted Josie's silence with, "*O bose moj*, I have put my foot in it. I do beg your pardon, Mrs. Utsumi. You see, I am very active now in Bombay for alerting all -- men and woman -- of the danger... if safe sex is not practiced."

"I am chagrined," responded Josie. "I fear I reacted as a Japanese. Everything is so oblique in our country. There's an English sxpression: We beat around the bush -- even asking for a glass of water."

"It eases my mind. What you tell me." said Alina. My years in the theatre...we call a spade a shovel -- to use and change an English expression. Sometimes for a day we have to strip down to the skin in the wings for a quick change. Modesty is out of place around a troupe of actors."

"Please be assured, Mrs. Mehta, I am not offended. It comes under the heading of cultural shock. One part of me is not used to such directness.

"Sad to say, there is AIDS in Japan. For too long it has been denied. Some young men -- if they can afford the cost, 4,000 in dollars -- go to a clinic in Hawaii for an HIV test."

This puzzled Alina, who waxed keenly interested in attitudes toward this spreading infection.

"No health clinics giving tests for HIV -- positive or negative?"

"Oh, yes," said Josie forcibly. "There is now government concern. So many street prostitutes in our cities. Desperate aliens from the Philippines and South East Asia. There is no such thing -- like Purdah as in India -- where women remain apart at home, but our young women would feel -- not guilt, but shame if they had intercourse before marriage. Young Japanese men -- now under much pressure in business -- take risks."

"It's poverty here that has led to widespread prostitution. I read in an American newspaper that AIDS will claim the lives of more people in India than in any other country. There is little or no blood screening. Ten million Indians will be infected with the HIV virus -- some experts say that by the end of the century, 20 million or 50 million will be infected. Most victims are in the city of Bombay."

Josie shuddered.

"Asia has the fastest growing epidemic in the world. When I learned that -- may I again call you Josie? -- I just had to do something. You agree?"

Josie nodded her head up and down vigorously.

"I must take you and the inspector to these slums where there is such degradation."

"You go there?" asked Josie in amazement.

"My husband disapproves, but I've organized groups of college students to penetrate these areas. As well as some Catholic monks -- there are Christians in India.

"Many Indians can not read, but still we leave flyers. More important, we hand out condoms -- explaining their use."

"I'm Christian, and I subscribe to the passing out of condoms in this age of wide-spread disease. But, Catholic monks?" asked Josie.

Alina shrugged. Then as if seeking a reaction from Josie, she said, "There's an old Portuguese Catholic church. A young monk has been most accommodating to me."

"How admirable," said Josie softly. "Are they being used -- the condoms?"

"I hope so. Men are such pigs," bristled Alina. "They threaten the girls -- some so young -- if they ask the men to use a contraceptive."

"It's for their protection, too," exclaimed Josie.

I feel ashamed now, thought Josie, that I've had such negative feelings about Alina. But, she does have a low opinion -- a hatred -- of men.

Unaware that Josie had company on the terrace, Kamala stood there in the doorway, "I feared you were alone, Josie. Do I interrupt?"

Before Josie could respond, Alina said, "By no means. Do join us."

Kamala had overheard all that Alina was saying about her work toward creating awareness of the threat of AIDS. Her emotions were drawn in two conflicting directions. On the one hand, she was truly moved by the Polish woman's commitment to do something dynamic about curbing the spread of this disease in Bombay -- even all of India.

On the other hand, she could not quite free herself of doubts about the Polish woman that stemmed from her first impression she had formed of her a year before. Alina and her husband Kursi had taken the adjoining apartment. Alina had rather forced herself on her neighbors, the Paranjotis.

`First impressions are valid ones -- much of the time,' said one of her teachers at the Rousseau school in Switzerland.  `As on an exam, the first answer to a question is usually the correct answer.' I'm eager to learn what Josie thinks when she and her husband have some moments alone with me. Josie is quick at sizing up people -- as I recall.

Alina invited the two of them to cross the hall to her apartment. "I'd like you to see the posters and flyers we've had printed. We've had some trouble with the Bombay tourist office -- even my husband's travel agency. `You'll drive away tourists. That's taking the rice out of our mouths!' is their cry. I scorn their greed."

Josie just shook her head. "How universal. Business blinding itself to what is a threat to all."

The caste system here in India strikes me as

such a sad phenomenon," said Josie, but..."We have the *eta*," said Josie. "Our people suppress even to themselves its existence. Our untouchables are now referred to by another name: *burakumin* -- common people. It's a futile euphemism. I am troubled by it."

"When a Parsi business group denounces our organization's efforts to combat AIDS -- I shout it out at my husband when angry, `It's not Zoroaster you bow to in the temple, it's Moloch -- greed.'"

Blood had risen to her neck and cheeks, negating, for the moment, her exceptional beauty.

Wishing to change the subject, Kamala interposed, "The Parsi community is much admired in India. No threat to Fundamentalist Hindus, since no one can choose to be a Parsi. Members of the Harijans -- the untouchables -- have never been admitted to the Parsi community."

Josie and the inspector had easily adjusted to living in an apartment, quite different for them, as they were used to a large house and garden. Their hosts made it easy. The Paranjotis, husband and wife, made them feel free to make their own schedule. They did not impose sightseeing on them. This was of importance to Inspector Utsumi, since he had agreed to help the Bombay police solve the serial murders of young foreigners.

Once again, Kamala and Josie were alone on the terrace. The luxuriant planting gave shelter from the yellow morning light. Despite the heat of the morning pressing down, the plants and flowers created an illusion of coolness, but no air stirred.

"You know what is on my mind, and I've not spoken of it," Kamala sighed as she said it. "Next year will be the 50th year of India's independence from Britain, and we have failed."

Josie made a gesture, as if to say, `Oh, no!'

"Yes, we have failed. I agree with Narendra that India is pockmarked with compromise."

Josie responded, "I've been reading your newspapers, *The Statesmen, The Times of India.* Few countries are as self-critical as India."

"True," said Kamala with a rueful smile. "But there is high-level corruption -- so brazen and with so little stigma.

"The decline in political standards began with Nehru's daughter, Indira Ghandi."

"How sad," murmured Josie.

"The Nehru-Ghandi family started the rise of Hindu Fundamentalism, the pandering to caste instead of overcoming it, the appalling corruption and refusal of the state to enforce the law," said Kamala, waxing emotional.

"I remind you of the *eta* we have in Japan. Parents of prospective bridal couples search the respective family lines without being troubled by the injustice of class discrimination," said Josie, hoping to comfort her friend.

"Dear Josie, I fear what you say is just cold comfort," responded Kamala. "And now the disgrace of these serial abductions of foreigners -- the killings.

In this Mahrashtra state -- where Bombay is situated -- the *Shiv Sena*. I've said to Narenda, the singling out of the Parsis, a minority, may be a revival of "The Army of Shiva'!

Josie shook her head, "I know nothing of your political factions, but it does interest me. Our *Ainu* to the north . . ."

Kamala interrupted with warmth, "At first *Shiv Sena* primarily sought eviction of South Indians. They looted and burnt down shops. The police, largely Maharastrian, did little to stop the violence. They won a significant number of seats in the city's governing body. A lunatic fringe was opposed to all minority groups."

"You do have a point, " said Josie.

"I could believe they are trying to drive the Parsis out of Bombay," said Kamala.

Josie wished to change the subject. "What each of us wants to talk more about is our home and children."

Kamala nodded her head in agreement and smiled, as she poured the green tea. She had chosen green tea because she knew that Japanese preferred it. At the white cane table, the two sat quietly, looking and smiling at each other like happy teenagers. The years that had intervened seemed like a few yesterdays.

"Time is subjective," said Kamala. "You and I pick up our friendship as if no time had passed."

"*Hai,*" sighed Josie. She was in full agreement with her dear friend Kamala.

Some people have divine tendencies, others demonic.
Bhagavad Gita

Chapter XVI
June 20, 1995

Josie and the inspector had settled in days before, but the opportunity was rare for Josie and Kamala to be alone and re-live experiences they had shared at their school in Switzerland. Despite the fact that there was prohibition in other parts of India, the Paranjotis knew enough visiting foreigners to be able to get alcoholic beverages as gifts from them. Feeling like schoolgirls doing something forbidden, Josie and Kamala raised their cocktails to each other, saying, "Cheers!"

"We've not made our plans for travel in India," said Josie as she smiled at Kamala.

"I confess, it is so good seeing you again that I am in no hurry to set out on a difficult journey. Besides, my husband is less accustomed to travel; he experiences jet-lag more fiercely than I."

"You and I traveled so much at a young age," commented Kamala. "Either we don't feel it -- or we ignore it, jet-lag."

Josie laughed, "Talking about it makes it worse. I find it does pass.

"I feel so at home here," said Josie, taking Kamala's hand and pressing it.

"I'm so pleased," said Kamala, smiling at Josie. "a lasting friendship is such a wonderful thing."

"Seldom," said Josie, "does the thought make me sad."

Mayor Paranjoti and Bert Appleton arrived at the apartment. Seeing the Mehtas on their terrace, he called over and asked the Mehtas to join them. A houseboy in *dhoti* served them drinks, and they chatted, exchanging the usual phrases of first introductions.

Although Kursi's travel business took him to Europe, both west and east, he was always surprised at meeting an American.

`I've never been to the States,' was a stock phrase of Kursi's. He always felt insecure in the presence of strangers. Americans are not like Europeans, was his frequent reaction.

In exasperation, Alina nudged him, whispering, "Americans *are* different. Why shouldn't they be?"

The Parsis, who had succeeded -- as had Kursi's family -- sent their children to England for university educations. Kursi Mehta looked upon those four years in England as the best. He was light complexioned, and had often been mistaken for English. He'd even taken up smoking -- a thing very much taboo in the Parsi community. Fire, as a symbol, was sacred. Fire in the temple is one thing; it is another when it is at the end of a match, was Kursi's rationalization.

Lacking something original to say, he would haul out his stock-in-trade of overworked phrases. If it a new acquaintance asked him, "How goes the travel business?" His predictable response would be: "You know, all work and no play makes Jack!" This would be followed by a loud guffaw.

That invariably was followed with, "I told my incompetent nephew, `To turn stumbling blocks into stepping stones, pick up your feet.'" To be sure that the man or woman to whom he was talking -- now glassy-eyed -- got the point, he'd pull up his trouser legs and mime mincing from stone to stone.

Chagrined, Alina would call to him, "Kursi, dahling, please get me a drink. You know the kind."

Kursi was likable, although at times he gave the impression of, not a diffident husband, but a flustered one. Unfortunately, he was one of those bores who never tumbles to the fact that he is a dead weight in a social situation.

Bert made conversation as he tried to figure out how best to present to Kamala Paranjoti -- as the mayor's wife -- that he needed more help from the mayor if he was to find Damon Rupert.

Alina leaned against a rattan chaise lounge, her chin lined up along her shoulder, as though she was slightly out of touch with herself.

It was an act. Alina felt a visceral attraction to this lanky American. She was a woman of contradictions; her high-handed contempt for convention and her genteel anxiety of being seen to flout it. Her wry humor masked her ambivalence.

By seeming to ignore him, she wagered that he would be drawn to her.

He's the type who thinks he is irresistible -- so like a man. *O lanjo!* After I've had him.

As if she predicted correctly, Bert walked over to her, "Mrs. Mehta, I hesitate to impose upon the mayor..." Alina broke off what he was about to say.

"You need something from those who are powerful?" Before Bert could respond, she added, "What we lack, we need. I'll get Kamala to speak to her husband. *Moj boze*, it's so easy."

"*Moj*...?" asked a startled Bert. "I appreciate your offer of help, but I don't understand...?"

"It's Polish: *Moj boze*. My God. In the theatre we swear a lot -- backstage. *Dac buzi moj zadek.*" I'm glad he doesn't speak Polish. 'Kiss my ass' in Polish -- that would get a reaction. She gestured to Kamala to come close to her, and whispered in her ear.

Alina rose and adjusted her sari. Nothing like making a man indebted, she smiled to herself.

Kamala went over to her husband. "Narendra, you already provided introductions useful to Mr. Appleton. Is there not more we -- you as Mayor -- can do to help him?"

At once he turned to Bert and the inspector, suggesting that he take Bert on a night-time tour of Bombay -- that he become more familiar with the city.

It was almost dark and the streets were clogged with people and traffic. The mayor's Ambassador car was held up by a long line of cars, trucks, and motor scooters. He became impatient.

"Let's continue our tour on foot."

The inspector recalled the day before, when the mayor, Paul and Zarina had walked in the area behind Malabar Hill. He had not understood, of course, the Hindi when a man in close quarters had been rude to Zarina. *"Tule aya Bahini nahit ka!"* said Zarina fiercely.

The mayor later explained to the inspector, "What she just said was that the masher was a madman and a scoundrel. The man persisted, and she said to him `drop dead.'  In fact she said, `*Ba-zawat gelas,'* -- go fuck your father. (Zarina would have been too embarrassed to translate this crude expression.) It worked. The man flinched and his face arranged itself into a scowl.

"These Hindi words are enough to tell the creep that she wouldn't be pushed around. Indian men tolerate some abuse from a woman if she is from a higher caste or if she is white, but not always."

He who deserves to be punished, must be
     punished,
He who is worthy of favor, must be favored.
       Gospel of Buddha

Chapter XVII
June 21, 1995

At the mayor's prompting, Inspector Utsumi invited Bert to share the temporary office space given to him by the police commissioner.

Detective Utsumi looked fondly at the cigarette burning between his fingers. He raised it to his lips and drew the smoke into the deepest recesses of his lungs before turning back to the mountain of paperwork on his desk. There were parts of his job back in Tokyo that he loved: learning about a mysterious death, squeezing information out of sources, bringing a killer to justice.

"A phone call, *sahib*," said a young policeman, poking his head into the inspector's door.

Inspector Utsumi looked up, but just for a moment. He said, "Give it to Bert Appleton."

Bert pushed his chair back from his desk and walked to the open door of what was now Utsumi's office. The inspector rarely closed his door in Tokyo. He was used to working in the midst of permanent bedlam.

The Bombay offices were modest cubicles

about five yards square, with high ceilings and flaking walls painted white at the top and yellow at the bottom. There were ceiling fans, a couple of filing cabinets, several ancient wooden desks with trays for paperwork and mail, and a couple of uncomfortable wooden chairs on the visitors' side of the desks.

Bert became more talkative than usual, completely unaware that Police Commissioner Zubin Varla had just come to the door and was listening to the conversation between the two men.

"India is a paradise for the sociopath," said Bert. "I keep thinking of a foreigner like Damon Rupert in this strange city of Bombay. A city that has exploded, I'm told, from two million to twelve million. They fill the streets and alleys, begging, fighting, cheating, stealing, clamoring for rupees. Never enough to keep them all alive."

The inspector interrupted, "I look at street. Crowded. Many people -- thousands. Faces...no names."

"I know what you mean, inspector. Thousands of nameless faces. Submissive. Trained from birth to be victims."

"*Hai.*"

"And where, you may ask, is the perfect place to commit murder?" questioned Commissioner Varla, making his presence known at last. "I will tell you: Bombay. It offers the most perfect victims. Sad for me to say it, but India is the only country in the world where you can kill someone and know that even if the body is found, no one cares. It won't even be noticed. Bodies are picked up off the streets every day. Nobody seems to care.

"I'll share with you my theory. The abductions and murders, so linked with the Towers of Silence of the Parsis, are the doing of the Shiv Sena."

"I'm all ears, Commissioner Varla," said Bert. "What is Shiv...?"

"As Bombay grew -- not by thousands, but by millions -- a nasty political movement here in the state of Maharashtra got started. Pressure for the Maharasta language predominated; then it was the steady influx of South Indians -- who poured into Bombay -- creating competition for jobs. They worked for less.

"Now Shiv Sena has it in for all minorities. They attack Parsis as well -- exploiting mob violence. Parsis are a minority -- I'm a Parsi. True, some Parsis are rich; they're industrious. But not all of us are rich."

"Envy!"" interposed Inspector Utsumi, who had been following the English of the two.

"Aha!" cried Bert. "I see what you're telling us. The abductions of foreigners. Being taken to the vultures of the Parsi community's burial place. Yes, their aim is to stigmatize Parsis.

"Exactly!" said the commissioner, pleased that he had found agreement with his theory.

"Bert reflected momentarily, "Does Mayor Paranjoti know of you hunch? Does he agree?"

"Hunch?" Oh, I think I understand. No, the mayor is convinced it's criminals, not political. It makes it harder to find the mastermind of these crimes that plague us."

"The profile Utsumi and I have come up with

is of someone who manipulates others from behind the scenes. Someone like Manson."

"Hmmm, a Manson?" puzzled the commissioner. He shook his head, revealing that he was unaware of `Helter-Skelter' and the American criminal Charles Manson.

Later that day, Bert was sitting in his cubicle of an office, consulting his file cards.

Bert's nightmare was that another young foreigner -- an American -- might be abducted and die before he and the inspector and Josie might catch the killer, or killers. The mayor was convinced that they were dealing with a serial killer, casing the luxury hotels. Bert knew there was a likelihood that they would strike again.

On the desk lay the Violent Criminal Apprehension Program (VICAP) information form. In an office with this heat and only a fan, he griped silently; I've fourteen pages and one-hundred-eighty-eight questions. I've been told by Philip Verdi that I'm to do a narrative summary. `Seemingly trivial particulars of unsolved murders may provide the clues that get the man -- or the woman' was what that Phil drilled into me.

"So Appleton is in far off India," said his friend Phil back in Quantico, Virginia. "The F.B.I. program offers help to detectives all over the United States." What the hell! Bert is an American."

"It was the U.S. Department of Justice that had set up the VICAP Crime Analysis Program initially," Phil rationalized. "Janet Reno is right on; she'd back me if there is a squawk."

Bert, as he sweated, filled out the VICAP form with everything he and the others knew about the disappearance of Damon Rupert, and the many he had learned about from Police Commissioner Varla.

From the manner in which he puffed on the cigarette hanging from his nether lip, even an amateur could have read his body language and expressed it in one word: stress.

He shook his head; ash fell on the cards in his hand. Without removing the cigarette butt from his mouth he blew at the ashes, intending to blow them away. The entire lighted end fell in his lap. He leapt to his feet.

"There's so god-damned fucking little to go on!" he muttered angrily, trying to push the burning embers to the floor before they burned the chair. "Shit!" he grumbled, stomping on the butt.

The Police Commissioner, a file folder in hand, heard the comment as he strode into the office area. Bert's colorful metaphor caused the commissioner to frown; he was not a smoker. But, he made no comment. He asked, "Any progress finding your young American? A Texan, yes? At Taj Mahal Hotel Intercontinental, I believe you told me. When you talked to reception, had they noticed anything? What was the young man's name? Was he nervous? Agitated?"

Still standing, Bert ruffled his stack of cards. Just as he was about to answer, the inspector and Josie entered the room. He waved gloomily, at the same time answering the commissioner's question. "All I've learned is that Rupert was last seen when he registered at the hotel desk. He was expected. The reservation was in order. He made no lasting impression on the evening clerk," said Bert. "I could have left at that point, but I didn't. I just stood there. Perhaps the pressure of my continued presence without speaking prompted some recall, because the clerk said, and I quote: 'Mr. Rupert spoke of the long flight. That he felt stiff. He said that he was going to take a walk after he had seen his room. I saw him to his room. All was in order. I left. That is all I can tell you.' From his tone of voice and manner, you'd have thought he'd told me some great state secret. Actually," Bert said, "that meant damn little.

"But then the second man at reception called me back. He said, `I was about to leave for the night. I saw that the doorman was having difficulty with a beggar who was trying to spend the night up against the hotel. What really got my attention was a car suddenly pulling away, making an illegal turn. The roaring noise! Black tire marks on the pavement.'"

"Were they there?" asked the police commissioner. "If we'd have had the monsoon rains, flooding the streets, they'd be gone."

"Oh, they were there all right," retorted Bert.

Both men suddenly remembered their manners, and each proffered Josie a chair. The inspector took two steps towards his assigned desk, then halted. To the commissioner and Bert, he said slowly, "I learned New York. Seminar. Look at evidence of crime scene. Make profile." He looked to Josie, "*Wakarimasu-ka?*"

In tune with her husband, she quickly grasped

the situation. "*Shujin* wants to explain further, in Japanese, as to what he has found out and what he thinks." The inspector spoke to his wife rapidly.

"The mayor, Paranjoti-san, has seen to it, as much as was possible, that taxi drivers have been questioned," Josie translated for her husband. "They were shown a photograph of Rupert-san that Appleton had in his possession. None had the young man as a fare."

"We've done all the usual. With no results. It is *so* frustrating!" said Bert. "Like the doorman; he says he was busy that night. He seems to remember a young American getting in a car, a car he must have called for, the doorman assumed." Bert threw up his hands in a gesture of pure frustration. "He could be our Texan, but there's no way to be sure." Bert wanted to let fly with a spate of curses, and probably would have had Josie not been present.

"From what the doorman described, the car may have been what we in the States call a gypsy taxi. It would be easier to find that fabled needle in the haystack than a maverick taxi in Bombay."

Bert removed another cigarette from the pack he had recently opened, then politely offered one to Inspector Utsumi, whom he knew was a chain smoker.

Josie waited politely until they'd finished lighting up, then got back down to the business at hand. "My husband has just come from the morgue. The mayor asked Tatsuo to accompany him," Josie explained. "The scene of the crime -- the death of the young foreigner -- was at the Towers of Silence. The corpse bearers at the Towers took the ravaged body out to the road -- quite a distance, I'm told. One of them called the police. The pathologist said it was obvious that the wounds had been inflicted by birds of prey -- vultures. A nasty sight."

"Let's put our heads together," said Bert. "You know the saying: Two heads are better than one? Well, we can do better than that. Translate, please, Josie. Let the inspector be mentor, and all of us will work together to try and construct a profile of the killer or killers."

"You'll never get to the scene of the crime," spoke up the commissioner. "Nobody, unless dead, gets to the Towers of Silence. It's forbidden. *Pavrita!*"

"So, we'll use our imagination," said Josie. All were silent for some moments, thinking.

"You know," said Bert, rubbing his chin thoughtfully, "if it is the body of Damon Rupert, then he was abducted in front of the Taj Mahal hotel."

"I see where you go, Bert-san. He young man, strong. Need more to...?" There was another rapid spate of Japanese between the inspector and Josie.

"My husband asks forgiveness," said Josie. "When he tries to speak English too quickly, or is frustrated, it interferes with his being able to get the proper words out. What he wants you to know is that in his opinion, it would have taken more than one person to force him into a car and overpower him. He was, after all, young and presumably strong."

"*Hai, hai,*" the inspector interjected. "We analyze possible scene."

There was another brief exchange between husband and wife. The inspector waved his hands, "You tell, *okusan*."

"The autopsy and the first lab tests," translated Josie, "revealed that the poor fellow had been rendered unconscious by an injection of cobra venom. *Shujin* and the mayor agree with the pathologist that the abductors are not likely to have been Europeans. Asians, most likely. Indians would probably know more about cobra venom."

"Cobra venom? That's damned exotic, eh, Inspector Utsumi." Bert was embarrassed that he'd let a cuss word into his conversation, and was too embarrassed to look in the direction of Josie. It didn't phase her in the least; she'd heard worse things in Japanese.

"So many drugs -- like chloroform -- obtainable, would have been my guess, here in Bombay. I came to know that most anything was to be had in Athens' pharmacies," added Bert.

"We've been told that the burial place of the Parsis is unapproachable; how was the body transported there?" puzzled Josie. "Were the abductors disguised, posing as corpse bearers? That -- if possible -- needs to be resolved."

The police commissioner nodded in agreement. "The blood type of the victim was that of a Caucasian. The coroner noticed that there was a smear of blood on one of the white bindings. The lab is to analyze the DNA -- to see if it differs from the victim's blood. Let's hope that the smear came from one of the abductors. Bombay has better facilities than most of the country, but it does take time, unfortunately."

"Perhaps it will tell us something, then again it may not," Josie translated.

"Taking a foreigner to -- of all places -- the Towers of Silence! It defies my imagination. Why do it?" exclaimed Bert.

"What killer or killers tell us?" said the inspector, who understood best Bert's American English.

"From cases we study at seminar in New York. There is puppeteer here -- like number one of *Bunraku* puppets. He control other puppeteers. Not control only dolls. Understand?"

Josie elaborated on her husband's metaphor of Japanese *Bunraku*. She did, however, have to translated the next bit of information. "Everything about the crime is telling us that the master criminal seeks domination, seeks to manipulate, and above all wants control. Bert-san will remember Manson and his `helter-skelter' group. He controlled. He was a master of mind control. We studied how he never killed. He always got others to do the killing for him."

"Boy, don't I remember that case," said Bert. "I'll never forget hearing about the murders on the news. Then, when they did find the killers...well, the case just kept getting more and more bizarre as it went along. The amount of control he had on his followers was just mind-boggling!"

"*Hai. Shujin* thinks the profile should include the possibility of a Manson-type personality," said Josie. "I agree completely." she said somewhat assertively. "Let's just say it's my woman's intuition," she said, blushing with embarrassment from having been so assertive during such a serious police discussion.

The mayor had arrived earlier, and had listened intently to all that had been said without comment. "We must be on guard," he said at last. "Counter to my wishful thinking, I feel in my bones that there are to be more murders. It strikes me that this has all been very carefully planned. If there are more murders at the Towers of Silence, the Parsi community will be deeply troubled. The Parsis are a significant, though small, community here in Bombay. Powerful. We are indebted to them for a Cancer Hospital and research institutes. Who and why would anyone wish to discredit the Parsis?" This question was followed by silence. No one spoke.

The mayor spread out police photographs of the body on the desk. He turned to Bert, "I know this is unpleasant, but since you have the photographs of Damon Rupert, perhaps you could..."

Bert took the unspoken challenge and studied the photos. He picked up first one and then another. "It's hard to say," he said at last. So much of the face is missing. For his sake -- Damon Rupert, that is -- I hope it's simply that he's taken off somewhere."

Shaking his head, he looked up and said, "No. I'm sorry, but there's just no possible way for me to tell if this is Damon Rupert. Since I can't be sure, I'll just have to keep searching."

All eyes in the room returned to the gruesome photos. They were thoughtful, stunned by the photographs. To lose one's life in such a horrible manner was a sobering thought.

I am most fortunate, the inspector thought, looking at the photos. I have allies. People who care, *okusan* Josie and this American, Bert Appleton. I am *ungaii shichi* -- lucky seven!

Pressure had been put on the pathology lab to determine the nature of the blood smear quickly. The report came back that it was not the blood of the victim or of a Caucasian -- it was Asian blood. DNA tests suggested it was blood of an Indian.

Hypocritical, proud and arrogant, being in
Delusion and clinging to deluded ideas,
Insatiable in their desires, they pursue
Their unclean ends.

Bhagavad Gita

Chapter XVIII
June 22, 1995
Later

Bert drove to the Malabar Hill apartment. He was pleased that he'd been invited again for drinks and dinner by Mayor Paranjoti, who wanted to talk with Bert about all the abductions. His mind flickered and rested briefly on what had transpired earlier that day.

Bert had studied maps of Bombay at the David Sassoon Library. Learning the layout of the city has been of some help, he mused.

Now he was exhausted, and it showed -- deep dark circles under his eyes. He could only hope that saying things aloud would help him remember them.

Arriving at the Paranjotis, he quickly parked his vehicle and made his way into the building. A servant led him into the apartment, where he saw and greeted the Inspector and Josie.

"We meet again."

The inspector rose, smiling, "Appleton-san. Come. Others outside on terrace. We join, *hai?*"

Bert followed the inspector as he ushered the way to the terrace, his thoughts dwelling on the missing Damon Rupert. He had asked himself, Where might a young American like Damon Rupert choose to spend his time? If he's on the run, he'd avoid the deluxe hotels, the kind his parents would have chosen.

"He must still be in Bombay," said Bert as he came out onto the terrace. His concentration had been so intense that he'd inadvertently spoken his thoughts aloud.

His face turned a bit red in embarrassment as he took in the raised eyebrows and questioning looks of everyone on the terrace.

Ever the lady, Josie smoothly took hold of the situation, performing introductions.

"Appleton-san, may I introduce you to the Mayor's daughter?" A simple hand gesture indicated that he join the two sari-clad women. "Indira, you've heard your father speak about Bert Appleton. From America."

Bert bowed slightly, saying simply, "Mrs. Paranjoti, thank you for having me once again in your home. I always look forward to these evenings. I'm coming to know your country -- through you and your friends."

Kamala inclined her head slightly in acknowledgement of the compliment. "It is a pleasure to have guests. I grew up in a large family. Many at the table reminds me of my childhood."

Josie then turned to Alina. "You remember the Mehtas. They live in the apartment next door."

Alina held her right hand out almost as if she were royalty to be bowed over.

Bert, used to dealing with many different situations, rose to the occasion admirably. He took her hand in his and bowed as he said, "I am most privileged to be in the company of *three* beautiful women."

"I'm pleased to make your acquaintance," Alina responded. "I find...people interesting." Though she had said `people,' Bert was virtually certain she actually meant `men.'

"Bert-san," said Josie softly, bringing his attention back to the others. "When you arrived on the terrace, you said, `He must still be in Bombay'. Damon, you think, must still be in Bombay?"

"*Hai*, you lucky?" asked the inspector.

Somewhat sheepishly, Bert said, "They say it's a sign of age when you talk to yourself." Everyone nodded, having heard that one before. "Actually," he continued on somewhat more seriously, "I will be out late tonight. I spent all of last night casing the cheap, cheaper and cheapest guest houses of Bombay, in search of Damon Rupert."

"Ah, yes," said the mayor. "The Criminal Bureau of Investigation received several calls from an American family regarding the missing Damon Rupert. Even before your arrival in Bombay.

"Our deputy superintendent of police, whom you've not met, has been burdened with pursuit of the serial killer. He's head of the Crime Branch. Yes, you should meet him.

"If I may ask, his family thinks he is still in Bombay?"

"I keep in touch with Interpol," said Bert. "No leads as yet."

Alina had been studying Bert -- admiring his height and handsomeness.

"Interpol? You men know everything. May I ask, what is Interpol?"

Bert turned to her, discerning her deep in shadow. His thought was: She must be kidding! A European, and she's not heard of Interpol? Oh, well...

"Interpol? Some days ago I was there: Lyons, France. I'll gladly tell you all I know about it. I may say, Search Group, Inc. would be high and dry sometimes without it."

Mayor Narendra spoke up, "If you'll excuse me, I'll greet my wife. Do make yourselves comfortable on the terrace. This terrible heat before the monsoon. One-hundred five degrees Fahrenheit today! But, the planting shades you. I'll have the houseboy bring you cool drinks."

With a gesture, he sent the houseboy on his way. The sky was fiery red, encountering the water of the bay -- as it began its descent to the West.

Before Bert took his seat on the hard *thakat* wooden platform, covered with white tapestry, padded with bolsters of heavy woven cloth that were piled against the wall, he gestured to a chair that Alina be seated.

In the act of sitting in a upholstered rattan chair, Alina changed her mind and joined Bert on the *thakat*.

As he leaned back against the cushions, stretching his long legs full length, he sighed, "I am tired. It's a toss-up as to which is worse. Tokyo's traffic, or Bombay's. Beggars everywhere, grabbing at me. Stepping around half-naked people asleep on the pavement. The heat and the humidity! The smells! And seeing food *fly*-infested!"

Josie caught Bert's eye, and she placed a finger on her lips. She did not want him to make a bad impression by dwelling on the negative side of Bombay.

"One needs to be Indian..." said Alina. She paused, as if to say more, but then suddenly she switched to another track. "You were about to tell me of your investigation ...that is, Interpol."

Investigation? Did she make a slip there? speculated Bert. Interpol it'll be. That's what I'll give her -- aplenty.

"In May, 1989, Interpol -- an acronym derived from International Police -- moved to new headquarters in Lyons, France, costing twenty million U.S. dollars. Interpol's boss, Kindall, told me! `People simply do not know what goes on through our efforts.' So don't be chagrined that you were ignorant of this International Police. Yes?"

Alina looked fully into his eyes, remaining silent, but smiling.

Quite the actress, mused Bert. Charisma -- that overworked word, but better than star quality.

"I was impressed," said Bert, luring his gaze away from the Polish woman. "It was like a scene from a James Bond movie. It's a complex granite and glass fortress -- impregnable. With the most advanced gadgetry of electronic security. Interpol operates through National Central Bureaus (NCB's) in each of its one hundred-fifty-eight member states.

"There is no such thing as an Interpol agent, only a law enforcement individual or individuals make arrests within their own country."

Alina was frowning.

"You may ask: What makes it effective, important to one hundred-fifty-eight nations?

"It is important as a clearing-house for information. If a national -- an American for example -- is murdered in a European or Asian country, a request for information may go out on the whole Interpol network. It can receive and transmit information within seconds.

"The fact that in most countries foreigners and nationals -- alike -- are registered with the police means that a pattern of movement is easily obtained. The exception is my own country. It's easy to get lost in the USA.

"I'm for everyone carrying identification and being requested to submit it to landlords, superintendents, hotels, motels, etc. The only ones who'd have cause to object would be the ones up to no good."

Bert was not indifferent to Alina's obvious attraction to him, and he was amused by her efforts. Still, he gave very little away.

"Forgive me, I'm on my soap box..."

"Soap box?" uttered Alina, more to herself. "Ah, yes. Hyde Park, London. Where they talk politics on soap box, literally or figuratively. Now I under-stand...

"You are here as a tourist?" asked Alina.

"You can say that," said Bert. At this point, Kamala joined them, accompanied by Paul Drake and Zarina.

After hellos had been exchanged, their cocktail orders taken, Kamala turned to Alina. Talk had moved on to the Parsi community, their Fire Temples. Alina fluffed off the questions put to her.

"Yesterday, Paul asked me about the Parsi Temple *Atash Behram* we had passed. As a Hindu, of course, I know nothing about the Fire Temples -- the rituals. Paul is a writer, Alina.

"I may be married to a Parsi," Kamala added, "but I can never become one. I am Polish Roman Catholic -- as is the Pope in Rome."

Zarina spoke up, "How odd that Paul has forgotten that I am a Parsi. Do I detect, Paul, male chauvinism? That a woman wouldn't know?" She laughed.

Paul hit his forehead lightly with his fist.

"We never talk religion. I was forgetting. Well, give. The others may be interested, as well."

"The roof of the consecrated chamber is shaped like a dome, to signify the dome of heaven. From the center of the dome hangs high above the fire a large metal tray, which is the crown for the fire.

"The fire is in the center of the room in a vessel, which stands on a stone slab known as the throne. The fire is fed by the priests with sandalwood and incense. Five times each day writings are recited in its honor."

Kursi Mehta had been standing in the shadows listening with keen interest to what Zarina was telling the others. He had come to let his wife Alina know that he had returned sooner than expected from his business trip -- a short one. Kursi welcomed the opportunity to take over conversations. He loved to talk -- often to the point of boring his conversational partners. He had a stock of banal phrases that sent him into a paroxysm of laughter.

"If I may add something of keen interest," said Kursi as he did a *namaste* with his hands close to his body in greetings to the others, "there is an elaborate and spectacular Zoroastrian ceremony in connection with the consecration of a Fire Temple -- and the sacred fire.

"I speak of the collection, purification and consecration of the fires. Sixteen different fires are required and have to be collected before consecration and installation."

Paul spoke up, "Is it possible that there are sixteen different fires?"

Kursi was enjoying the attention of his audience. He looked at each of them in turn, and then said, "The first fire to be collected is from a burning corpse."

"A burning corpse...!" said Alina as if shocked.

"It must be obtained, then," said Paul, "from one of the Hindu burning *ghats*, where Hindus are cremated. Right?"

Kursi nodded his affirmation.

"Other fires to be collected are from a potter, a brick maker, a goldsmith, a baker, a soldier -- others -- and from the chief citizen of the town. Guess what fire is the most difficult to obtain?" asked Kursi, enjoying creating some suspense.

Most were shaking their heads, not having an idea as to which fire it could be.

Zarina spoke up, "Fire from lightning. It is the most difficult to obtain. Fire from lightening which has struck a tree or a house."

Kursi smiled and looked approvingly at Zarina.

"Lastly, there must be fire from the home of a Zoroastrian priest or layman.

"Union of all the fires takes place when ceremonies in honor of the righteous dead have been completed.

"For the next thirty days priests recite from the writings in honor of the divine powers. Then the hallowed fire is removed to the consecrated chamber in the Fire Temple."

The opinion of most was that Kursi Mehta was likeable, after all.. On this occasion they had enjoyed listening to him, and there was a polite round of applause. He smiled and did a *namaste* and exited for his apartment.

> That middle path . . .
> Opens the eyes, and
> Bestows understanding
> Which leads to peace of mind,
> To the higher wisdom,
> To full enlightenment.
> *Gospel of Buddha*

Chapter XIX
June 24, 1995
Bombay, India

Two weeks had passed. The weather was hard on the inspector, but he went each day to the police office.

One night over dinner with their hosts, the inspector and Josie talked of their projected trip to Bihar and Sarnath in Varanasi -- once known as Benares.

"It was at Bodhgaya that the Buddhist sat under the Bo Tree and attained enlightenment. A descendent of the original tree still flourishes today," said the mayor, who knew his Indian history very well.

He continued. "Then the Buddha came to Sarnath to preach his message of the middle way to find nirvana. You'll see there, inspector, I suspect, magnificent stupas erected by the great Buddhist emperor Ashoka."

Inspector Utsumi was finding the air-conditioning of the mayor's spacious apartment too much for him. He had perspired so heavily out in the city that he'd come back to the apartment twice to change his suit and shirt. In Tokyo, Commander Okubo's office on the floor above him had an air-conditioning unit; it never gave him a twinge of envy that he had nothing of the kind for his smaller office.

"For my husband, it's the contrast with the hot, humid weather of India."

Shall we have our coffee, then, on the terrace?" asked Kamala.

The inspector gave a vigorous nod of agreement.

Josie said, "I'd never before had coffee with the fragrance, essence of roses. It's overcome my disinclination to take coffee in the evening. I find it something very special."

Kamala smiled at Josie, "Wonderful, Josie. Our cook Sita Devi will be pleased when I tell her. She's a simple woman from one of the villages. She learned to read in a missionary school, and she is intelligent."

"An excellent cook," said Josie.

"The country people amaze me," continued Kamala. "They have an almost incredible `grape-vine' which gets news from one village to another with uncanny speed. It's been more than a century, but of late man-eating wolves have been killing -- more than twenty -- children in the state of Uttar Pradesh. It's been in the Bombay papers and television . . ."

"Uttar Pradesh . . ." puzzled Josie. "India *is*

a sub-continent -- alongside small Japan. I'm sure I don't know where that is."

"It's a stretch of the Ganges river basin, three hundred-fifty miles from New Delhi.

"I bring it up because Sita tells me the villages are convinced it is not wolves, but werewolves. Half-man, half wolf-creature. The superstitions of village life."

What Kamala was telling Josie caught the attention of Narendra, her husband. "In all seriousness...as I was having my coffee this morning cook told me a relative had seen, with her own eyes, a wolf grab a four year old boy. Having grabbed him, it rose on two legs until it was a tall man!"

"Yes, she claimed it then wore a black coat, a helmet and goggles." The mayor laughed. "I scolded her for believing such nonsense."

"How did she take it?" asked Kamala.

"You choose not to believe it, but all servants eavesdrop. Our cook became very serious, telling me that it was werewolves taking the murdered foreigners to the *Dakhma* of the Parsis. `Werewolves and vultures work together!' She was adamant," concluded the mayor.

With a shaking of heads, the three of them made their way to the terrace through the sliding glass doors.

On the terrace of the Paranjoti's penthouse above Malabar Hill they were seated in cane chairs around a bamboo coffee table. They could look due east, right across Back Bay to the curve of Marine Drive and the Bombay skyline beyond.

"To your left you can see Chowpatty Beach," said Kamala. "This is the scene of the annual Ganesh Chaturthi Festivals. As an important part of the festival large images of the Elephant-headed god Ganesh are sent afloat and are immersed in the sea."

"It's unfortunate that it's not the time of the year for the festival," spoke up the mayor. "Changing the subject," he said, "in my younger days I'd run along Walkeshar Road -- not quite to the Hanging Gardens -- to Kamala Nehru Park. The Towers of Silence, where the Parsis expose their dead to the vultures, is in the area. Not being a Parsi, I've not been able -- nor do I choose to -- get close to the Towers of Silence."

As they sipped their coffee, there was silence. The dying rays of the sun gilded the waters of Back Bay.

"Malabar Hill is an expensive residential area," said the mayor, breaking the silence. Putting down his cup, the mayor continued, "It is a little cooler than the sea level parts of the city, and we have pleasing views."

"It's well worth the money -- an apartment here on Malabar Hill," said Kamala. The jingle of her gold and silver bracelets gave emphasis to what she had said.

Were she not my dearest of friends, reacted Josie silently, I'd take umbrage at her boasting about where they live. Then, she caught herself. She sighed, with the added thought, Japanese overdo modesty -- often false. Gold and jewels do suit Kamala -- her dark complexion show them off wonderfully.

Kamala turned to Josie, wondering what caused her frowns. She coughed slightly and said, "At school you were always reading theatre magazines sent to you from Tokyo. I was envious that I could not read Japanese.

"I had wanted very much to be a dancer. My heart had been set on learning *Bharata Natyam* -- a form of Indian dance.   It is one of the oldest documented dance forms in the world, a blend of pure lyric movement and pantomime drama. But, as the child of a diplomat father moving about Europe, the dance that was available to me was ballet.

"What about you, Josie, have you kept up your interest in theatre?"

This is one of the occasions that the inspector followed the English fully, for the mayor's wife spoke slowly and distinctly out of consideration for her guests. "Kabuki. I like most," said the inspector.

"I'm hoping ultimately to get my husband accustomed to the slower pace and simplicity of the Noh theatre," said Josie.

"We have been supporting a contemporary theatre in Tokyo. I overheard Alina Mehta saying to Paul Drake that she hoped to act in one of the Bombay theatres. Kamala, are there theatres that perform in English? She does have a lovely voice, and she had had a Polish-American who taught her English, so she's bi-lingual."

"Oh, yes, Josie," Kamala replied. "There are English speaking theatres in Bombay. What got you interested in a Tokyo theatre that does modern plays?"

"I can now tell you, Kamala, something that

happened a long time ago. In the library of our Swiss school," Josie said, "I had come upon a volume of Ibsen's plays. His heroines became my heroines, so vivid were they for me."

"I seem to remember there was a period when you were keen on reading plays, Josie," said Kamala.

"As a Japanese woman, I had empathy," Josie went on, "with how these Ibsen heroines resisted the role of women assigned to them -- in the 19th century.

"In 1975 I saw the play *Hedda Gabler* in London. Father had gone off to Washington for meetings respecting our trade with the United States. He anticipated that those meetings would be long and tense; he proposed that mother not be there with him."

The inspector interjected, "Your father has temper. I see him get Kobe-beef red -- in the face."

Josie responded in agreement, "He suppresses it, but mother is terribly sensitive to his moods. He knows it upsets her."

"There was time you away from Japan. When, I don't remember. What year?"

"*Shujin*, you must not have missed me much. Not to remember. You had gone to Hokkaido -- not to play golf. Nothing as agreeable as that. It was the summer of 1975," responded Josie.

"*Hai...*," he interjected drawing out the syllable of his yes. "It was troublesome arson case. Half a village burned to the ground. Not arson -- after all..."

"You spent weeks to determine the cause. The irate villagers were set on it's having been started by a retarded youth. Could have been tragic were it not for you," said Josie as she lightly touched her husband's arm.

Embarrassed, but silently pleased, he said gruffly, "Thatched roofs in remote villages...dry! Like firewood. Whole village can go up -- in flames. Few men left can thatch a roof...perhaps that's ok."

"Oh, *Shujin*. I so delight in the old villages -- so like the ones in the woodblocks of Kuniyoshi. One day never to see thatched roofed houses..." murmured Utsumi's wife. She turned at once to something cheerful -- picking up the thread of her story.

"You were away, and I went with mother to London. There was much talk among mother's friends of Glenda Jackson's performance as Hedda at the Aldwych theatre.

"I laugh now to think of how Lady Orpen and others said -- with seeming relish, `You'll never get tickets. Sold out, the whole season -- I've heard.'"

"You did see it?" asked Kamala. "From what you said earlier I was led to believe that you had."

"Dear Kamala, we did see it. At the tea was Suria Saint-Dennis; she came over to mother and me, saying quietly, `My husband Michel, I'm certain, can get you house seats. Name the day.'

"The performance transcended the experience I had had from reading it," she smiled and continued. "The inspector had not suspected that I decided to translate the play into Japanese -- working from the English. I was sanguine that I could do it."

"*Hedda Gabler*," said Kamala. "We have BBC videos sent to us.. Quite some time ago I recall watching the tape of the play. I got the impression from the interpretation of the leading actress that Hedda was more sinned against -- shall we say -- than sinning?"

Josie's response to that was immediate. "The director of the Haiyu-za asked that very thing."

"Did you agree?" spoke up Indira.

"No," said Josie deliberately. "I cited the fact that the talented writer Loveborg, who had conquered his addiction to alcohol, was goaded into taking a drink by Hedda, and then urged by her to go on a spree with Judge Brack and her husband."

"Might not that have happened -- an alcoholic going back to drinking without her tempting him?"

"Perhaps, but I could recall for you the plot, that in addition to taunting the young writer down that self-destructive path of alcoholism, Hedda burns the manuscript of his work. She had been trusted with his manuscript -- it had come into her hands!"

"What a terrible thing to do," said Kamala softly.

"I had my way with the obstinate director of the Haiyu-za by showing him that in a volume of Ibsen's letters, Ibsen had referred to Hedda as *demonic*.

"On the strength of that, the director of the contemporary Tokyo theatre convinced the actress playing Hedda in my translation."

"Didn't you feel the need to know Norwegian -- the language of the original?" asked Kamala.

"After I had translated it from the English version used by the Glenda Jackson production which had been published -- I found it in Harrods' book section. I compared it with a French version. But, not wanting to risk being taken to task by the critics, I bought a Norwegian-Japanese dictionary and an English-Norwegian one," replied Josie.

"I had lived with the play for months. So much preoccupation with it that I often felt as if I had written it: *Hedda Gabler*. Shameful of me to have such a thought."

Kamala laughed, thinking: Feeling shame, not feeling guilty...how Japanese!

"You speak of the Critics. Did you gamble that a theatre in Tokyo would put it on the stage?" asked the Mayor, having become interested now in Josie's recital.

"Yes, it was a gamble, but not much of one." interjected Alina, entering the gathering. "The director of the Haiyu-za -- a theatre doing contemporary and western plays -- had been accused by an actress who claimed the director had slapped her.

"My husband is a theatre buff -- knew the theatre's director. By talking to the actress, he learned that the director had simply whacked her on the ankle with a fan. It had been a hot day."

The inspector who had -- to his amazement been following his wife's English -- interposed, "Inexperienced actress. I said, `It is custom in Noh correct actor like this. Director pays you compliment.' She was impressed. No complaint to acting union."

Josie had no need to translate into English what Utsumi had said. The Paranjotis laughed.

Not Alina. "I would have sided with the

actress," she spoke up. Having just come in, she had heard only the last of the conversation.

Not hearing the comment from Alina -- or ignoring it -- the Mayor commented loudly, "That would have put the director under quite a bit of obligation -- to you. Yes? Inspector Utsumi?"

"*Hai!*" was all the response from the inspector.

Josie had warmed to her story, and went on. "I took *Shujin* to a performance -- the opening. It did not take great persuasion to get him to agree to accompany me to the Haiyu-za. You can imagine how great was his surprise when he saw my name in the program..."

"*Ha-chan*, I had no hint that you were an author," said the inspector, speaking in Japanese to his wife.

Josie tapped him lightly with her fan -- as had the Noh actor who had instructed her at the Kita school of the Noh. "*Do itashi mashite, Shujin.* Not author. Just translator." She reverted to English, "I beg pardon of my husband for correcting him. He still thinks of me as a Japanese housewife. I told him one can be both."

There was an uncomfortable prolonged pause. Kamala broke the silence with, "I think it is now time for afternoon tea. Or, is it to be cocktails? The sun is over the yardarm."

All felt relaxed, and conversation resumed. Except for Alina. She moved about restlessly, picking up one art object after another without looking to admire them. One she obviously did not like, a small carved wooden statue of Shiva, holding the *lingam* in his hand. "Ugly!" she said to herself, shuddering slightly as if mortally offended by the very sight of it.

She dropped it into a wastebasket and smiled. Josie had noticed, thinking, What a thing to do. How pleased she seems. A strange woman. I can feel the tension within her; pacing this living room as if it were adjunct to the tiger house of a zoo.

> By sustained effort
> One comes to the
> End of sorrow.
> *Bhagavad Gita*

Chapter XX
June 25, 1995

Indira's excuse for coming so frequently to her father's apartment was expressed as her wishing to see her half-brother and half-sisters -- Kamala's children. After playing for a short time with them she'd slip away to visit with Alina. Each week, she spent more and more time in the Mehta apartment.

Alina was a good listener, it had been an important part of her training for acting professionally. She carefully chose moments when she'd support Indira's wishes to be independent, to defy her grandparents. Alina encouraged Indira to see her beloved Parsi friend, Maneck Dalal.

The covert meetings with Maneck had been going on for weeks. To escape the smothering heat of summer, they'd walk on the beach or as did other lovers recline on a grassy spot in the Hanging Gardens.

One night when they were lying close on the grass, kissing, the arousal became too intense for Indira. She rose up and turned to Maneck.

"What is a Parsi marriage ceremony like? Is

it different, Maneck, by much -- from a marriage between Hindus?"

He continued to lie beside her, on his back, staring up at the stars. "It's one of the most important events in a young man's life.

"I was a witness not long ago at a marriage. I'll try to remember how it went..."

"Please do," Indira said as she took Maneck's hand in hers, then kissed his fingers.

"Bride and groom sit side by side; parents and relatives sit behind them. My parents would sit behind me, if I were the groom.

"As the witness, I stood beside the couple -- as did other witnesses. Two priests stood in front, and then the ceremony began.

"The priest asks the witness -- that was me -- on behalf of the groom's family: `In the presence of this company that has met together in the city of Bombay...'. How does it go? I'll try to remember. `In the year...of emperor (I don't remember his name)...of the Sassanian Dynasty of Iran...say whether you have agreed to take this maiden' -- I don't remember her name, since I didn't know her, but I did know the groom. I'll use your name: Indira. `In marriage for this bridegroom in accordance with the rights and rules of the Mazdayasnans, promising to pay her two thousand *dirams* of pure white silver and two *dinars* of real gold...?'"

"How odd," said Indira as she turned to look fully in Maneck's face. "A Hindu bridegroom expects a dowry from the parents of the bride. That is different. But do go on."

"Then the witness from the bride's side is asked: `You and your family, with righteous mind...' (there's more, but I don't remember) `agree to give this bride in marriage to... (it was my friend Darab). The bride's witness replied: `I have agreed.'

"They say the most crucial part of the ceremony is when the priest turns first to the groom and then to the bride and asks: `Have you chosen to enter into this contract of marriage up to the end of your life with righteous mind?'"

Indira's response was, "That does make marriage a very serious matter."

"The priest asks this three times and three times both the bride and groom must reply: `I approve.' Neither groom nor bride had refused to answer 'I approve,' so there was no interruption to the marriage."

"You've been telling me this in English," stated Indira.

"Indira, as you well know, I'm not a priest. There was much for the couple to memorize, for the entire ceremony was recited in Sanskrit," replied Maneck.

"Sanskrit!" said she. "That does surprise me."

"It was told to me that in the early days of our settling in India, Sanskrit was the language of educated Hindus.

"The priests recite the benedictions and throw grains of uncooked rice on the bride and groom to symbolize prosperity and plenty. The ceremony concludes with a final blessing."

Indira laughed, "I thought that was typically

Western. When I was at the university in England, I went to several weddings. They always ended with the guests throwing rice at the departing couple. How amusing."

Making no comment on that, Maneck continued, "The priests were presented with cashmere shawls and cash. After the bride and groom had embraced their parents, they left and went to the Fire Temple to pay their homage to the sacred fire.

"I'm told prayers were said, and sandalwood and incense offered to the fire, and a ritual was recited."

"Do they go off then on their honeymoon?" asked Indira.

"Not yet," replied Maneck somewhat impatiently. "They return to meet their guests, and when the guests have departed the bride goes to the groom's house. She holds a small lamp in a small, protected silver vase.

"The light must not go out on the way to her new home. At the threshold the husband awaits the bride. He either lifts her over the lintel or she crosses it, right foot first. The little wick lamp is kept lit in the bridal chamber all night."

"When you said the couple go to the Fire Temple...it made me feel very sad..." said Indira as she pulled slightly away from Maneck.

He sat up and slowly withdrew his hand from Indira's. "I forget sometimes you're not Parsi," said Maneck.

Indira turned to him. Taking both his hands, she said, "But Parsis have been marrying here in India for years -- Hindus, even Europeans."

Maneck stood up. "It's getting late. I should get you back to your father's apartment." He helped Indira up, and in silence they walked to Malabar Hill. He did not accompany her in the elevator, but said his goodnight softly, adding, "I'll call you in a day or two." He turned away and left.

Once in the elevator, Indira began to sob convulsively.

Days later Indira received a letter from Maneck. In it he told her that he had to think long and hard about the two of them. He said that he was aware that for centuries in India, where there was great diversity of peoples, that there had been mixed marriages for centuries, he found it hard to tell his family that he wanted to marry a Hindu girl.

`I know what you will tell me, that we all look alike -- with the same brown skin: Hindus, Muslims, Parsis, even the Jews of Calcutta, of which there is a substantial number. Europeans always think they are simply Indians.

`I've been wanting for sometime to go with a young doctor friend to districts in the interior -- the villages. There have been reports of both typhoid and cholera. Having grown up in an affluent family, I feel it's time for me to do -- as they say -- good works.' He closed the letter with: `Ever with affection, Maneck.'

Word came two months later that Maneck had sickened in one of the villages and died of cholera.

As soon as word of the death of Maneck reached his family, they went hurriedly to the village. Fortunately, it was not at a great distance from Bombay. They had him packed in ice and brought back to their home. A corner of a room had been washed and a clean sheet spread on the floor. A priest was sent for. He lighted the sacred fire and fed it with sandalwood and incense while chanting prayers in a low tone.

At the moment of Maneck's death, no Parsi relative or friend was there to sit beside his corpse and whisper the four lines of prayer in his ear.

Before his body was wrapped in torn white strips a prayer was recited. Once bathed, no one was allowed to touch him. A wick lamp was lit and placed at his head and two persons sat beside the body, repeating a prayer.

A short time later two men, trained for the work, came to the house. They put on clean white garments, recited prayers as they lifted the body and took it into the living room and lay it on a marble slab. His arms were folded across his chest and his legs were stretched full-length and tied together at his ankles. A white shroud was passed all around the body, only the face remained exposed.

Two priests arrived and recited prayers. Friends and relatives filed past the corpse and paid Maneck their last respects.

Headed by priests holding the *Paiwand* between them, the funeral procession moved to the gates of a Tower of Silence.

At a prayer bungalow beside the Towers of Silence the families devoted four days to mourning.

Indira took no part in this. She was too broken with grieving, and she was not Parsi.

Having lost all discrimination
They follow the way of
Their lower nature.
Bhagavad Gita

Chapter XXI
June 28, 1995
Early Morning

Not quite a month had passed, and the mayor hoped that that was the end of the abductions and murders. The Bombay police were less sanguine, and Tatsuo Utsumi agreed with them.

Utsumi was enjoying keeping up his English, and he said to Bert, "Josie has expression in English: `Lull before storm!'"

"Very apt," agreed Appleton. "There must be a similar Japanese saying, eh?"

"*Tabun*," said the inspector, cogitating, as he grabbed a small towel off of his desk to wipe the sweat off his face. "Sorry, I speak Japanese. I'll give question some thought."

"That power failure, yesterday," said Bert. "It's affected our fans. They're not working. They didn't do much -- in this heat. Almost a month and no monsoon. They say it gets worse: the heat and the humidity."

Not far away, in the back yard of the Sodawalla Baag, Nusswan and Varun had hunkered down, sitting on their heels. They ignored the trash and the filth all around them. They were too preoccupied.

"I miss the money," said Nusswan, communicating that largely to the air in the space before him.

"It has been a month," said Varun. "I miss the excitement. Don't get me wrong, brother and I have missed those rupees, too," the youth added quietly.

Nothing was said for awhile. "You and your brother? Are you game? We do another one?" asked Varun.

Nusswan didn't respond at once. He turned to Varun and looked him in the eye.

"You and Arun don't understand. You couldn't!"

"What? I don't get you," spoke up Varun.

"The risk is the same for all four of us," added Arun.

"It's not that! You're forgetting -- we're Parsis."

"So?"

"Once dead, the body is unclean. Within three hours it is rotting. Physical contact with the corpse can be harmful.

"You Christians bury -- put the body in the ground. We're told by the *Dasturs* pollution lasts for fifty years. The earth becomes defiled."

"I could never understand why you Parsis don't use the *ghats* -- burn the body. Hindus do. Now that my brother and I are going back to being Hindu, we'd want that to happen. Funeral pyres."

"You're stupid! Why are our temples called Fire Temples? Well? Okay, I'll tell you. There's eternal fire in the temple; it's sacred."

"So?"

"Make the connection," shouted Nusswan out of exasperation. "It's sacred! Sooo...we don't pollute fire by burning bodies!"

"Gee, thanks. I get it. But, you're not so bright," said a defensive Varun. "So far, the guys we've abducted haven't been dead. Just out!"

"If they were to die -- that cobra venom...," said Nusswan.

"Ah, now I understand. That one we ran over. He was dead all right, and that's why you left all of the handling to Arun and me. Now I get it."

Nusswan picked up a small stone and threw it at a cat who happened to come within hitting distance. When the cat was out of sight, he looked at Varun, bringing the subject back to what was really on his mind. "Its the money that interests brother and me. I could do without the danger and the risks."

"Oh, it's more than what you're thinking," responded Varun. " I told you that we've decided to stop being Christians. We've returned to our roots. We're Hindus. We worship Kali."

"You Hindus have so many gods. Just who is this Kali?" asked Nusswan.

Now Arun was exasperated, "Don't you

remember? At St. Thomas, the lecturer on the British in India. The history period. The worshippers of Kali: the thugs."

"Yeah, sure I remember," recalled Nusswan. "The bands of thugs were put down. All that's left of them is the word. It turns up in those comic books."

"Each time we took a foreigner, alive or dead, to your Towers of Silence, Varun and I think of it as an offering to Kali. I'll show you a postcard I have of her -- the one in the famous Kalighat of Calcutta. You'll see: she's black, and around her neck a string of skulls. Destruction! She's the goddess of destruction."

Nusswan scratched his head, "If that gives you satisfaction..."

Rustom had quietly come up behind them. "One man's meat is another man's poison. Right, fellows?"

He looked directly at his brother. "I've got news for you. The *Dastur* of the Fire Temple gave me permission to go to the Towers of Silence alone -- without mother. I hung around until it was real late. As I suspected, the *nasesalars* take off. I followed them."

"What did you find out?" asked Nusswan. "Anything?"

"You can imagine what it's like for them with those creepy vultures perched on the walls, waiting for a body.   Once the mourners are settled in the bungalows for the night, they take off."

"Enough suspense! Where do they go? What were they up to?" asked Varun. he always shuddered at just the thought of what went on out there. Those stinking birds!

"Unless you're satisfied with the money you've had, we can plan another kidnapping." He rubbed his chin thoughtfully, "In fact, a lot of snatches."

"Hey! Wake up! Finish the story. Where do the stupid corpse bearers go?"

"I have discovered they're hooked on morphine. I acted as if I knew where they could get anything they wanted, cheaper fixes than what they had been getting."

"Do you?" asked his brother Nusswan. Thought Nusswan, my brother talks like an American movie!

"Do -- I -- what?" Rustom said in a slow, deliberate voice.

"Do you know where to get drugs cheaper," said Nusswan somewhat more hesitantly at the coldness in his brother's voice.

"No. Of course not. But I did get their attention. I shared some heroin with them. It's stuff I bought from that creep that hangs around St. Thomas. As soon as they were stoned, I told them how easy it would be to earn some really big money. That we'd take all the risks. All they had to do was make it safe and easy for us. I convinced them that they'd just be doing their job. They bought it. Hah!"

Arun and Nusswan jumped up shouting and kicking up their heels, rejoicing over the news. The thought of the money made them impatient to get at it.

"Varun," said Rustom, "get your brother Arun

to bring the car around. We won't park in front of the Taj this time. One of the smaller hotels, I think..." Rustom had clearly established himself as leader.

As long as one has a body,
One cannot renounce action altogether.
Bhagavad Gita

Chapter XXII
June 28, 1995
Later

The Paranjotis were proud of their country and enjoyed sharing their city with guests and visitors. There were many activities for them; it was just a matter of deciding what they wanted to see and do.

Kamala had proposed to the Utsumis, "Let's go to see a dance troupe. They're to perform out beyond the city limits of Bombay. Do ask our other friends to join us." Kamala had taken classes at Darpana Art Academy from a teacher of *Bharata Natyam*; she had longed since a child to be not a ballet dancer, but an Indian dancer. Seeing the dance troupe perform was something she truly enjoyed.

As Kamala had promised, all were driven outside Bombay to where the Indian dancers performed.

Once the dance had begun Paul was aware that modern dance of the West had proved to be a catalyst for this young troupe of Indian dancers, but they had not severed their roots to indigenous dance forms.　They used some masks, body paint and costumes and traditional music.

All were entranced as the troupe danced there under the boughs of a huge tree on an improvised stage.　As they danced, Kamala, in a stage whisper, commented, "This troupe has fused elements of free-style movement with classical Indian dance."　Paul nodded his head in agreement, since it had been his observation as well.

The performing was wild, passionate, and yet sure.　It mattered not that the episode from the epic *Ramayana* was largely unfamiliar to Paul.　Zarina whispered to Paul, "Hindu epics are crowded with many characters -- Gods, demons."

At the university, the comparative literary course had only touched lightly on the Asian classics. Now Paul wished he'd read them, for the bronze beauty and strong bodies of the female and male dancers kept his gaze fixed on the stage.

"This will go on for hours.　Shortly, torches will be brought in to light the stage," said Mayor Paranjoti.　"Have you had enough?"

Kamala had to repeat his question.　Paul and Inspector Utsumi and Josie had been caught up in the phantasmagoria of color, strange music, and mesmerizing movement.

The inspector was too polite to say he'd had enough.　The highly spiced Indian food had not been agreeing with him.　One look at his face and the eyebrow he'd raised slightly was a subtle cue to Josie. She reacted immediately.

"Too much of this and I would be hypnotized

into a coma," said Josie. "Please forgive us, but *shujin* and I still suffer from jet-lag," was her lame excuse for their choosing to leave early. Josie turned to Paul Drake. "We three have traveled about the same distance; you from the west, and we from the east. Have you been having difficulty sleeping? a radical time change?"

"Yes," responded Paul. "It's affect on me is that I want to lie down and sleep at all hours."

Jim Taylor -- one of the Americans at the writer's seminar -- had been invited by Paul Drake for the dance event. Midway through the program, Paul became aware that Jim seemed to have disappeared.

Had Jim had gone off to get something to drink at a stand outside the performing area? Paul puzzled. By now he should have come back.

Jim's disappearance nagged at Paul. He turned to Zarina and said, "Where do you think Jim could have gone? I don't see him anywhere. He planned to return with us."

Zarina turned her head from side to side, as if she might spot Jim among the standees at the side of the bleachers. She rose from her seat, but her searching glance was without results. She shrugged her shoulders.

"Who knows? He's an adult, Paul. Let's not worry. Jim may have accepted a ride back into Bombay from one of the other Americans here."

"It is possible," Paul conceded reluctantly. "There are quite a few of us Americans attending this seminar. I haven't met all of them."

Zarina's face brightened and she smiled at

Paul, "You agree? He most likely has gone back to Bombay...He's staying at your hotel? Call him at once when we return."

Paul pressed her hand, "I'll do just that."

Josie had overheard their verbal exchange. "Do you think he would leave without telling anyone?" She did not make known her other thought, I would not have thought him rude. He is the guest of the mayor.

By this time, the others had become aware of their conversation and concern for Jim Taylor. The mayor frowned, "There have been too many disappearances of late. All have been foreigners: European or American."

The mayor's remark increased Paul's anxiety. "I'm going to go look for him." Without another word he stood up and made his way beyond the bleachers. Zarina and Josie followed him.

They scanned the stands. Some spectators had started for their cars, into which the three of them peered.

No Jim.

By then the program had ended. The remaining spectators were making their way hurriedly towards the parking area. It was evident that they were concerned about the long delays getting onto the highway.

Still no Jim Taylor.

The mayor and Kamala joined them. They walked slowly and silently to the limousine that had brought them from Bombay. The mayor was shaking his head as he looked to his wife Kamala. He was perturbed. Kamala smiled reassuringly, but he could tell that she too was worried.

Paul said, "I know his room number. When I get back to the hotel I'll give him a buzz."

The card of Mayor Paranjoti to the Bombay Commissioner of Police had been an `open sesame' for Bert Appleton. As he sat in the office he shared with Inspector Utsumi, a dhoti-clad servant brought tea. Word came that a body had been found on old Faulkland Road, renamed Patthe Bapurao Marg. The commis- sioner said with disgust in his voice, "The Kamathipura area is known for its sexual activity -- prostitutes in human cages.

"It is an American who has been found. The passport on the body identifies him as Jim Taylor." The police commissioner turned to Bert.

"It's not the person I'm looking for," Bert said, "but may I accompany you to the Bombay morgue?"

The commissioner nodded.

When the plastic cover was pulled back, Bert saw that the victim had been handsome, a tall, well-built man of about twenty. His light brown curly hair was wet and stuck to his face. He had full lips and a generous mouth.

"Poor fellow," commented Bert.

As the commissioner pulled the sheet back over the body's face, he said, "Tourists *will* go into these dangerous areas."

Bert the investigator was not prepared to

accept this simple explanation. He had noted that bits of stone and reddish dust had become embedded in the skin of the corpse. Bert had read the textbook *Forensic Geology*, by Raymond C. Murry and John C. F. Tedrow. He knew that the FBI had a number of geologists who consulted the book. "There's the Geological unit of the Smithsonian in Washington, D.C.," Bert said.

He paused a moment, absentmindedly rubbing his chin with one hand. Bert asked the commissioner, "Is it possible for me to send samples of the grit and pebbles from the body of Jim Taylor?"

Eager to please the likable American, the Police Commissioner had an attendant scrape detritus off the corpse. "Will that do?" he asked as he handed to Bert a matchbox of earth.

"Perfect!" Bert exclaimed.

Bert was not adverse to parading some of his expertise as an investigator. "Once the minerals we have collected are sent to Smithsonian, they'll be washed and sorted out and made ready for power x-ray diffraction; then for the electron microprobe; and last, for the cathodoluminescence. That is a cathode-ray tube which shoots electrons into the sample we've sent to them."

"So mineralogy can play a role in crime detection?" said one of the policemen sharing the office, although he was overwhelmed by all the technical words.

"Yes. Definitely. You can finger-print soil samples from a crime scene," said Bert. "Two rocks a hundred meters apart can differ. The role of geology is to tie the person or the body to the place. The samples we send will help us place the crime scene -- hopefully, within a couple of miles. No question they will be consistent with the minerals of a locality."

Bert knew that a survey might bring forth a hefty-sized bill.   But, as he had said to the commissioner, "This may prove costly, but I think it's something that the Ruperts can afford, even if it is *not* their son. They'll never know -- I hope."

Within forty-eight hours the report came back that the pebbles were of limestone and brick indigenous to India. What was most significant, they said, was that mixed in with the pebbles sent to them was the excrement of vultures.

"The Towers of Silence have been construct-ed of stone and brick," said the Police Commissioner. "It was a Parsi friend who told me it was built to be impervious to the pollution of dead bodies."

They still maintain with complete
Assurance: 'Gratification of lust
Is the highest that life can offer."
                    Bhagavad Gita

Chapter XXIII
June 28, 1995
Evening

As Kamala was dropping Paul and Zarina at the Taj Mahal Intercontinental Hotel, she said to them, "Tomorrow I'm expected for tea at the studio of a sculptor. He lives some distance outside of Bombay. He's English."

Josie brightened, "An English sculptor? Living here in India? I'm trying to think of what his name may be. I went to a one-man show in London some years ago. Of an English sculptor from India."

"That must have been years ago," said Kamala.

"I'd like for all of you to go with me. Is it yes?" asked Kamala. She turned to her husband, "Might it not be possible for a car and driver to take us?"

"He came as a tourist to India," said the mayor. "I'm told he wanted to visit the Ajanta Caves, to see the frescos -- and to nearby Ellora for the Kailasa of stone carved from a mountain as the home of the god Shiva. He had thought our temples -- the sculpture -- would be a catalyst for his work."

"He had said to me, `I've grown stale,'" added Kamala.

The Utsumis and the Paranjotis waved at Zarina and Paul as the car headed away from the Taj Mahal Intercontinental hotel.

Next Day

The mayor had put a car and chauffeur at his wife's disposal. Kamala, Josie and the inspector, and Zarina and Paul travelled together for the visit to the sculptor. Kamala talked at length about him and that they could anticipate a warm welcome.

There before the threshold of his house and studio was a man sprawled on a wooden frame -- strung with rope -- that was less than a foot off the ground. They were taken aback. Was he indifferent to the arrival of guests?

"It's the sculptor, Peter Findley," whispered Kamala. "When he awakes I'll make the introductions.

Dozing, his mouth was agape, Findley was showing nicotine stained teeth, which were huge.

Their approach did arouse him, and he jumped up, rubbed a massive hand over his face. He was unshaven and his *dhoti* rumpled.

He laughed to cover his embarrassment, saying, "Pray forgive me. I worked through the night and, I confess, I had forgotten your visit."

He pointed to the simple framed wooden bed,

" A *Charpoy*; Indians are realists. The closer you are to the earth -- sleeping -- the cooler it is. Heat rises."

It struck him that here he was the host, and he was muttering non sequiturs. Fully awake now he raised his hands, pressed together, to his chest, first in the direction of Kamala and Zarina. Turning to Paul, he grasped both his hands and squeezed them. Paul winced. Kamala introduced the inspector and then Josie, her long-time friend. Peter made the *namaste* with his hands in their direction.

"Welcome!" he shouted as he spread wide his arms. He was huge and every nerve in his body tingled with vitality.

Once the amenities were out of the way, Peter said, "I'll have the tea set out in no time at all. My houseboy is off. Each morning I see him painting an elaborate symbol on his forehead. Today he asked for a day off to spend the day at temple. He tells me he's a devotee of Vishnu."

Kamala said, "I was not aware that today was a special day devoted to Vishnu?" She was honestly cogitating as to whether there might be a festival she was unaware of.

"I suspect he has been romancing some girl in the village," said Peter. "I don't mind. He's young."

Their host waved that they proceed into his house. It was apparent that quite recently the inside walls of his house had been white-washed. "Make yourself at home."

Curious, Paul and Zarina stepped down into his studio. Close behind them were the mayor and Josie.

"His work has changed," she said. "India would seem to have cast a spell on him."

Paul, who admired greatly sculpture, said, "He hasn't hacked at stone, in my opinion. He's liberated from stone an imprisoned figure. His work makes me think of Michaelangelo's Slaves in Florence, otherwise entrapped for all time in Carrera marble."

Stepping through the door of the studio was a sari-clad woman. The light was dim, the unknown woman was not a surprise to the others, but it came as a shock to Narendra. It was Alina Mehta.

"Peter asked me to call you for tea," she announced quietly.

The Paranjoti party left soon after the tea.

That evening, a frustrated Alina drove away in her Porsche from Peter's studio. He fretted. He walked in his studio and around his sculptured pieces, muttering in a low voice to himself, as he would pound his fist or rub his forehead.

"It's the drinking. I know it is the drinking. I've become impotent," he said aloud to himself.

"What's to do about it?" He stopped suddenly and stood death-still. "By jove, I've got it. It's what the lowliest of Indians do." Now worrying that his houseboy might hear him talking, he placed his hand over his mouth. He knows enough about me already, was his thought.

He went into the room that served as his office. He stood looking at the shelves of books in disarray. His lips formed the word, `No'. He dug down deep into the large drawer of his desk. Impatient, he scattered papers on the floor in all directions.

He came up with an Asian journal. Under his breath he said, "Ah! This is it," Peter was a slow reader; he'd never been corrected of sublingually saying each word he read.

I'll gamble that that slob shopkeeper can put me in touch, ran his reflections, with the swami and his cobras. I'll have to pay him -- the pimp. He'll stick me for as much as he can get. Oh, well, it may be worth it. He can bargain with the swami.

As Peter had anticipated, the shopkeeper, whose name was Nari, was accustomed to setting up sessions with the swami, who lodged in a shack behind one of the brothels. Nari saw to it that he got a fee for the use of his back room.

Peter Findley's rendezvous was for late that night, for Nari used the selling of trinkets and tobacco as a front for his more lucrative dealings in smuggled pornography. He felt the need to keep a low profile, for the police made periodic swings through Dharavi.

Peter knocked two times, followed by three quick raps. I wonder if the slob knows that his appointed signal is the opening of Beethoven's third symphony, was his idle thought as he waited. I'd bet good money he has never heard of Beethoven. The door opened fully, without revealing who had opened it. Peter stepped into total darkness, as the door slammed shut behind him.

He had been sweating profusely from the heat and humidity. Late hours brought little coolness.

Anxiety caused his jacket to be drenched with sweat. Before taking a step, he closed his eyes to allow them to refocus to the absence of light. A sweating palm grasped his and pulled him to the door at the rear of the little shop. Once through the door, he was aware once again of the dim bulb hanging from a cord in this room that served as storage space.

Gradually, Peter discerned there in shadow the swami seated on a thin cushion. On the floor beside him was a large burlap bag. All was quiet, and Peter realized that now he was alone, standing there before the turbaned man whose gaze was seemingly fixed on the floor before him.

Peter cast his thoughts back to the article. It had convinced him that after he had recovered from the venom, he'd have the sexual appetite and prowess of a twenty-year old. A sure cure for impotence, he'd said to himself.

The swami's lad had appeared noiselessly. Using no words, he mimed that Findley was to kneel on the floor before the swami. The second he was down, he began to shake from nervousness. Suppose it kills me, was the sudden thought. I can leave. But, at that moment the strong hands of the assistant held his shoulders as if in a vise.

The swami seemed to have awakened, and under his breath he began chanting mantras. His movement then was sudden, and he shook from the bag a coiled cobra. With a stick he prodded the snake to uncoil and to come closer to him. Irritated, the beast raised its head, with hood flared. With a stick the swami pinned the creature to the floor. Findley watched, transfixed, as the swami swiftly and deftly slid his hand right behind the jaws of the cobra.

So rapt was Peter's attention on the hands of the swami, he was scarcely aware of the pressure exerted by the young man kneeling squarely behind him, forcing him down and close to the master. He was paralyzed by fear, and when he was told to extend his tongue, he was like a robot taking directions, doing as he was told by the forceful young man.

The swami got up on his knees, all the while holding the cobra with both hands; he closed the gap between him and Peter. Slowly, the head of the snake was moved ever closer to the extended tongue. In a flash the fangs bit deeply into flesh before it. In shock, Peter felt little. He started to pull away, but the lad held him firmly as the cobra pumped venom into red and glistening tissue. With a swift movement, the swami lifted the snake and the fangs left the tongue.

Peter collapsed, and the youth let him lie, shuddering supine on the wooden floor. Only the shopkeeper was aware of the silent departure of the swami and servant. Nari had been through this time and time again. He knew that Findley would be out for many hours. The very last thing he wanted was to have someone unconscious in his shop -- or possibly a corpse. He walked over to the church.

As advised by the article, Peter had arranged with a young lay missionary at the nearby church to check on him at the shop. His scam was that he sometimes was prey to an epileptic seizure. The shop-keeper Nari was most happy to see Peter Findley carried out and making the trip in the care of the young American across to the Catholic church. There was a dormitory behind the church where Findley was to recover from his blackout.

Blinded by their strength and passion,
They act and think like demons.
Bhagavad Gita

Chapter XXIV
June 28, 1995
Same Evening

In the street, Paul Drake stood for a moment trying to make up his mind where to eat. The night before he'd gone with Sam O'Leary, of the seminar, to the *Tanjore*, in the Taj Mahal Hotel Intercontinental. He had enjoyed the traditional Indian food and thought the sitar music and classical Indian dancing an eye-opener. It was wonderful.

It was expensive, and he was thinking now of going someplace cheap. He'd been told that the *Kamat Hotel* had excellent vegetarian food, *and* it was air-conditioned upstairs. He'd had a surfeit of curry -- much as he liked it.

He'd not written to Janis Peacock, as he had promised.

His next thought was, if I had a quick meal, I could write a letter -- it would be more than a postcard to her. It's too hot to eat much. I can see why all are talking about the heat and hoping for the coming of the monsoon.

As he set out he looked around for the man who had been following him earlier in the day. After what had happened to Jim Taylor, it made him feel anxious. His anxiety was heightened by the fact that he had not as yet received a letter from Janis, giving him any news as to what had happened to Damon Rupert.

"It makes me fidget," he groused to himself. "India is so different from anything I've known. Culture shock, they call it. Right on. I sure have it."

A car turned the corner behind Paul. Its glaring headlights picked him out. He was down near the water's edge. It passed him; a shabby old cadillac. It was going slowly.

Suddenly, a few yards ahead of him it, it came across the road to the curb and stopped with a screech of the brakes. The doors opened and four men got out and stood across the pavement facing him.

I'm cornered, he thought as he sized up his situation. I'll have it out -- better than diving off into the water. I've seen how polluted it is.

Paul walked towards them.

Something is very wrong, he realized. They make no effort to let me pass. He made to squeeze past the monument. The end man moved over slightly to block his path.

"Excuse me," Paul muttered.

Now they formed a semi-circle, with him as the center.

"You, Paul Drake?" questioned the one -- obviously the ringleader. Three of them seemed like poorly garbed young laborers.

His heart thumped against his ribs. Paul muttered, "*Acha*, but please excuse me. I wish to return to my hotel."

The bold one turned his head and nodded to the others. They moved, closing in on him. It was done in complete silence. Paul looked around wildly. It was late, and they were there alone by the monument to the Gateway to India.

There was a gap between the pair of them. Paul dived for it frantically, but as he did so he felt two hands grip the front of his shirt. He was flung back violently against the monument. A fist hit him in the stomach. Another blow landed on his mouth.

Paul fell to the ground, and they began to kick him. Then, without any explanation, the four youths suddenly stopped and jumped back into the vehicle. The car started up and sped away. Paul did not realize it, but a police car had come around the corner.

Paul slowly got to his feet and braced himself against the monument, taking in great gulps of air, listening to his heart hammering in his ears. He knew that he could not stand there indefinitely.

He decided to go back to the hotel -- not eat anything. He wanted to lie in a cold tub of water.

Then I can rest a bit, he thought. His legs had begun to tremble violently, and it was all he could do to walk the short distance to the hotel.

❖

"We made it. Whew!" said Rustom as Nusswan parked the car some distance from the Baag Sodawalla.

"Cobra venom is tricky," said Rustom. "You know what I've been hearing about Peter Findley? From Nari the shopkeeper?"

Nusswan came out of his trance.

"What did ya hear?"

"What," said the other two, like an echo.

"It's an old Hindu thing. Laborers, especially, they go to a swami with cobras. The snake has been milked, so it's just a small amount of venom -- just enough to put the fellow in a coma. When he comes to, he feels like a new man -- sexier than ever."

"*Are Bapre*, I've heard something like that. But what about Findley?"

"He got too much. That young American at the church said Findley died in the dormitory of the church. He fears someone paid off the swami. Someone had it in for Peter Findley," summed up Rustom.

"Probably knew too much for you-know-who's comfort!" added Nusswan.

Rustom nodded his head in definite affirmation.

Paul made it to the hotel, and at the desk he asked for the key to his room. He'd spoken in such a low, strangled voice that the clerk had to ask him a second time what his room number was. He got the key and made his way to the elevator and to his room.

The red light on the phone was blinking. He had a message. Alina Mehta urged him to come to the apartment. She did not disclose why.

Paul was suffering from shock. He didn't want to be alone, so somewhat reluctantly, but with resolution, he took a taxi to the Malabar Hill apartment of the Mehtas.

Half a cigarette was burning in the ashtray, and Alina went to stub it out. But, then she changed her mind and put it in her mouth. It isn't too chic to be seen with a cigarette in one's mouth, she thought. It makes me look hard? "*O lanjo*! Then as if a curse in Polish were not enough, "Shit, shit!" This is India," she spouted.   Not giving a damn, "Here there are worse sights than a woman smoking."

Paul stepped out onto the terrace, and Alina turned to him.

"I feel the need of some air. Escape from this heat. Can I entice you to go on a walk with me?" asked Alina. "As far as the Hanging Gardens?   It's just a good walk from Malabar Hill. No, I'll have you drive the Porsche."

Paul nodded with awakened enthusiasm. They set off.

On the way they decided to go to the beach, where they walked on the sand. Both gazed out onto the shining, opalescent sea. Alina listened to the sounds of people having fun on the beach, children laughing. "They're noisy," she said, with scorn, "But it does seem cooler here. It's an illusion, of course."

"Every place has its negative side. I suppose it's possible to vacation in India -- without getting into too much trouble," Paul said with irony. "Tourists flock here not knowing any better."

On their way back to Malabar Hill, they entered the Hanging Gardens. "This is cool and comfortable here in these lush gardens," said Alina. Without a word, they reclined on the grass. They gazed in silence at the stars overhead.

"You plan to spend a lot of time here -- in India?" Alina asked.

For a long time Paul didn't respond, so she opened her mouth to speak. But Paul turned toward her, put a finger to her mouth. His lips formed the word, `quiet.'

He had heard a noise from the other side of the garden, a rhythmic, panting sound. He peered through the darkness, trying to see what was going on. He saw a man and a woman, both naked, but he couldn't tell who they were. The woman was on top, riding the man slowly, deliciously.

"O moj boze," uttered Alina, in Polish. Then, "Oh my god," as if shocked -- which she was not.

Paul watched for a minute, then looked away. One of Alina's breats brushed against his arm. It turned him on. She didn't say anything. Not even did she smile. But her face was close to his and the invitation was so clear. He appeared embarrassed, but *he* was smiling. She snuggled a little closer until her face was touching his chest, as she pulled apart his open shirt.

Alina hesitated for only a second.

It was a delicious sensation for Paul to feel the top of a woman's tongue along his breastbone. He responded by letting his hand caress the back of her head.

"You have such lovely hair. So fine. It's like spun gold," Paul whispered. He drew into him the scent of the intoxicating perfume she had brushed into the curls and waves of her locks.

She drew him closer to her.

Paul hesitated, but the he put his arms around her and gently kissed her. Alina responded by thrusting her tongue between his lips. Suddenly they were all over each other. It was pretty disorderly -- there in the Hanging Gardens. He slipped his hand beneath her sari and caressed her breasts until he felt her nipples harden. Alina moaned softly, the sensation of his touch was heightened by the Polish vodka they had drunk. He moved his hands slowly downward, his fingers tracing the soft curve of her belly, following the natural descent to the delectable vee at the top of her thighs.

He worked her sari loose and spread it around her like wrapping paper. She saw the way he looked at her, and she savored the feel of his eyes on her body. Her hand glided to his waist and she busily unhooked his belt and slid down his zipper. Paul lay there beside her, kissing her again, and again.

Alina pulled him against her and kissed him hard, shocked by the immediacy of her own need. She reached between his legs, took hold of him, and guided him into her, eager to feel him inside her, to keep him and hold him there...so that no one else could have him. Their sudden movements became furious and out of control. It was marvelous. Nothing, nothing could have prepared Paul for this.

When it was over, Paul lay on top of Alina with her legs locked around his waist. He felt as if he should be exhausted, except that he wasn't. He felt great. Oh, he had tremors of guilty feelings.

Alina's expression was that triumphant look she beamed out to an audience on curtain calls. She burst out laughing. Her cheeks were burning.

Paul was puzzled. "Are you all right?"

"Never better!" exclaimed the actress. "It *is* hot -- even here in these gardens."

They lay in each others arms. Both feeling relaxed and intimate.

Paul broke the silence, "What is it like being an actor?"

Alina just mewed, not having a ready answer. Paul had it in his nature to be persistent. He liked, insofar as possible, to get inside another person's psyche. What made them tick. "The few actors I've known seemed respectable, settled."

"Stuff and nonsense," uttered Alina. "It's a facade. Or, the actor was seldom employed as an actor. More often, likely as a waiter," added Alina rising on one elbow.

"Actors are said to be like crossword puzzles in which there are no words to fit the clues. An actor's personality is made up of the parts an actor plays.

They are the persons they mirror. Someone I read said: `Make-believe is their reality; thus an actor can look upon reality as just so much make-believe.'" She took time to reflect. "How true that is."

"That's both cynical and harsh," responded Paul. "You're an actress, you tell me, but you seem very real to me."

Alina laughed long.   "You believe that. Maybe I play many parts...." Then as if she had second thoughts, "These precious moments have been very real."

Before he could press for more answers to questions of his, Alina lay back and asked him, "Why a writer? You tell me, Paul Drake."

"Now the shoe is on the other foot. I'm too young to be original, and I've asked myself that very question. I sense that an actor is impelled to act as it is the nature of water to run down hill."

Alina was nodding in agreement.

"Why do I write?" asked Paul. "Reading famous authors who have posed the question, I find repeated as an answer: There is an urge to write -- one is born to write. If said person as writer does not, he cannot live. That would be my answer, too, Alina."

"Take the writer. Does he -- do you, Paul -- use experiences of people and places, awareness of yourself, your loves and hates to fashion in a novel a picture of life?"

Paul sat up. "It is getting late, or I would elaborate on what you have just said. How true it is, however. For the writer, everything is grist to his mill. Especially, is he, himself."

Slowly they walked from the park to Malabar Hill. After a quick embrace, Paul struck out for the return to his hotel.

Those who are swept away
By the pursuit of pleasure and
Power are incapable of
Following the supreme goal.
                    Bhagavad Gita

Chapter XXV
June 30, 1995

I'll be able to resume my career as an actress, was a thought that played over and over like a broken record in her thoughts.

She had asked Kursi long ago in Poland when they first met, "What kind of theatre is there in Bombay? Is there theatre?"

At first he felt offended, taking her remark as a put-down of Bombay -- the most important Asian city next to Tokyo, in his opinion.

"Bombay is the number one city of India, and India is more a continent than a country," he said with emphasis. He wanted to establish that.. "As a matter of fact, we have theatres performing in English!"

Alina's ears would have pointed -- if she were canine -- as did those of her cherished pet dog.

"Ah," she said there at the dinner party in Warsaw, drawing out the sound of the `h.' From that point on she turned on the charm whenever she had Kursi's attention. She thought of the urbane and quick-witted Millamant, a heroine of Congreve's *The*

Way of the World, a role she'd played to acclaim at the National Theatre of Warsaw.

Much of her stellar performance as Millamant was lost on Mr. Mehta. She suppressed her irritation and her appraisal of him as insensitive. He may prove useful, she thought.

Kamala had graciously obtained a letter of introduction to the director S.R. Ray, of the National Center for Performing Arts, Bombay. She presented it to Alina.

"It's off Madame Cama Road, not far from our Malabar Hill -- by car," said Kamala. "Would you want me to take you one day?"

Alina was rather flip in her response. "Not necessary. Paul Drake has agreed to go with me. I've persuaded him to pose as my agent." As an afterthought she said, "Thanks, anyway."

Although Kamala was rather taken aback by her attitude, she reminded herself, That's Alina. I might as well get used to it.

Mr. S. R. Ray had been a minor diplomat, but he had been brought back to India for incompetence. "I can't refuse to see her, can I?" he said briskly to his assistant. The letter of introduction does apply pressure, ran his thoughts. We always need those patrons.

Alina and Paul expected to be invited into his office, but he stepped out into the hallway.

Knowing he was being rude, he gushed, "What a pleasure always -- to meet a star of the European stage. Warsaw, was it?" The latter was said condescendingly.

Alina was about to respond. She bristled. Paul got in a word before she could speak. "Madame Alina Crezmar had also performed at the Royal National Theater, London."

"Ah, yes," said the director, "with the National Theatre of Poland."

"Madame is bi-lingual. She is fully at home in English. As an American, I can attest to that," interjected Paul.

"Hmmm, very interesting. I do have her letter and her *curriculum vitae*. He pronounced the `v' as a `w.' He was showing off his foreign education.

"She mentions a play she would like to star in with our company. I'll suggest it to our board."

"When do they meet -- your board?" said Alina between clenched teeth.

"Not until after the monsoon," said Mr. Ray. He paused, then he added, "Mrs. Mehta, might there be in the Parsi community a possible patron? Eager to see you in the play you propose?"

Before Alina could respond to that, Paul said tactfully, "I'm sure Madame Mehta will discuss that with her husband.

"I know -- as does Mrs. Mehta," said Paul, to be diplomatic and to escape, "that you are very busy. May we call you in some days?"

"Please do!" said S. R. Ray, and ducked into his office:

As Paul had anticipated, Alina fumed angrily for the next twenty minutes.

Once in the Porsche, Paul tried to assuage her, "You must know, Alina, at a first meeting -- even a first audition -- nothing is decided."

"Don't speak of auditions. I am a star," said Alina in her most stagy voice.

"Of course," agreed Paul. "I've had to send a manuscript of my work repeatedly to agents. One doesn't ever score immediately."

Before Alina could erupt once again, Paul interposed, "Do come with me to my hotel. You'll find the bar and having a drink there just what the doctor ordered."

Alina nodded agreement. She was too angry to be kind to Paul. She muttered, "The whole world: males. Nothing but male chauvinists!"

Alina burst into the Paranjoti apartment -- as was typical of her. She recited how badly she had been treated by the producer. Before Kamala could say a word, Alina turned -- sobbing -- and flung herself out the door.

"I do feel sorry for Alina," said the mayor. "I can identify with her disappointment. I've had my share. A life spent in politics."

"Sorry for Alina?" asked Kamala. "She freed herself from a country, Poland, which she had come to dislike. Kursi is a devoted husband; he refuses her nothing."

"Quite right, but you know how much being on the stage means to her," replied the mayor. "I had already learned from our young writer friend, Paul Drake, that she achieved nothing by going to see that theatrical producer."

"Ah, yes. Now I understand. I, too, feel sorry. How patronizing of the producer to see her in the hallway -- not in his office. I shall certainly tell Indira, whose friend provided the letter of introduction. Her husband is a patron of the theatre, I hear.

Next Day

Alina did not take easily to rejection, and she viewed her meeting with the producer of the English language theatre as just that. She fumed. She smoked. She paced the floor of the apartment, going from room to room. Kursi was away on business. If he saw me like this, she thought, he'd throw me out. I must get hold of myself.

She decided to devote some time and energy to her AIDS awareness project. She had cultivated Father Francis in the old church in Dharavi. "I'll go there!" she said aloud with resolution. She slammed the door of the apartment, and punched repeatedly the bell for the elevator. "Damn, it's hell to park the Porsche in that slum. Oh, well, I'll go to confession, and use it as an excuse for parking in their courtyard."

She left the church's confessional booth, having said little to the father, except that she'd just had a fit of anger. Her penance was very light -- ten *Aves*.

Alina's early religious training was deeply ingrained in her. She felt compelled to do her penance. It seems easier here in the sanctuary, she reflected, I'll do the *Aves* here -- I don't want to forget to do them.

She settled into a pew and knelt. Ten was not a great number; she was soon finished and became aware that a priest was praying in the same pew. *Is* he a priest? she questioned herself. In the heat before the monsoon, I guess he is allowed to dress comfortably?

The handsome, sturdy young man -- Caucasian, with bright red hair -- was wearing a short-sleeved shirt and thin linen trousers. Being of the theatre, she smiled. He's dyed his hair. I wonder why.

Although her head was bowed, Alina had been observing him. He is a priest, she thought. It gives me a rush. Ah, that American-slang expression of Paul Drake's -- but it is apt.

At that moment the young man raised his head from meditation and pushed his shirt back into his jeans. He had sensed, rather than saw, that someone was very close to him. It could have been the scent of Alina's perfume, *Joy*, the most expensive French perfume, according to ads. The actress liked the luxurious feeling that she was moving in a *nuage* of fragrance. Like most Polish actresses, Alina enjoyed sprinkling the few words of French she knew into her everyday experience.

He rose and made his way to the altar, where he began to arrange things there.

She rose and bolted for the confessional.

In the booth, Father Francis was startled. "Daughter, you again?"

"Yes, Father," said Alina, pretending to be

distressed. "I have sinned. I had lustful thoughts about the young priest who came and sat next to me as I was saying the *Aves*."

"Who could that have been? A young priest?" asked the Father.

"He went to the altar -- just now."

Father Francis turned away and drew back the curtain on his side of the confessional. He chuckled softly to himself as he looked to the altar.

"There's no priest there. It is just Damon, our new lay missionary. An American, who has such energy for good works," said the padre.

"Oh, Father, I'm so relieved," said Alina. "Damon is his name? Unusual."

Moj Bozie, what I had hoped for, she mused. "His surname?" The Father ignored her question, and revealed his impatience.

"For penance, now a rosary. It is best to leave the church now and do the rosary at your home."

Alina did as requested, and slowly made an exit. But she lingered in the shade just outside the entrance to the church.

He is energetic and eager to do good works, mused the actress. I'll see to it he joins our group for Awareness of AIDS. She did not have long to wait, for the young man had opened the large portal of the church and almost bumped into her.

"How stupid of me. I should have been more observant. Do pardon me," said he.

"Hello. Father is it?" she said cheerily. Alina could shift moods with lightning speed. There was no response. She rushed on, "I was hoping we would meet.   Father Francis urged me to make your acquaintance. It's Damon..." she lingered over his given name, hoping he would take the hint and supply his surname.

He frowned, and did not give forth his full name.   He knew dying his hair had not been an adequate disguise, but he had had to show the church office his passport. At that time, he had requested anonymity.

That doddering old man, Father Francis! He's like a sieve with whatever's told to him," grumbled Damon to himself.

"Excuse me, padre?" said Alina, knowing full well he was not a priest.

"Sorry, but I'm a lay person, not a padre," he said somewhat apologetically. It had been quite a while since he'd had any kind of extended conversation with a woman, and he began to unbend a bit. "I guess you can tell by my accent that I'm an American. If you know anything about the States, you probably detect the drawl." He stood up to face Alina.

Alina took it all in, and inwardly was very pleased with the encounter. "I marvel at your casual clothes. I find...," she stopped there, but rushed on with, " just right...this oppressively hot weather. Or, does it make you feel that you could be back in...Texas, was it?"

The American laughed long and hard. "If you could see what is trickling down my back and legs! Dallas can be hot as an oven in summer, but Bombay right now seems as hot as...words fail me. I heard Father Francis say that before the monsoon, Bombay is a circle of hell that Dante omitted." He looked to Alina to see if she was amused. He need not have worried, for Alina was having some warm and stimulating fantasies. She'd love to see those rivulets coursing his bare body.

"I've been a Catholic all my life, but I've never known what is expected of a lay missionary. What brought you to India? You an American. So much I'd like to know," burst from Alina.

He lifted his gaze. He was fending for time. "It's so dusty and hot here. I have one of those miserable headaches closeness and heat bring on." He could tell she was disappointed, but he wanted a break from dull chatter. He wanted to see her again. "Another time. If you agree. We could continue our conversation?"

"I'm so pleased that you said that," said Alina. "You may have seen AIDS posters here in this area...you know, urging awareness -- the use of condoms." She had chosen to add that to see if he would blush. No, she thought, he's no baby. Ah, those Americans.

"Let's see," he said, mulling his schedule over in his mind, "I don't have any classes day after tomorrow. Can we meet then? I'd like to help. We are bound by vows of poverty. I can't take you to lunch."

"I did tell you that we share the same faith, so I well understand. It would please me very much to take you to lunch. Shall we say that I pick you up here at noon? You may have seen the Porsche in the courtyard...?"

"Indeed, I noticed it. It made me think of the one that stands in the garage back home." He paused and took her hand. "I feel as though I should know your name. First names will do."

"How remiss of me not to have told you right off. Alina -- that's my
name. And yours? No breaking of vows, I trust?" said she, smiling coyly at her new conquest -- she hoped.

"Damon," he said simply. "A name I've never been fond of, but I'm stuck with it -- been in the family for ages." Before she slowly withdrew her hand, she gave it a slight squeeze. Damon turned and walked away.

Alina sat in her car for a spell. She was deep in cogitation. Why does that name seem to ring a bell? It's unusual, and I know that I've heard it somewhere.

To renounce one's
Responsibilities is
Not fitting.
Bhagavad Gita

Chapter XXVI
June 30, 1995
That Evening

The mayor was attracted to Alina. His wife Kamala sensed it, but she was accepting because her husband was always honest with her when he strayed. Kamala comforted herself by thinking, Well, he'll grow up.

How prophetic!

Josie was alone in the mayor's apartment. I'm sure that is the elevator I hear, was her surmise. She waited, thinking it may have been Kamala who earlier in the day had gone with Indira to visit Indira's grandparents. Her step-daughter, Indira, was resisting an arranged marriage. Kamala had hoped she could help them avoid a painful confrontation.

Perhaps I should look to see if they forgot their key, thought Josie. As was her wont she opened the door quietly. Quite near she saw Narendra Paranjoti slowly easing open the door to the Mehta's apartment. She withdrew, feeling perturbed as to what to do. Nothing, she decided.

Josie sat in the dark on the terrace. Out of feelings for her friend Kamala Paranjoti she was depressed.

Just inside, a few feet inside her door, stood Alina. "Good to see you, mayor!"

"Likewise, Mrs. Mehta," replied the startled Mayor Paranjoti.

"And now, Mayor, I'm going to shoot you."

"Don't point that...gun at me. It's against our laws to possess one. I should report you."

Alina, taken aback, lowered the firearm. "That's what should come of your sneaking in here."

Paranjoti still stood in the half opened door. "Stop this right now."

Alina laughed. It was theatrical. "It's a stage prop. But it's real. Bullets, too." As she walked slowly to the door leading to the terrace, she turned, saying, "Very well, you may come in, mayor."

"I'll take that from you. We'll have no more of this." He placed it on a small table by the door.

Turning her back on him, Alina complained, "What in God's name do you want me to do with myself?"

"You've not had a visitor? Paul Drake?" asked the mayor, as he took her by the shoulders and turned her to face him.

Alina removed his hands and stepped out onto the terrace. The only light was that spilling out from the Mehta living room. "Not a single person.... All are in the country, I guess," said Alina abstractedly.

"In the country?" puzzled Narendra, following her out onto the terrace. "No one of my family would have gone to the country. Kursi -- your husband -- is not at home?"

"No. Right after lunch he went away on business. Was he to expect you?" She knew the mayor would not have entered as he did without knowing full well that Kursi was away.

"Hmmm. Should I have known that?" Alina was making him feel uncomfortable. "That was stupid of me."

"Why stupid?"

"Right after lunch, you say. In that case I would have stopped by earlier." He looked meaningfully at Alina.

She crossed the room, as if taking stage. "You would have had no one here at all. I've been in my room since lunch."

"And the door not a bit ajar so I could have talked with you...privately."

"You forgot to arrange that," said Alina, following it with a laugh. She was enjoying the way it was all going. So unexpectedly. Not that I haven't seen Narendra Paranjoti undressing me with his eyes, she thought to herself.

"That too was stupid of me."

"So, we'll just have to settle down here -- and wait. Kursi will not be back for a while."

Paranjoti responded, "Don't worry. I can...be patient." Once Alina had seated herself in a high backed rattan chair, the mayor sat, drawing his chair a few inches closer to her.

They looked at each other.

Alina broke the silence,"Well?"

In the same tone, the mayor said, "Yes?"
"I spoke first," uttered Alina.
Drawing his chair still closer, "Let's have an intimate chat -- as friends, Mrs. Mehta."

Having overheard that, Josie was about to withdraw from the Paranjoti terrace. She was feeling most uncomfortable overhearing their conversation.

Leaning back in her chair, Alina put space between her and Paranjoti. "Doesn't it seem like an eternity since the last time we talked together? A few words last night and this morning -- but they don't count." This was said as if by rote.

Josie hesitated. Why does this seem more than vaguely familiar to me, she thought. She returned to her chair in the shadows of the terrace.

Paranjoti frowned. "This morning? Am I forgetting? There was conversation last night, but it was in the midst of dinner guests. I agree with you, they don't count."   He continued to look at her questioningly.

"You mean like this? Between ourselves? Just the two of us?"

What he said was like a cue. Alina smiled enigmatically. "Yes, more or less."

"Of late there hasn't been a day when I didn't wish you were back in Bombay. You back from your trip to London -- if it was London." He was hoping she'd confide in him where she had gone.

"Bombay. I was wishing the same," said Alina looking away from him.

"You? I thought you'd be so happy to be away -- escaping the heat while we suffered and hoped each day for the monsoon. Was it a marvelous trip?" prodded the mayor.

"Oh, you can imagine!"

This secretly pleased Narendra. "You and Kursi had a good time? In London?"

"There's nothing my husband likes better than...lining up groups for travel. *Vacations to India. Goa!* The beaches are polluted -- I'm certain. I've never been there, of course." All had been said by Alina as if she were improvising.

Paranjoti was shocked by such an attitude from a wife, "After all, it is his business."

"*Moj bose* , that's true. So there is nothing wrong with it -- but what about me! I've been so dreadfully bored!" she said, flinging wide her arms as if acting for more than an audience of one.

❖

Josie was not one to eavesdrop. But listening to this dialogue -- that is what it seemed like to her -- had her mesmerized.

The mayor was a bit taken aback by the drama of it all, "Bored? You mean that? Alina...?" He gestured as if to take her hand. Alina skillfully avoided contact between their hands by fussing at her bodice for a handkerchief.

Josie made a difficult but firm decision.

Alina frowned. She was disconcerted by the way Paranjoti had replied. It was not quite what she wanted. O, well, she thought, I can't expect it all to fit -- exact. It's happened before.

He was studying her. She seemed oddly out of the conversation he thought he was having.

Turning to him, Alina murmured "everlastingly."

"Kursi is a good sort," said the mayor. The chap did enable her to escape from a communist Poland. He married her, were the thoughts he did not voice.

Alina turned away, speaking carefully. "Dear friend, Kursi Mehta is a specialist."

"Your husband a specialist? I confess I don't understand." He frowned.

"And specialists aren't at all amusing to travel with. Not in the long run, anyway."

The mayor decided to ignore her use of `specialist.' "Your husband is a businessman. Travel -- and the one you love."

Alina raised her hand, palm out to her forehead, "Ha! Don't use that...sentimental word."

The mayor was shocked. "Mrs. Mehta. I say..."

She rose and walked to the doors leading from the terrace. She turned, lifted her head and laughed as if playing to the house. "Just try it yourself. Listening...to...morning, noon and..."

"I use that word of yours `everlasting,'" said the mayor. Where is this leading, he thought.

"Alina, I heard voices," Josie called out as she entered the Mehta's apartment. "Your door was slightly ajar. I just walked in."

Alina took her time to respond. "Something I can do for you? Josie? The mayor was about to leave. As a foreigner in Asia, I needed some advice." She came boldly to the center of the room as if taking center stage.

I shouldn't be adverse to lying, thought Josie, since she had been caught in the act of doing just that. "I'd made some tea. I find that a cup of hot tea -- oddly -- makes one feel the heat less."

"How true," spoke up Alina, having actually taken in very little of what Josie was saying.

"Narendra, perhaps you will join us in a cup of tea?" asked Josie. He blushed, and Josie had to suppress showing the bit of pleasure she felt in having given him a twinge of guilt.

Kursi Mehta entered. Now Alina was more than pleased that Josie was there.

The next morning Josie began discussing with *Okusan* her reaction to Alina Mehta. " She seems to be always on stage." The inspector's only comment was, "Her voice is fascinating -- even seductive." Josie's suppressed thought was, Ah, you men. You're much alike. She did not tell him what she had overheard last night when Narendra had been in the Mehta's apartment.

The inspector was distracted and did not press Josie for more of her impressions of Alina.

Josie moved to stand directly in front of him. She had found that it worked -- getting his full attention. "I had a dream last night. I'm doubtful that there is any connection..."

"Don't be too sure, *Ha-chan*. You may be forgetting how prophetic was my dream of that incense burner. How right you were that dreams may be trying to tell us something. You recall?"

Josie had hoped that he might bring up that dream. "I was in Norway -- in the dream. That is as much as I can remember now. I should have written it down as soon as I was up."

"Did your parents ever take you to Norway?

I've always wanted to sail into some of the fjords. Mysterious and beautiful," commented the inspector gazing over the head of his wife.

"Never Norway. My father would only consider visiting countries where he could speak the language. He was comfortable with French and English. He could be stubborn."

Throughout the day a wish for associations to her fragment of a dream kept nagging her. It's like the tongue never ceasing to wiggle that loose tooth in one's mouth, fussed Josie to herself.

They are truly wise
Fettered no more by
Selfish attachments.
Bhagavad Gita

Chapter XXVII
July 1, 1995

Josie liked young people. Paul Drake and Zarina Sabavala together seemed so right. Josie missed her daughter away in the states pursuing a university degree. Her first motivation to spend time with Zarina was to learn more of what life was like today on a college campus. Josie had urged her to come more than once for tea.

The two women now settled in the Paranjoti's living room where the air conditioning enabled them to escape the heat. Neither had spoken of the coming of the monsoon. It had become threadbare as a topic of conversation.

"You know, Mrs. Utsumi, that I am a Parsi." Josie nodded that she well knew that. "Something my father was telling me is much on my mind. Young foreigners have been disappearing."

Josie could not resist interrupting, "Mayor Paranjoti and my husband are much involved in trying to solve these serial crimes. Has your father something to add to the investigation?"

"As a leader in the community, he has learned that more than one foreigner has been abducted and carried as if a deceased Parsi to the Towers of Silence.

The first man died of wounds inflicted by the vultures before he could be rescued. Father fears that there is likely to be more of this, foreigners murdered.

"You know of the Towers of Silence -- the reason why they serve a need of the Parsi community?" asked Zarina.

"Kamala has told me much, as has Kursi Mehta," said Josie. There was more now for Josie to think about.

Alina got from Kamala the telephone number of the police office, saying, "Do you, by any chance, know how I can reach Inspector Utsumi? He does have an office somewhere in Bombay, doesn't he?" She knew perfectly well that he'd been working out of the Police Commissioner's office.

"I gave it to Josie yesterday," said Kamala. "She'd have it."

"I thought of that, but she went shopping with Indira -- I think."

"Very well, I'll look it up," said Kamala who had been busy with her children. She returned shortly with a slip of paper in her hand, which she handed to Alina.

"Here you are, Alina. Now if you'll excuse me...?"

"Of course, Kamala." Alina was most often remiss in thanking people, and she quickly exited without thanking Kamala.

Back in her apartment, she headed straight for the phone. With one hand poised on the receiver, she glanced up, noting her reflection in the elegantly etched mirror hanging over the telephone table.

"There's really no need," she said somewhat wickedly, making a face at herself, "for Kamala to know that what I really wanted was a meeting with that handsome Bert." Her hand slid from the receiver as she continued her day-dreaming. "There *is* something about an American man that stirs my blood. Just like that lay missionary." She gave a wicked stage laugh.

Her thoughts turned to her encounter with the young American male who'd made the blood rushing through her veins feel like liquid fire. "What was his name? Ah yes," she said, smiling, as she began to dial.

Her call for Bert Appleton was transferred. There was a wait. She heard a lot of talk -- loud talk -- in the background. When he did not come to the phone immediately she began to drum on the table with a pencil.

"This is Appleton," came a male voice at last. "Who's calling? Is it local?"

Now Alina played the seductress. "Bert, do forgive me for disturbing your
investigation. But, I may just have a shred of something that may prove useful to your search."

"You must be kidding!" said Bert in amazement. "Right now, you're talking to the most frustrated man in Bombay, so if you've got something to say that's even remotely helpful, I'd love to hear it!" When she didn't reply immediately, he added a quick, "Please?"

"Did you say you were frustrated?" Alina gave a low and sultry laugh. "It's the heat, you know. Just bear up. The monsoon -- so they say -- will come eventually. Relief at last."

Bert rolled his eyes and made a face, his eyebrows moving up so that they almost touched his hairline. He brought his free hand up to massage the back of his neck -- his temples were beginning to throb. She goes on and on, thought Bert in frustration...reminds me of Mary Lou!

"Look, did I hear you right Alina? You think you know something about this guy I'm looking for."

"Yes," Alina said, deliberately making her voice sound a bit stiff.

Bert sensed his abruptness might have offended her, and he needed any shred of evidence he could muster. He changed tactics and in a much more jovial tone, said, "Say, I've got an idea! What do you say to my taking you for cocktails at my hotel?"

"Well..." she said coyly.

"Great!" Bert exclaimed. "How about 7 p.m.? Is Kursi in town? Bring him along."

"No, Kursi is on the road as much as if he were a traveling salesman."

Alina stayed in the ladies room of the hotel, because she wanted to be ten minutes late. She wanted to `make an entrance' for the benefit of Bert and the other patrons at the cocktail lounge. As she did so, she reminded herslef there would probably be no applause. Well, she consoled herself, it's just a bar.

The waiter took their drink order. After an exchange of banal civilities had been disposed of,

Bert abruptly said, "Well? I'm all ears. I need a clue or two, Alina. What do you have?"

Alina placed her gloved hand on Bert's hand, the fingers of which had been doing a rat-ta-tat-tat on the glass table.

"Are you familiar with Dharavi?" Before he could answer (she knew what she was doing was maddening), "There's a treasure of a church there, built ages ago by the Portuguese."

Bert started to get up, feeling he'd had enough. He was in no mood to play games with anyone, even a beautiful woman.

Alina played her ace. "Does the name Damon have any significance for you?" she said with slow deliberateness.

Bert would have dearly loved to deck her -- woman or no -- right there in the cocktail lounge. "Damon Rupert is the man I'm looking for. Where is he? Have you met him?"

"I do AIDS awareness work. I've had unprecedented cooperation from the churches."

She could see that his neck had turned red. Sensing that he was angry and getting angrier by the minute, she gave him her best smile. "Dearie -- "

Dearie? Dearie she calls me? Jeez! he thought in frustration.

"Try to be patient! I have to tell it my way. Besides, it may mean nothing."

Bert had begun to fume again, his neck turning from red to purple. A cigarette, he thought, I need a cigarette. NOW!

He'd tried to quit smoking, and up till now

had done fairly well, but this was too much for him. He needed a cigarette. Before Alina could continue, he held up his index finger. "One minute, please?"

He turned and asked the man sitting at the next table (smoking contentedly, damn him!) if he could have a cigarette. The gentleman had noticed Bert's red neck.

"Quit smoking recently?" he said as he proffered the pack for Bert.

"Shows that much, does it?" replied Bert apologetically. He took a single
cigarette from the pack. The gentleman with the cigarettes smiled softly as he whipped open an elegant gold lighter.

Bert gratefully accepted the silent gesture gratefully, lighting the cigarette quickly. He inhaled deeply, threw his head back as he exhaled.

"Thanks,"' he said to the stranger. "You're a lifesaver!" He gave a quick snappy salute before returning his attention to Alina. She had not liked being interrupted in the midst of her story. That much was evident by the expression he caught on her face as he turned around, which she quickly masked.

"Where were we, Alina?" he said as he exhaled again. "Ah, yes. AIDS awareness. Church. Dharavi. Damon. Right?"

Alina fumed inwardly, but nothing of it showed on her face. "Yes. Exactly." She leaned forward slightly.

"There's a lay missionary at the church -- an American." She paused to let that little tidbit sink in. Bert's raised eyebrows showed he was at last interested.

"By chance, I met him. We spent several minutes talking. His name is Damon." With an added air of innocence she added, "Unusual name, isn't it? I've even had lunch with him. He's young and attractive. I'm sorry I didn't succeed in getting his surname," she said, looking up at him from beneath lowered lashes. "You see, Bert, I was thinking of you."

Bert leaned across the table and kissed Alina. "Bless you! I think this may be just the lead I've been looking for." He stood up so fast that he nearly knocked his chair over. "Let's go to Dharavi. Right now." He turned and strode towards the door, confident that Alina would quickly fall in behind him. As they exited the hotel, Bert asked the turbaned doorman to get them a taxi.

"Taxi, *wāllā, āgyā dēnā,*" cried Bert, mustering up the little Hindi he could recall.

"Sahib, your taxi will be here momentarily," said the doorman in precise English. He couldn't wipe away the smile from his face that came from the foreigner's effort to speak Hindi.

The driver of the taxi plunged in among the cars moving in the direction of Dharavi.

"In time, I'll lose my mind over this infernal traffic," said Bert.

"Use your horn!" Bert shouted at the driver, who ignored him.

It was getting late, and the church was locked. Bert pounded on several doors, but to no avail.

"Mr. Appleton," said Alina coolly, "Come back tomorrow -- early. These religious men retire early and rise early. As a Catholic, I know."

"Damn, damn, damn!" Bert exclaimed angrily.

Alina turned, and headed toward the waiting taxi. She called over her shoulder, "Your Damon Rupert will not have vanished into thin air. Come to my apartment for a nightcap....That's what you Americans say, isn't it?"

Disgruntled, Appleton joined her in the taxi.

"Kamala, I do hope you understand," said Josie as she came to the breakfast room.

"Understand what? Josie dear. I'm sure I will," responded Kamala as she smiled at Josie.

"Fortunately, I am Japanese, so I understand. The fact is that the inspector is suffering from homesickness." Before Kamala could comment, Josie felt the need to explain. "Yes, homesickness. So common when Japanese are abroad. Years ago, when one of the Rockefellers created the Japan Society, they frequently invited distinguished Japanese to the United States. All expenses. So generous."

"I would say it was generous," interposed Kamala.

"Ah, but what they had not been aware of was the malaise I refer to: homesickness. For one or two it was so severe, they committed suicide. The famous translator of plays of a great English playwright was found in his hotel room before it was fatal. In each of these cases they were traveling alone," concluded Josie.

"Josie, how fortunate it is that you are here with your husband. Is there something Narendra and I can do?" asked Kamala.

"You've done so much -- wonderful hosts. No, there is nothing needed. He would deny it was homesickness. It is the western-style bed, the heat -- please do not be offended -- the wonderful but highly seasoned food," She held up her hands to stave off a rejoinder from Kamala." It is none of these. He's a tough old bird -- to use that American expression. Once we travel, or we have located the serial killer -- that's a high priority for your husband. He'll be fit as a fiddle -- there I've used another one." Both laughed.

"We'll just let him sleep. If you agree. I've told him that I choose to get up early each morning. I don't divulge what I do each morning. I simply say, `It's cooler, mornings,' continued Josie.

"He accepts that? What is it you've been doing, leaving the apartment almost before it is light?" Josie put her index finger to her lips and smiled at Kamala conspiratorially. Then slowly shook her head from side to side. She was not telling. Truthfully she hated keeping secrets from her dear friend. But she was simply playing a hunch. Kamala would worry that it was dangerous.

Josie had bought a large map of Bombay; the lettering was in English. How fortunate, she had thought. She had located the Hanging Gardens, and deep within or near where the Towers of Silence stood. She knew she could not approach them. The location and the taboo she had learned from Kursi Mehta.

For several mornings she had stood in the Hanging Gardens and observed Parsi mourners with the bearers carrying on a bier the dead person to be left at the Towers of Silence. Her persistence and patience paid off. That morning she had seen four bearers with a bier. But no priests.

Without giving Kamala a full explanation of what she had in mind, Josie proposed that Kamala take her where she could do some research. Kamala took her to the David Sassoon Library at 152 Mahatma Gandhi Road.

"This is a remarkable library," said Kamala to Josie. "It was founded by the British.

"Don't be put off by the fact that this street is run down. It does front onto Jehangir Circle. Once we're inside you'll find it is helpful. You wanted more information on the Parsi community?" asked Kamala.

"Yes," Josie said, "I find I'm very much interested in this community." That was all she chose to divulge to her friend at this time.

Kamala excused herself, saying that she wished to do some shopping She would come back for Josie in an hour. As Josie was acquainting herself with the library, she was delighted to come upon Bert Appleton.

Bert spoke first, "This is indeed a pleasure to find you here, Josie. I hope you don't mind my always calling you Josie?"

"By no means. I feel as does my husband, the inspector, that we are the very best of friends -- in fact old friends," said Josie.

Both made a certain amount of small talk when Josie spoke as to what was really on her mind. "Mr. Appleton -- Bert -- I have been going early in the morning down close to the Hanging Gardens, where as you know one can see at a distance vultures hovering over, I'm told, the Towers of Silence.

"From something that Zarina Sabavala had said, I have been observing any processions that are taking corpses to the Parsis' burial place. Is it possible that you would accompany me in the next few days? Then I can explain to you what has piqued my curiosity. What I have prompted me to come here to this library to do research on the Parsi community."

Bert hesitated. Then he explained to Josie, "Tomorrow, I shall be away from Bombay. I must go down to Goa, on the coast. It may be that I will locate there our possible runaway Damon Rupert. Many people -- among them young Americans -- are into drugs and are living on the beaches there in Goa. I *must* go."

"Oh, of course, I do understand. That is your first responsibility," said Josie, ever thoughtful and polite.

"But I assure you, said Bert, "I am most interested in what you are doing. I'm aware of the work your husband, the inspector, and the police commissioner have been doing. Once I've returned from Goa, it's a date. We will go, and I will see about filming what may be there to be seen."

"I'm going to ask Zarina Sabavala if she will join us. You agree?"

Bert nodded his full agreement.

Even a wise man acts
Within the limitations of
His own nature.
Bhagavad Gita

Chapter XXVIII
July 4, 1995

Very early in the morning, Zarina Sabavala set out accompanied by Bert Appleton and Josie Utsumi.

"I want to film any morning burial processions making their way toward the Hanging Gardens and the Towers of Silence," she told her father.   Her father had entrusted to her his video camera. "The leaders of the community are dead set on getting to the bottom of this use of the Towers. We have prospered in India -- are respected -- because we have been ever law-abiding," said Zarina's father, Sir Jehangir Sabavala, sententiously. He was tall and his most prominent feature was a beak-like nose. His relations with the English had been of the best; he continued to admire them. He had been knighted. His Oxford accent and his tailored suits attested to his identification with them. His beloved Zarina had to be unusually persuasive to get his consent to her going to a university in the United States.

Josie was the first to touch Bert's shoulder and whisper to Zarina, "I've looked through my bird-watching binoculars. I'm convinced these are the four I saw last week. They're all in white, but no priests."

Zarina gasped and immediately lifted her father's camera and aimed it at the iron bier carried by the four men. Almost at once they were lost to view by trees.

"Yes," said Zarina. "That was at least three minutes of film footage." Turning to her two companions, "I'm new to this. I hope the focus was set for that distance! " She shrugged. "My father will project what I shot. He thinks he may identify them if they are *nasesalars*."

The three returned to the Paranjoti apartment.

Zarina did not take time to remove the video cassette out of her father's camera.

The day proved to be a festive one; it was Kamala's birthday. She had invited not only the inspector and Josie, of course, but had asked Bert Appleton, Paul Drake and Zarina Sabavala and the Mehtas to help celebrate the day with their children. With her husband the mayor at the head of the table all the guests were seated. As the luncheon was drawing to a close, Kamala proposed to take all of them sightseeing.

"It would give me great pleasure to take you to visit some of the temples of Bombay. I can explain which gods the temples are devoted to.

"What day is today?"

Josie spoke up, "It's Tuesday. I'm sure of that."

"Tuesday, oh, I was forgetting Tuesday is a special day for a visit to the temple dedicated to Hanuman, the Monkey God," said Kamala.

"He is in our epic the *Ramayana*," added the mayor. "To Hindus the monkey is the physical incarnation of Hanuman -- a god. As such, he is a symbol of duty, devotion, and love.

"Hanuman is a very popular deity and is worshiped all over India, especially in villages. An the anniversary of the monkey god's birth, it is celebrated all over the country. People visit the temples where the idol is given a new coat of vermilion mixed with clarified butter and then richly decorated. Most often the *Ramayana* is read on this occasion." The mayor added, "I fear I bore you."

As if with one voice, the guests said, "No!"

"Please go on. I'm sure all here are most interested to know more," added Josie.

"Very well. There are a few more things that I'm prompted to add. Many people feel more comfortable addressing prayers to this ape-god Hanuman as being easily approached. Shiva or Vishnu may seem like terrifying divinities. Hindus look to lesser gods for intercession. As Kamala has said, Tuesday is sacred to Hanuman, so you'll find that the shrine is thick with weekly favor-seekers."

A barefoot servant wearing a *dhoti* approached the table and bowed deeply to the mayor.

"We must all go at once," said the mayor as he rose from his chair.

Kamala arose, and said, "Narendra's car and chauffeur is below waiting for us."

Once they were all seated in the large limousine, Kamala warmed to her role as guide.

"As Narendra has pointed out, Hanuman is a god, a monkey god. To harm a monkey would be a sacrilege. Hindus and the priests of the temple would simply stand aside and do nothing, no matter what damage the monkeys might do to personal property.

"It's been known for monkeys to go on a rampage before they return to the trees. When this happens, Hindus consult their priests for an interpretation of the portents."

Seated in the front seat of the limousine, Kamala, fortunately, was largely oblivious that whispered conversations among her guests meant that they had only half heard what she had been telling them about Hanuman. Once within the temple, Zarina became fascinated by the numerous monkeys who were playing there amidst them.

She turned to Paul and said, as she handed him the camera, "Oh, do take
some footage of this temple area. It's easily copied, and think of how interesting it will be for the Utsumis' friends in Tokyo."

"How do I turn on the camera?" asked Paul of Zarina.   Bert, standing nearby, was holding the camera's instructional brochure Zarina had given him and handed it to Paul.

"Oh, Paul, I need help!" cried out Alina. "I've twisted my ankle." Paul hesitated. Zarina asked me to use her camera, he silently procrastinated. Now it's Alina.

"Paul!" came from Alina with the dipthong 'au' of his name stretched to a wail. "Get me a chair. A bench, anything!"

Galvanized into action, he rushed to her side. He had put the camera on the nearest balustrade. Unaware as to what had happened, he eased Alina down onto the steps. She wrapped her arms around him, giving him a kiss of gratitude full on the mouth.

Zarina let forth a cry of anguish. "The monkey! It has the camera." She turned to Bert, then to Josie. "What are we to do? My father's camera..."

Indeed, Hanuman had snatched up the black box. He sniffed at it, turned it around in his hands. He was about to take a nibble at the leather. He was startled and alerted by Zarina's cry. He leaped to the upper reaches of the temple.

All now looked up and were wildly gesturing to him to come down. This provoked from the mischievous monkey shrieks back at them. It was joined by other curious monkey Hanumans.

Kamala stood there, shaking her head. She hated those who utter in like situations 'I told you so,' so she waited until they gave up trying to persuade the monkey to come down and return the camera. Zarina turned to her with her hands spread in a pleading gesture.

Kamala reminded them, "There is nothing any one of us can do. Nothing. No point in finding one of the priests of the temple." She put her arms around the young woman, who was now crying."

"Your father will understand. He knows as well as we Hindus that here the monkeys are held sacred, images of the God Hanuman. I'm sure he has read the *Ramayana*. We cannot do anything to retrieve the camera. It would be sacrilegious."

Bert, with raised eyebrows, looked to Josie. Neither spoke.

If you egotistically say, "I will not
Fight this battle," your resolve will
Be useless; your own nature will drive
You into it.

Bhagavad Gita

Chapter XXIX
July, 4, 1995
Evening

Josie and the mayor came out on the terrace and saw Paul and Alina engaged in conversation. It was intense. Paul was being urged to going with Alina's Parsi husband to the Fire Temple. Both realized that the American had fallen under the influence of the charismatic and assertive actress, Alina.

Alina exclaimed, "Yes, courage -- yes! If one only had that."

"Then what?" Paul asked.

Alina heaved a deep, long, dramatic sigh. "Then life might be bearable."

Inwardly, Josie groaned. I believe I recognize this scene from Ibsen's play, she thought.

Paul was silent. He thought silence the best response.

Josie kept up the pretense that she was listening to the mayor, who was in a talkative mood.

Alina's expression brightened. "Paul, you

really must talk with my husband," she said looking directly at Paul. "He promised me something."

"What?"

"Well...Since you are a writer, I wanted you to go with my husband to the temple."

"You can't be serious!" interjected Paul. "I've been told that here in Bombay only Parsis may enter the temple."

Alina pointedly ignored what Paul had said, maintaining her eye contact with him. "In Iran, it's possible. Yes, there are still Zoroastrians -- in small numbers -- in remote areas in old Persia."

"Go to the Fire Temple," said Paul meditatively. "No, no. I don't really think the risk is worth it."

Alina lowered her head slightly and fluttered her lashes a bit, "But if I insist?"

Josie felt it was most definitely time to step in. She did not like the turn the conversation was taking. She caught Paul's eye. "There have been those terrible deaths. Several ending at the Towers of Silence," said Josie -- forcibly.

Turning her back on Josie, Alina directed a coy look to Paul, "Poor me. Then I have no powers over you at all."

"It's just too obvious that I'm a foreigner," Paul, shaking his head. "That I'm an American."

"I know of two Parsi authors -- living now in Canada. When they return to Bombay -- as they often do -- they're still Parsis, but they look and dress no different from you, Paul," said Alina.

She reached out one delicate hand to touch his arm. "Seriously, I really think you ought to," said Alina. "A unique experience! The chance of a lifetime! Writers thrive on the new and exceptional."

Paul did not answer at once. "What makes you think so?"

"It's common knowledge. Everyone knows that writers need the stimulation of new experiences." She laughed, "They are new-experience junkies. Everything is something more to draw upon when writing. Do you deny it?"

"What about your husband? Has Kursi agreed to risk it?"

Alina laughed rather theatrically. "Kursi Mehta! You think he can resist *my* asking anything of him? Not at all," she sniffed contemptuously.

Kursi Mehta, deep in conversation with Kamala on the far side of the terrace, had not been listening to the exchange between Paul and his wife. When Alina addressed him directly, by name, he wandered closer. Alina reiterated her plan that Kursi take Paul to the Fire Temple.

Kursi nodded, "Yes, I agree it can be done. It's no problem, Mr. Drake. We're about the same size. I'll outfit you from my closet. I have many conservative suits. We Parsis come in all shapes and sizes. A black rinse to your hair, perhaps.

Alina spoke up, "That, I have. It covers the few gray hairs I have." She perused Drake, taking hold of his chin. "You're handsomely tanned.

"Hmmm. I'll squirt some lemon juice in each eye," added Alina.

"What!" exclaimed Paul.

"The sting lasts a second," said she, patting his cheek. "When I played an Arab damsel in a film -- a terrible film -- the director insisted on it."

"I still don't understand," said Paul.

"Take a close look at Kursi's and also the mayor's eyes. The whites of the eyes of dark-skinned people are darker than yours and mine. We're Caucasian."

Paul shrugged. "Okay," he said. "But..."

Kursi interposed, "Then I'm sure you'll pass -- also since you are accompanied by me."

"With Kursi, they'll be no question," asserted Alina.

"I admit, I am curious -- " Paul said.

Alina could sense he was beginning to weaken. "Of course you are. Paul, do say yes."

He took a deep breath, and expelled it noisily, ready to agree. He opened his mouth, his lips were shaped for `yes'. Then he hesitated. It was difficult for him to dismiss his reservations about the risk.

"No, no," he said, shaking his head. "Josie agrees..." But Josie had left the terrace. "It's too great a risk," Paul said with conviction

"If not for your own sake -- for the sake of others..." said Alina with raised eyebrows.

"Others!" Paul exploded. "What others? It's obvious to me that the Utsumis have not urged me to go, and there isn't anyone else about to go, so I repeat, what others?"

"Well...people," said Alina, trying to think fast. "The mayor. What about the mayor? He might think you're not very bold. Not sure of yourself." She smiled sardonically.

"I have no wish to insult our host, but I don't really care what he or anyone else may think of me." Paul looked fiercely at Alina.

Ah, Alina thought happily. I'm getting to him.

She pressed her advantage. "I saw it so clearly in the mayor -- his reaction." She shook her head sadly. "Kamala's reaction...Just a short time ago," Alina said softly.

Distressed, now, Paul asked, "Reaction? What did you see?"

"Contempt. When you declined going with my husband to a Parsi temple, I saw contempt on their faces."

"But it's such folly -- " Paul started to say.

Alina interrupted him, "Yes, 'tis folly to be wise. I saw the mayor smile and glance at my husband."

"Are you saying, I don't dare? That I'm a coward? A...a chicken?"

Alina shrugged. "Not I. It's the way the mayor sees it."

Josie had returned to observe and listen to them. She was troubled. What was Alina up to? She's acting a part, playing a scene, thought Josie, one I think she's rehearsed. The way she holds herself. She doesn't look directly -- most of the time -- at Paul, or anyone. It makes me shudder, but I can see why the role continues to attract fine actresses. Were I to close my eyes, I do recall the dialogue of that play of Ibsen's -- and where it's headed. Josie felt a sudden chill in the heat.

❖

On the way to the Fire Temple with Kursi Mehta, neither had any impetus to converse. Doubts about what he was doing clouded Kursi's mind. I'd better keep my attention on the road, he scolded himself silently, if I'm to survive this hideous traffic.

Anxiety had taken hold of Paul; there was a tightness in his stomach. For once he had forgotten the heat of the night, which rose from the pavement in waves.

But, once Kursi parked the car, and they walked up to the imposing portals of the sacred place, the writer in Paul took over. Now he tingled in expectation. What an opener for a novel, he thought. Age-old rituals! What will I be seeing? I've no idea.

Paul kept close to Kursi Mehta, who walked into the temple very slowly. He was solemn, and only nodded to those he knew.

Paul chose to act as if accustomed to the place. He waited a beat, and then did exactly what his companion was doing.

All seemed to go well. The two of them removed their shoes before entering the outer hall of the Fire Temple. Before a special vessel, Kursi washed his hands and face with consecrated water. As did Kursi, so did Paul.

With a covert nudge, Kursi had Paul facing east. Paul kept his head down and moved his lips silently, as his companion performed the *Kusti* ritual. Kursi had seen to it Paul had covered his head -- as did all men and women. Keeping close to the other worshipers, the two of them entered the inner room, built around the consecrated chamber where the sacred fire was housed.

Kursi whispered close to Paul's ear, "Only the priest may enter." He pointed to the consecrated chamber. As worshiper, Kursi's first action was to bow down before the fire and place his head on the marble lintel which separated the consecrated chamber from the rest of the room. Paul followed suit. All were fully attentive to what they recited. No one was aware that Paul simply moved his lips. Keeling close to Kursi, Paul rose from his knees as soon as the others did. As is the custom, the priest offered each some cold ash from the sacred fire. Paul almost slipped up, but Kursi maneuvered to face him, showing him to place pinches of the ash between his eyebrows and at the base of the throat.

It was then that Paul recalled what Zarina had told him. The ash and the act were both symbolic. 'It is a reminder that the individual will one day be reduced to dust, and it is a gesture of humility before God, that all are equal before Him.'

Kursi covertly broke in two the large sandalwood and handed half of it to Paul. The two of them gave sandalwood to the priest. Kursi had bought the sandalwood outside the gates of the temple.

The priest left the sandalwood on the marble lintel.

Kursi whispered to Paul, "It will be placed on the fire as an offering from us as worshipers."

Kursi picked out a quiet corner of the room in which he knelt and prayed silently. Paul did likewise.

A simple devout ma, Kursi was caught up in prayer -- so much so that he soon forgot about his companion Paul. He had much on his mind -- his travel business had worsened. Once he'd ended his prayers, according to form he went to the marble lintel and placed his forehead on it, reciting a short prayer. Fully rested and relaxed, he rose to leave. He did not want to call attention, but he looked to the left and right. Trying to be casual, he turned around slowly. He became somewhat anxious. There was no Paul Drake.

He tried to comfort himself with the thought, he probably left earlier.

On this path effort
Never goes to waste,
And there is no failure.
Bhagavad Gita

Chapter XXX
July 4, 1995
Later

Events of the last week had begun to take their toll. Two years before the mayor had had a minor stroke. It worried Kamala.

"Your getting ill will not help the situation, Narendra. You have delegated responsibility to the Bombay police."

"You're right, as always, my dear. I must remind myself that the Inspector and Josie are my greatest help."

"Don't forget Bert Appleton," reminded Kamala. "Please, let us lie down -- despite the early hour. I'll put a cold, wet cloth on your forehead."

The mayor sighed , arose from his easy chair and followed his wife, as might a tired child, to the bedroom.

The inspector and Josie were deep in thought on the terrace. They had failed to be aware that their hosts had quietly absented themselves -- as they were sitting together, looking at the lights of Bombay on the opposite shore of the bay. But, in fact, they were not seeing nor reacting to the city.

Josie had kept to herself, but she strongly suspected who had set up these serial murders. She was not alone in being disturbed that young Drake had been persuaded by Alina to go with Kursi Mehta to a Parsi Temple.

As is often the case with married couples, the inspector seemed to have read his wife's mind. They conversed softly in Japanese. He followed her out the apartment door; waiting for the elevator they plotted what they must do.

"I'll go ahead," said the inspector. "Appleton-san is waiting for me in his car. You'll find us seated at that canteen near the Crawford Market. I know that Kursi was taking him to the largest of the Fire Temples. It's buried in a cobweb of crowded lanes."

"Less risk for the two of them. Being large," added Josie as she kept pressing the button to get the elevator.

"Bring with you all that we may need -- if happens what we fear," said Utsumi in English as he stood holding open the elevator door.

"Oh, I so hope no harm comes to that young man," responded Josie. "I'll get there, *Shujin*. I'll ask Kamala to have her driver bring me to you. If there is a problem, it'll be a taxi -- I've taken them before."

Josie arrived. The foresight and patience of the three waiting at the canteen was rewarded. They saw Paul leave the temple. He began to walk briskly in the direction of his hotel.

"Now we can relax." said Bert.

Josie raised her hand to caution him to stop talking. She whispered, "See those two young men? They rushed out of the temple. They've been joined by two others. One is pointing after Paul Drake."

"I'll be damned!" said Bert. "Excuse me, Josie, but you're so right. They're piling into that wreck of a car."

The inspector jumped up, and said something excitedly to his wife. Josie translated, "Shujin says, `We must follow. Those fellows are up to no good. I fear for Drake-san.'"

Bert led the way to where he had hastily dropped the car. He stood there looking puzzled, for it didn't seem to be where he had parked it.

"There it is. Jammed in, now. Carts and cars. Jesus H. Christ, could there be a worse time?" Because he had cursed, he turned away from Josie.

She shook her head and smiled, thinking, I'm glad he said it for me. I wasn't born yesterday.

The street was clamorous. They stood before an alcove set into a house festering with rot from neglect; the ground floor accommodated stalls and one or two stores. The largest group of male laborers crowded before one of the stalls. The ones in front were making purchases. The haggling held up those behind. They were becoming noisy, protesting in Hindi -- Josie and the Inspector assumed.

"It's a *paan wallah's* stall," said Bert. "I knew at once. It's a vice common to Asia."

"*So desu-ne!*" said Josie, reverting to Japanese. Bert looked puzzled. "Over there by the gutter I saw several men spitting jets of red -- saliva?"

"The thick wads in their cheeks are betel leaves," explained Bert. The red splashes -- from chewing betel -- you've seen on buildings all over the city. It's their maroon spittle."

"I wondered what they might be eating," nodded Josie. She gave a shudder "Ugh!"

"The wallah has smeared a paste on the leaf and wadded it up for the purchaser. They're the ones we have to get to if we're ever to get the car out of here," said Bert. He grimaced as he looked at his watch.

"We get them to move," said the inspector. He turned to Josie. "You have rupees?" The three of them pressed forward up to the wallah's stall; Josie peered into the store.

"It's closed!" she murmured. "There is usually someone who understands English. How frustrating," said Josie. "How I wish I knew some Hindi words."

As if the wish had spawned what happened, a child came out of the crowd, "You want something?" he said in understandable English.

"Bless you," cried Josie. She knelt down right in the scruffy street to be on the child's level. She explained simply, "We must get our car out." She pointed. "It is very important. Go up and tell those men. Please? We must get our car out. We give them rupees." She thrust a ten rupee note into the boy's hand.

He stood and stared at it. Josie turned him around and gently led him up to the men who were intent on getting their leaves with betel paste. It was their 'high' for the end of the day. One pushed the kid aside and spat a red stream onto the pavement.

The boy was clever and persistent. He tugged at first one and then another sleeve, shouting in Hindi. At first no reaction.

He proved, however, to be a gifted child. Bombay is a Babel of languages: Marathi, Gujurati, Tamil, Telugu, Sindi, and Kanada. Muslims speak Gujurati as well as Urdu. This one must be Muslim, he thought, so I'll try Urdu. That did get attention. From a couple of Hindus as well.

Tightly between his forefinger and his thumb he held up the rupee note Josie had given to him. That did the trick. They listened.

Joined by her husband, Josie and the inspector both held up rupees spread in their hands as if the rupees were playing cards. There was a rush to clear the way for the car. Bert almost got knocked down by a cart heavily loaded with huge sacks of rice.

Once all three were in the car, which Bert had left running, he slammed down the feed and the car left tread marks on the pavement.

I am death;
I am what is and what is not.
No one who does good work will ever
Come to a bad end, either here
Or in the world to come
Bhavagad Gita

Chapter XXXI

The omnipresent traffic slowed Bert immediately. Were it not for Josie beside him in the front seat, he would have let loose a blue streak of curse words such as only a Green Beret soldier has at his command.

They learned later what had happened. Leaving the Towers of Silence, Paul had walked rapidly, and he had almost reached the Taj Mahal Intercontinental Hotel when a car pulled alongside him. He heard someone calling to him in English from the vehicle. Without too much forethought, he asked himself: Might it be one of the seminar fellows?

He stepped up to the car. The fact that it was beat-up didn't alert him. Most attending the seminars had little. They rented anything that had wheels. Rustom was seated to the right of the one driving. He opened the car door slowly Paul leaned in to learn why they had called him.

At once he realized it was no one from their group, but for him it was too late. The two husky

Christians had jumped out, pinned down his arms and shoved him into the back seat.

Paul cried out, but din of traffic and people crowding the sidewalks blanketed his cry of `Help!' Varun had ready the syringe with the cobra venom and jabbed the needle brutally into the American's shoulder. The spasms incapacitated him totally.

So much time had been lost, there was no hope that Paul's three friends could catch up to the car -- despite the wreck that it was. They searched for Paul as they headed toward Paul's hotel.

"Let's check at the hotel. He may have reached it," suggested Josie, as she hoped against hope. "The doorman is still on duty."

"Yes," said Bert, "It's the one I spoke to about Damon Rupert. He recognizes the Americans registered in the hotel."

No luck. When questioned, the doorman's response was immediate, "I've not seen Sahib all evening. I came on duty early afternoon. Sorry. Something wrong?"

Bert gave him some coins, appreciative of his concern, but he did not respond to his question. No need, thought he, to stir up the management of the hotel once again.

He turned to Josie and the Inspector. Josie had been in the lobby at the house phone for calling guests' rooms. "I asked for his room by number. I let it ring. No answer," said Josie. "I say let's go to Zarina. She said she'd be waiting at home. She was worried."

The inspector had said something to her in

Japanese. "Shujin thinks that if at all possible we should have Zarina involve her father," said Josie to Bert.

They headed to Bert's car. All the while he kept talking. "He is a leader in the community -- her father. She told me as much. He, and he alone as a Parsi, can find out at once -- I hope -- if a body has come to the Towers tonight."

The inspector spoke up, "There have been so many disappearances. I fear now...the hereditary pallbearers...paid off." He does find the English words when he feels a desperate need for them, thought Bert.

Zarina had already aroused her father. He realized at once how important was the life of this young American. When the Utsumis and Bert had arrived at the Zabavala home, they learned that Sir Jehangir Zabavala had obtained word that no burials had taken place in the last forty-eight hours. "We are a small community," he added. "Since the number of vultures has diminished, I regret to say some of our co-religionists use the modern crematorium."

"So many new apartment buildings on Malabar Hill encroach on the wooded area surrounding the Towers," said Zarina sotto voce to Josie, "that the people living there have begun to complain. They are upset greatly when the birds drop unpleasant things on their terraces."

Unprecedented though it was, with the support and cooperation of Sabavala père, they made their way past the sandalwood shop at the bottom of the hill, now closed due to the late hour. Dimly outlined were small dwellings, bungalows.

"These are *bungalee*," explained Zarina in a hushed voice. "They serve for the traditional four days of mourning of a Parsi family. Of course, now there is no *afargan* fire for the burning of incense." She gestured that they proceed. Zarina's father had stealthily gone on ahead.

There was dense foliage, a tangle of vines, and undergrowth. A small animal ran in front of the four of them. Of all people, Green Beret soldier Bert froze, cried out in a husky whisper, "It's a rat!"

"Not a rat at all, Appleton-san," teased Josie. "I'm certain it was just a squirrel, and it scampered away to safety." Bert hung his head in embarrassment.

"See vultures...up in trees. Sticking out necks. Make me shake," whispered Utsumi in Bert's ear; and he nudged him.

They're all nervous, thought Zarina. They all know how forbidden it is to be even this close to the *Dahkma*.

"Only twice, as a small child, have I been here," she whispered. "For grandparents' funerals. So, I shiver, too..." She wanted to put them more at ease.

"Father has told me that the paved path ends in gravel as it continues uphill to the entrance to the tower. He knows, because the approach to the tower is for male mourners only. The three of you had best wait on the veranda of the prayer *bungalee*. Where the women mourners remain behind."

"Are the corpse bearers up there within the tower?" asked Josie.

"Perhaps, and if all of us were to trod on the gravel path," cautioned Zarina, "the crunching noise could arouse them. Most unfortunate for us.

"Father thinks -- and hopes -- that they are ignorant of their involvement with the abductors having been found out. "

Overhead the vultures were encompassing the area, flying lower and lower, and at length alighting in the trees and on the stone wall of the tower.

Sir Jehangir Zabavala suddenly appeared, startling all of them. Zarina rushed to him.

"I now know that it's possible for Zarina and me to place ourselves in the shadows close to the entrance to the *Dakhma*.

"Make as little noise as possible. And patience, I beg of you," stressed Zarina's father.

Bert nodded, saying softly, "It's the waiting game. *That*, soldiers know about. Your brave daughter told us to listen for the sound of her high pitched whistle. We'll come on the double."

They waited anxiously. Josie was aware of the weight of the backpack on her shoulders. She had anticipated what she might need on such a night. It had been her hope that she might rescue Jim Taylor...the others.

Hours passed slowly. They strained with listening. Every once in a while, Bert ventured a few steps farther up the path, hoping for a glimpse of the two Sabavalas. Nothing. He returned to wait with the others.

Zarina had wisely brought with her the whistle she had always carried with her when she ventured out from the Barnard College campus.

At length, the twittering of birds in the trees made the inspector aware that day would soon be breaking. "Look up to the sky," he said to Josie.

"It is getting lighter. I can make out clouds," she whispered back. "Oh, I hear the signal. It's Zarina's whistle. The bearers must be approaching the Towers." She started to lift the backpack. Bert grabbed for it.

"No," shushed Josie. "I may be in India, but I am still Japanese. I would feel ashamed were I not to carry it."

Bert nodded, knowing he had met more than his match. "I guess I do understand," he said. "No officer, even in the American military, carries a package. His wife carries the parcels."

To be sure that the whistle had been heeded, Zarina and her father had moved some paces away from the tower ramp. Taking the lead, Bert saw the iron bier pass within the gates of the tower. Fortunately for the would-be-rescuers, the nervous youths and the *nasesalars* failed to secure the gate.

Everything happened at lightening speed in the miasma of putrid odor that hung over the place despite the fact that there had been few recent burials. The four youths in white hung back while -- in white with caps of white -- the corpse bearers of the *Dakhma* removed the white strips of cloth covering the body on the bier. There lay Paul Drake, unconscious and defenseless.

Josie gasped as she quickly removed a large black Sony `boom box' from the backpack. Her training in theatre as a *deshi* at the Kita Noh school had come to the fore. She had rehearsed and tested the cassettes when she was alone in the Paranjoti apartment. The inspector lifted it to her shoulder. All was in readiness.

The vultures, unaccustomed to the presence of so many people, held back, simply making chicken-like cackling sounds. Then suddenly, with a whirring of their wide and heavy wings, all the vultures rose en masse. Their hanging directly overhead was terrifying. The men in white scattered as the birds of prey made to descend on the body tied to the bier.

Bert and the inspector moved closer to Josie. She was intent on what she had to do immediately. She felt frozen to the spot, but she forced her fingers to act.

Sounds of hideous howling, coupled with barking like laughter, rent the air. The vultures had settled close to the bier. There was a pecking order among the birds, so there were seconds before they were poised to attack.

"More volume!" shouted the Inspector to Josie. He had said it in English to his amazement.

Josie's response was automatic. Deafening sound of jackals rent the air. The vultures, to a bird, rose in the air like airplanes on maneuver. They took flight to the trees from which they angrily flapped their wings. The racket they made was almost equal the amplified sound of jackals.

Paul was suddenly aware of shaking his head. The movement worked to dispel his feeling of being heavily drugged. His head throbbed and his eyes hurt him. The stench of the *Dakhma* persisted, but of that he was mercifully unaware, and he had no realization of where he was and what he had escaped.

Zarina was the first to get to Paul. She stroked his forehead, while Bert and the inspector lifted him. Josie went to Zarina who had begun to sob convulsively.

Assured that the young man dear to his daughter had been rescued, Sir Jehangir greeted the police officer -- a Parsi -- and his men. They had captured the eight men in white who had been fleeing.

Okusan has been keeping something from me, ran the thought of the inspector. If I am wrong, we know only a little more tonight. Who is the puppeteer?

Those whose desires are
Fragmented, who are
Selfishly attached to the
Results of their work, are
Bound in everything they do.
Bhagavad Gita

Chapter XXXII
July 5, 1995
Early Evening

Bert and the inspector, with Josie beside him, were standing close to Alina Mehta, who was leaning on the arm chair there on the terrace. The sun had just set over the Indian Ocean, and the light was beginning to fail. The breeze was slight. Alina shuddered.

"What were you saying about Paul Drake, Inspector? That he'd not been attending the seminars for the last two days." It was less of a question, more of a rhetorical statement.

"You urged Mr. Drake to go with your husband. To the Parsi Fire Temple," said the Josie softly, but accusingly.

"What did you just say?" said Alina, stalling for time to phrase a response.

"With my husband." She said the word `husband' without concealing the scorn she felt.

"What prompts you to ask that of me? It

could very well have been my husband. Suggesting it." For the first time, her face had taken on a pallor.

"That explanation is most unlikely," said the Josie. Turning to her husband she repeated in Japanese what she had said to Alina. Then she sat in a chair, where she could face Alina Crezmar, actress. "Kursi would have had to have been talked into it. He is a Parsi and knows the risks of a non-Parsi just stepping inside the temple."

"I see..." said Alina almost inaudibly, but it was in fact a stage whisper. Josie smiled, thinking, the gallery would have heard it.

"Paul Drake was here two nights ago," said Josie.

Alina had fixed her gaze upon the evening traffic on the sea drive. Their flashing lights seemed to have mesmerized her. "Two nights ago...hmmm," she murmured softly.

"No question of it. He had been invited by Kamala and her husband, the mayor. She told me that Paul Drake had indeed been here, that you and he were deep in conversation. Paul left with your husband."

Alina said without hesitation, "Yes, it's true. I want Paul to do things daring -- for his writing." A small sadistic smile appeared, a feral twist of the lips. "An adventure -- to witness the rituals in the Fire Temple."

The mayor continued, "From what your husband has told me, as is the practice, Drake was beside him. Kursi lowered his head to the lintel. Minutes passed. Kursi raised his head, no Paul Drake. Had he disappeared? Or left without saying anything to your husband?"

Josie interjected, "How frightening for Kursi that he had put himself -- a Parsi -- in great danger...his taking Paul into the temple."

"He did it as covertly as possible," said Bert. "Kursi searched the temple, but there was no trace of Drake. He had no choice but to tell us. Paul had not reached his hotel. Paul had been abducted."

"Do the police know," asked Alina, "that I urged Paul to go with my husband?" She bunched her fists.

"No, Alina," said the mayor. "They won't as long as I keep quiet."

"And if you don't keep quiet," asked Alina. "Then what?"

"Your lawyer could always say that it was your husband's doing."

"My husband!" said Alina. "That nothing."

"People propose, but don't disclose," said Bert succinctly. "You understand that English expression?"

Ignoring his question, Alina said, "What may happen?"

"Well, Alina," stated the mayor. "There'll be a scandal. Another foreigner has disappeared. And if you're not arrested you're sure to be deported."

"Sent back to Poland?" Alina said in a strained voice.

"What is it you're so deathly afraid of?" said the mayor. "Poland's no longer communist. Like Russia, I daresay, there may be chaos."

Josie turned to the mayor, "There'll be questions. All the disappearance of foreigners, yes?"

"All those -- disappearances," said Alina,

turning away. "They're no concern of mine."

Not perturbed, Josie spoke directly to Alina's back. "You have to answer all the police's questions. You sent Paul Drake to the Parsi temple. We all heard you, Alina."

Then Josie turned to the inspector and speaking in Japanese to him she said, "You agree?"

Utsumi nodded and at the same time formed with his lips the affirmative: *hai*.

"I hadn't thought of that," said Alina softly.

"There's no danger of deportation, Mrs. Mehta -- as long as I keep quiet," said the mayor to Alina. He smiled just for Alina's benefit.

"So, I'm in your power -- mayor," said Alina, staring at him. "You have a hold on me from now on."

Josie turned to her husband, and said softly in Japanese, "Listen closely to her manner of speaking. It's as if she's delivering lines of dialogue from a play -- that it's not Alina speaking."

"Ah," said Utsumi, nodding. "The actress!"

The mayor leaned forward, whispering softly to Alina, "My dearest Alina, believe me -- as mayor -- I'll not abuse my position."

Alina lowered her voice, but said histrionically, "All the same, I'm in your power. Tied to your will and desire. Not free, not free then."

Alina rose and paced. Her hand went to her mouth in an overdone gesture, "No. I -- I can't bear the thought of it. Never!" With a melodramatic gesture, she exited from the terrace.

The mayor, Josie and the inspector quickly followed her into the house.

The mayor, catching the inspector's eye as they went inside, raised his hands, with both palms before his breast, and said mockingly, "*Namaste*. Women usually adjust to the inevitable."

Josie's hackles began to rise. She turned fully to the inspector and made a face of disgust. "I know for sure this time what the mayor is up to," she whispered in Japanese. "Poor Kamala!"

The inspector put his finger to his lips to caution her. He rolled his eyes in the direction of the door.

Alina had positioned herself under flattering lighting, but with her back partially to the door, and was unaware of the newcomers.

Paul Drake, accompanied by Zarina, entered silently, ushered in by Kamala.

The mayor made a half-gasping, half-choking sound of astonishment.

Alina turned quickly at the sound. She was disappointed, in shock. The blood drained from her face. She shook her head in disbelief.

Kamala stepped forward. "Paul, I must confess I'm not surprised. Josie and the inspector told me you had been rescued. Please, Josie, tell how Paul now is safe and here."

Utsumi shrugged, "*Hanashite, okusan*. We tell all now."

"Paul had found the strain of being in the Fire Temple too much for him," related Josie. "Is that right, Paul?"

He nodded agreement. "I'm terribly sorry, Kursi, I didn't whisper to you that I was leaving. All I could think of was getting out of there."

"We saw you leave," Bert filled in. "What a time we had getting my car out! Jammed in by carts and other cars...We're much indebted to a kid who not only spoke English, but other languages as well."

"And it says in the Bible: `a child shall lead them.' He disentangled us, bless him," interposed Josie. "We feared the worst when we found out that not only wasn't Paul at his hotel, but the doorman hadn't seen him at all. The doorman did say he thought he'd seen an American getting into a car some distance from the hotel."

"From his description, it sounded like what we'd call in the States a gypsy cab," said Bert.

"So Paul had been abducted, but what confounds me is how you managed to get to the *Dakhma* -- the Towers of Silence," spoke up the mayor.

Kamala turned to her husband, "Josie told me about that. It seems Zarina and her father were waiting for them by one of the towers. A signal had been arranged..."

Josie felt the need to elaborate. "The pallbearers carrying Paul unconscious on an iron bier had been admitted to the tower by the four hereditary bearers."

"The inspector, Josie and I," added Bert, "rushed in to find, as we had anticipated, a comatose Paul Drake. The vultures had begun to circle and to hover over him. I was frantically trying to come up with an idea about what to do, because I had been kept in the dark..."

"It was *Okusan*," blurted out the inspector, who had been taciturn up to now.

"Well," said Josie, "I reasoned that all creatures are fearful of something. Based on that premise, I went to the library of the University of Bombay to research what a vulture might fear. I learned that they fear jackals."

"What good was that? How were you, Josie, to come up with jackals?" asked Kamala.

"We're all exhausted. It's a long story -- for another time. But, I will give you a shortened version. I had sent to me by Express International Mail from London audio cassettes of the howling and, yes, laughter of jackals. Our daughter Yoriko had made me a present of a portable tape recorder."

"*Okusan* has many music cassettes," interrupted the inspector.

"Josie, dear" said Kamala, "that express package came days ago. I was curious, but I didn't ask you what was in it. Now, I am truly inquisitive. Had you anticipated the need for tonight?"

Despite the stressful night that Josie had been through, she mustered a laugh. "I can't see into the future, Kamala, if that's what you mean. Not at all. No. If you remember, I told you about that early morning I'd been down by Old Ridge Road, observing what burials were headed toward the Towers. I must confess that I had the impossible fantasy that if I suspected it was an abducted person being taken to the Towers of Silence and not a dead person, I'd rescue him. With my tapes of jackal laughter, I would drive off the birds. I had absolutely no premonition that Paul had been set up to be abducted!"

"Oh, Josie!" exclaimed Kamala.

"You will all, no doubt, have a good laugh at

my expense," said Josie, her usual good natured self.

"Oh, no, Josie," said Kamala quite seriously. "I think it was a terribly brave thing to even think of doing. A lone female against those horribly, vicious birds. Ugh! I shudder to think of it."

Josie had not meant to upset her friend, so soothed her by saying, "It was just a fantasy, Kamala. Tonight I learned just how impossible it would have been for me -- a single person -- to save anybody, let alone my getting anywhere near to the Towers themselves."

Inspector Utsumi had his gaze fixed in a particular direction, which Josie suddenly became aware of. She turned to brush ashes off the lapel of his jacket, as she usually did. It enabled her perceive what had his full attention. Alina stood there, apart from the others. It was obvious that she was so tense that she could have posed for Lot's wife, turned to a pillar of salt.

"Inspector?" said the mayor. When the inspector did not react to his call, he called out, "Josie." When she didn't react either, he raised his voice, "Josie!" She turned to face the mayor slowly.

"The *Nasesalars* -- the attendants -- should have prevented you from entering the grounds. And, as if that weren't remarkable enough, you were able to actually reach and then enter one of the burial towers. Beyond belief!"

Utsumi had been listening carefully. He spoke in Japanese to Josie, who then translated, "The attendants had been subverted with money for drugs. They were hereditary, but new to the responsibilities of the Towers. And carelessly, the gate through which Paul was carried had been left ajar. Fortunate for us."

The inspector added in English, "I tell Josie. Much volume. It drive off vultures."

Bert finished the story. "The vultures settled in the trees, flapping their wings in agitation. The sound of the howling jackals did it -- frightened them away."

Zarina spoke up, "They're to be punished. Those young men -- all eight."

Alina was taking it all in, but as if in a trance.

"It's a miracle," said the mayor, "how you, Paul Drake, escaped the fate of the others."

"He almost didn't," said Josie. "There was a lot of traffic. Under normal circumstances, we would have caught up with Paul, who had walked away from the temple and Crawford Market."

Kamala shuddered. "What kept the vultures from attacking Paul immediately?"

"By this time, Paul, you were coming to from the injections," said Josie. "Fortunately for you, you were only given enough to make you unconscious, not kill you. The corpse bearers..." Josie paused momentarily when she saw Paul shudder at the mention of the words corpse bearers, then continued, "The corpse bearers had removed the cloth covering you. Naked, you were very vulnerable. The vultures were silent, but their heads had been thrust forward. Zarina's father tried to restrain her, but she was like a tigress defending her cubs, absolutely fearless. She rushed to your side."

Alina's eyes burned with fury as she looked at Paul. "Here you are -- alive! What is it, this curse?

That everything I touch turns ridiculous and futile?" Alina turned slowly and began to walk away from them.

"Wait!" Josie called after Alina. "There is something else. More to reveal."

Alina, caught up in her fears, didn't seem to hear Josie.

"The four youths Peter Findley rounded up for you, Alina, have been arrested. They have confessed. We know now that it was you who set in motion the serial killings of foreigners. I found it so hard to believe that your obsessions, your misanthropy would lead you to this . . ."

Josie wasn't sure, but from the look of fear in Alina's eyes, she knew that the actress realized she had been unmasked. Josie would later swear that she saw Alina's personality -- her grip on reality -- visibly snapst that moment. She was a cornered animal in the last stages of a breakdown.

The only response from Alina, however, was spoken theatrically -- as if it were a line she'd memorized for a play. "I'm tired. I need rest. I'll go to the studio."

Kursi took a step toward her, intending to detain her.

The mayor waved to him to desist. "Poor woman, she needs to collect herself," he said.

Soon music of a piano could be heard playing wildly. It caught the attention of everyone present.

"Alina's playing my piano," said Kamala in astonishment. "She's never done that before. How curious."

"What do we do now?" asked Bert. "Narendra? Inspector? Can she be brought to justice?" No answer was immediate.

"The youths may agree to testify," responded the Mayor at last, "but a clever lawyer will be able to discredit their testimony. I've learned that it was Peter Findley who recruited them. They claim never to have seen fully the person who hired and paid them."

"Well," said Bert, "I can promise you that Peter Findley won't be of any help. The police commissioner told me Peter is dead." At their looks of astonishment, he continued, "He died from an overdose of cobra venom! Seems he was seeking an aphrodisiac."

"So," said the inspector turning to his wife, "no conviction. *Hai?*"

Josie reacted with, "Hmmm..."

Just then a single shot rattled the air.

Kamala cried, "In the study..."

Kursi rushed in. Alina lay there lifeless at the piano, her head on the keys. She had shot herself in the temple.

"I'll be God-damned," cursed Bert.

"She took Hedda Gabler's way out. Inevitable, I suppose, when you think about it," said Josie. Her face had turned quite red from the feelings she was suppressing. "It was the role she had always wanted to play -- and had been enacting here among us."

Shocked and not listening, the mayor said

unknowingly -- exactly as if he were Judge Brack of the Ibsen play -- "People don't do such things."

A sweeping wind made the terrace doors rattle. Bolts of lightning streaked across the sky, their flash illuminating the room, making all unreal and ghostlike. The thunder was intermittent, but the heavens opened and crashing torrential rain pelted Bombay. The wind and the plunging cataracts of water made no exception of fashionable Malabar Hill.

From the terrace the earthy smell of wet earth and growing things was suddenly whipped by gusts of wind into the apartment. There were slapping sounds on the awnings. Kamala ran to close the terrace doors. Bert jumped up to rush to Kamala's side.

"She would have been flung back into the living room," cried Josie, astonished at the sudden stormy intensity.

Kamala smiled, as she brushed drops of water from her arms. The mayor came to her side.

"Kamala, is this the monsoon?" asked Josie.

"Yes, my dear friend. It will be many months before we will be able to put from our thoughts all that has happened here tonight," said Kamala, "but this warm cleansing rain is most welcome."

Afterward

The decisions of life are many branched and endless.
Bhagavad Gita

September 10, 1995

The monsoon had come and had ended. I could not be in India without a visit to Ahmedabad to see my dear friend Mrinalini Sarabhai, one of the world's great dancers. She had written to me that she hoped I *would* come and see *Natarani*, Darpana's amphitheater on the banks of the Sabarmati River.

There at the airport was Mrinal. When I embraced her, kissing her, she laughed delightfully, "Now, Jack, you know we in India don't display affection publicly. Do you wish to shock these people all around us here at the airport?"

All that had been said was followed with a smile. I knew she was pleased and happy to see me. I admired her flexibility.

"You were to Bihar and Sarnath. So your postcard said," said Mrinal.

"I've learned from travel in the past that if I try to encompass everything, I remember little. I was eager to take the time to reflect what had happened in Bihar and Sarnath twenty-five hundred years ago. In Bihar, the Bo tree was still there."

"From a sapling of the original tree,"

corrected Mrinal. "It is fantastic.

"Happy as I am to see you Jack," sighed Mrinal, "I thought you would hold off coming until the year 2002."

I was astounded. "For heaven's sake why, Mrinal?"

"Every ten years a great festival brings in tens of thousands of people who travel to the south of India to see the great statue of Gomateshwara. It is thought to be the tallest statue in the world."

"Tell me again. A statue of . . .?"

"Gomateshwara, one of the most venerated Jain saints. The spectacular ceremony is performed once every seven years. Pilgrims saw the last one conducted in 1995. A scaffold is erected above the image. Thousands of pots of milk, saffron, coconut milk, poppy seeds, almonds, gold coins and other substances are poured down over Gomateshwara," said Mrinal.

"That must be a most impressive sight."

"It is. The sight of the monolith's features being inundated in changing colors with every application is a memorable one," said Mrinal reverently.

Mrinal's eyes brightened. "At the very bottom of the card you said the most extraordinary coincidence occurred there -- Varanasi. Well . . .?" She lingered on the word as we settled ourselves in her Premier car. She told the driver to drive to her home.

"A series of murders in Bombay put off Inspector Utsumi's and his wife's travels to Bihar and Varanasi. How ironic it was that it had been these visits that persuaded the inspector to travel with his wife to India."

"I read from newspaper clippings -- sent by friends -- that a remarkable Japanese couple were in Bombay, staying with the Mayor of Bombay and his wife."

"Splendid," I replied. "You have some of the background."

"Do go on," pled Mrinal.

"So that I would know for sure that I was in India, I stayed in Benares -- excuse me, Varanasi -- in Clark's Hotel. Hotel Clarke's Varanasi, I recalled from my previous visit, is the oldest hotel here, that it dates back to the British. It had only a few air-conditioned rooms then. In the large modern extension, there were ample air-conditioned rooms. How pleased I was to discover that the hotel had a swimming pool. Small wonder that it's considered to be the best place in town to stay.

"After a nap I had tea in the lounge. There, I noticed a beautiful Indian woman and a handsome man. He was American -- I assumed. They were seated close together, and they couldn't seem to take their eyes off each other."

"Ah, young love is such a beautiful thing," sighed Mrinal.

"What had brought them to India -- to Varanasi? I pondered. Then the young woman responded to the hotel page -- 'A message for Sahib/Memsahib Drake.'"

"Well, many American men come to India these days on business. Some fall in love here, and marry," interrupted Mrinal.

"Yes, of course," said I to Mrinal. "I was curious, though. He didn't seem the businessman type. As an American, I think I know. Moreover, the young woman spoke English with an American accent!

"I went up to them, saying, `Excuse me. We seem to be fellow Americans. Please, join me for tea." They accepted.

"At first, I thought them shy. But that evening as I dined alone, I came to the decision that they seemed to be withdrawn. `Grief?' I asked myself.

"Soon, I won their confidence. They relaxed -- with me."

"Jack, you are affable." Mrinal paid me a compliment. "But I want no cliffhanging. By the look in your eye, there is much for you to tell me."

There was: all that I had been told had happened in Bombay and at the Tower of Silence.

Mrinal shook her head when I told her of a Polish actress shooting herself in the Mayor of Bombay's apartment.

"There are two types of actors -- in my experience," said Mrinal. "There are those who are always on stage; then there are those who fade into the background."

"You would know," I replied.

"Your actress Alina Crezmar, from what you've told me, is one of the former. I remember reading about this suicide..." Mrinal said.

"Paul Drake told me of all that had been sorted out after his rescue and after Alina's suicide."

Over dinner at Mrinal's house, I was able to add what had been told to me.

"Before turning in for the night, I went to the desk to ask for any messages and letters. Inspector Utsumi and wife were there, about to register..."

"Inspector! Josie-san! How pleased I am to see both of you."

"Jack Royce," said Josie. "You, here! In India."

The inspector was dealing with the porter who had their luggage.

"After our visit now to Sarnath, our stay in India ends," Josie informed me. "We almost missed seeing you. Are Paul Drake and his wife still here? They told us that they were to be at Clark's Hotel."

"Indeed they are. Early this morning, with our guide Mr. Gupta, the three of us made the boat trip on the Ganges," I explained.

"Do tell us all about it," said Josie. "*Shujin* and I want to do it."

"I'd love to, but I can see you are just arriving. I've had dinner, but perhaps we could share some conversation over coffee or a drink, if you'd like."

"That would be wonderful. Just give us half an hour to freshen up?"

"*Hai,*" said the inspector, joining in the conversation. He'd been busy tipping the porter who was to take their luggage to their room when Jack had first spotted them. "The plane ride was a long one," Utsumi continued, saying to his wife in Japanese. " I am most hot. I need a fresh shirt! India is very humid." Josie translated.

As the three of them rode the elevator upward toward their floors, they discussed when and where to meet. All agreed thirty minutes was plenty of time to shower and change. They decided the lobby was a good place to meet.

Later, Paul and Zarina joined them. There was small talk about airlines, flying, and travel in general as they waited to be served on the terrace. Once the waiter had left, Josie picked up the threads of the conversation she and Jack had been having earlier about the boat trip on the Ganges.

"Tell us all about it," said Josie.

"Ahhh," said the inspector approvingly. "Good...research a place...before visit. No surprises. I dislike surprises." At Paul's raised eyebrow, he explained further. "Too many surprises...job."

Paul nodded that he understood. "Yes, inspector. I imagine you probably have more than your fair share of surprises in your police work." Paul spoke slowly and the inspector seemed to understand Paul's English.

"Well," Paul began, "I can tell you that Zarina turned her gaze away from the burning ghats. Devout Hindus -- as you may well know -- wish to be cremated there."

"*Hai, wakarimasu.* I understand. I buy good guidebook," said the inspector, producing a small book from his jacket pocket.

Josie gently nudged the inspector with her foot, under the table.

"So sorry, Jack-san," the inspector

apologized, "Go on, please. I promise not to interrupt again."

"No problem. Anyway, everyone is impressed by seeing the devout Hindus bathing in the Ganges, filling their highly-polished brass vessels with the river's water to take to the Golden Temple."

"Where?" asked the inspector.

"The Golden Temple. It's up a steep street of stairs, which are wet with the water spilled from the brass vessels. The devout make their way into -- I should tell you -- what remains of the Golden Temple. Mr. Gupta told us it had been destroyed by the Muslims centuries before.

"The Golden Temple is, in fact, across from its original spot. The unfilial son of Shah Jehan -- who built the Taj Mahal -- destroyed the original temple and built a mosque over it. Non-Hindus are not allowed into the temple. The Shiva *lingam* was removed from the original temple and hidden to protect it from Aurangzeb, son to Shah Jehan. This Golden Temple was built in 1776 by the brave and noble *Rani* Ahalya Bai of Indore, and three-quarters of a ton of gold was used to plate its towers.

"Since no one of us is Hindu -- Zarina Sabavala is Parsi -- none of us was able to enter the present day Golden Temple. Mr. Gupta pointed to a sign that requested non-Hindus not to enter."

"Of course," said Josie.

"It didn't matter. Mr. Gupta took us to a grille that enabled us to look into the interior of the temple. The devout Hindus were pouring Ganges water over the *lingam* of Shiva. It is a stylized phallic symbol.

Shiva, in one of his facets -- we were told -- is the god of creation."

The inspector nodded his head and asked his wife to translate. "These phallic symbols are to be found still in the Japanese countryside -- fields to assure fertility. I've never seen them in our temples -- Buddhist or Shinto."

"What startled and amused me," said Zarina, "as we looked through the grille into the interior of the Golden Temple, was that sacred cows -- attracted by the flowers in the temple -- were milling around among the pilgrims and munching on the flowers."

Josie had been reading their guidebook on India. "As sacred animals, of course, no one shooed them out. Right?"

"Right," said Jack. All three laughed good humoredly at the mental picture this conjured up.

I paused for breath from telling Mrinal all that had happened, and by this time we had reached the end of a meal.

On the veranda, Mrinalini's houseman served us coffee. As I had hoped, it had a subtle fragrance of rose. Mrinal urged me to continue. Bats flitted around us. Twilight had ended.

"I informed the Utsumis that Paul had told me all about the case that had been solved in Bombay," I resumed telling Mrinal.

"My curiosity has been aroused. I wish to know all, Jack."

The inspector ordered crab cakes. "Credit must go where credit is due. One of *okusan's* English expressions. Credit is due her," said the inspector, turning to his wife to translate.

Josie's face had flushed from her husband's praise, but she did as he asked. "He added that I am to tell you how the serial killings were solved."

Jack turned to Josie. "At what point did you suspect that Alina was up to something? Was it early on?"

"I wouldn't say it was early on," said Josie, "but my first impression of her was that she was, shall we say, always on stage. She was an actress, of course, but I've known many actors. They give it a rest. In short, quite soon I was aware of false notes."

"I will confess, Alina could be overpowering. Seductive. "I've told Zarina everything," said Paul as he held out a chair for his wife. "We have no secrets, True? Zarina?"

Zarina, blushing with embarrassment, nodded yes.

Paul took a seat next to his wife. He continued, "I would have thought Mayor Paranjoti would find Alina solemn, even dull."

"None of us really knew the true Alina Crezmar Mehta -- the actress," interposed Zarina.

"*Okusan,*" said the inspector, "tell Jack-san...you hear...Alina and mayor...over on terrace. *Hai?*"

Josie grimaced. "I will give the impression I eavesdrop . . ."

"We know you too well, Josie. Tell Jack," urged Paul.

"Very well. I saw Kamala's husband, the mayor, stealthily opening the door to the Mehta's apartment. I regretted what I had seen. I retreated to the Paranjoti's terrace. I had not anticipated that the two of them, Alina and the mayor, would move out onto her terrace. I could not help but overhear them. The situation distressed me terribly."

"That must have been hard," said Zarina.

"Narendra and Alina were talking loudly."

"Josie," Jack interrupted, "I'm puzzled. You did overhear what they were saying to each other. What did it seem to tell you?"

"She was playing a role. The feelings she expressed were not her own. all was insincere -- overly dramatic. Do you understand what I mean?

"As I listened, it came to me: without his knowing it, Kamala's husband, the mayor, was behaving as does the character Judge Brack in a scene written by Ibsen. Like the Judge, the mayor was bent on seduction.

"His being *on the make* set off Alina's obsession with playing Ibsen's Hedda Gabler. Due to my familiarity with the play -- which I had spent months translating -- I realized that not only did she covet the role, but she couldn't resist playing it." Josie, pausing to catch her breath after such a long explanation, looked at the group.

Paul spoke up, "Did you detect that Alina had masterminded the abductions?"

"Oh, no. Not at all," responded Josie. "But,

I decided then and there to observe Alina closely. It fascinated me that she was confusing what was happening around her with a role she was bent on playing. I confess I was increasingly troubled by Alina. I was picking up ominous clues."

"We're forgetting about Bert Appleton," said Paul.

"He was in India!" Jack exclaimed. "Yes, Paul, tell me."

"The mayor was convinced that he had been abducted," said Zarina.

"Bert?" Jack asked.

"No, no," said Paul. "Bert had been hired by the parents of the missing American writer Damon Rupert. I was sent to the seminar in India in his place. The very night he disappeared, a young American -- who had left his suitcase in the lobby before registering -- had been abducted. Bert told me all this.

"For the longest time all thought it was Damon who had been murdered that night."

"Did they ever learn who the young American was?"

"Oh, yes," interposed Josie. Then she turned to Paul and gestured that he please go on.

"June had almost ended. Our thoughts were much on the heat and when would the monsoon come! Finally the Mormon Church made inquiries..."

"That's the Church of the Latter Day Saints?" interrupted Jack, who had a propensity to `dot the I's'. "When young Mormon men turn nineteen they go out as missionaries to convert -- the most receptive and even the reluctant ones."

"Yes, yes," replied Paul with some irritation. "They contacted the Bombay police through Interpol. Their young missionary Matt Namen had arrived in Bombay on the same plane as Damon Rupert. He was listed as a missing person for the longest time.

"His fellow missionary's visa had been held up; he was to arrive some days later . . ."

Not wanting to forego his talent to amuse, Jack again interrupted, "I've heard that, like nuns, they always travel in pairs." Even Paul joined the others in a laugh.

"Mormon missionary James Hoover arrived; he couldn't locate his partner Matt, Paul continued. He caught the next plane back to the states. Bert said, `I suspect the young lad never wanted to be a missionary.   To be weighed down with godly responsibilities -- and miss his youth.'"

"What had happened to Damon . . . . That is his name?" asked Mrinalini.

"Once everything had been sorted out," I replied, "young Rupert *had* wanted to disappear. He was in flight from his parents -- as Bert had suspected. He had met the parents!

"Alina, not meaning to, had led Bert to the small Catholic church which had become Damon's hideout. He'd dyed his hair red."

"If that was all, not much of a disguise," commented Mrinal.

"He thought he could at once become a monk -- with a robe to be added camouflage. There was a priest -- no one knew his motive -- who housed the young Texan. Even let him go about in that slum area Dharavi in a monk's habit. The priest's fantasy may have been that he could convert this Southern Baptist to Catholicism.

"Bert talked Damon into a change of mind. As Bert had suspected, the young man had had his fill of religious austerity -- and the Catholic padre."

"This was a sudden decision, you say?"

"Very sudden." Jack leaned forward a bit conspiratorially, "From what I have heard, it seems his decision to reconsider any vows of chastity coincided with the attentions of a beautiful woman...Alina?" Jack raised his eyebrows.

"How awful, Jack."

"No, I swear. Every word is the truth!" said Jack as he made a cross-my-heart-hope-to-die gesture.

"He decided he'd had enough and returned to Texas -- escorted by Bert Appleton."

"What about Paul? How did he survive the vultures and the Towers of Silence?"

Jack continued his story with, "Well...as Paul tells it..."

There on Hotel Clarke's terrace, Paul said as he took Josie's hand in his, "You saved me."

I turned my full attention to Josie Utsumi.

"How did you rescue Paul Drake?"

Josie spoke to me at length. "Dr. Matthew Torrence, formerly of the London Royal Zoological Society, was the one to whom I turned -- he is an authority on jackals and hyenas and has been asked recently by the Encyclopedia Britannica to do the new entries on these scavengers.

"At length I reached him. I asked Torrence-san what was it that vultures were afraid of. He consulted an ornithological colleague. `Any birds of prey competing for tasty rotten morsels, jackals and hyenas would drive away.' As he quoted to me the bird man, Torrence-san couldn't resist a hearty laugh.

"He mailed me, International Express from London, cassettes of the cries and howling of jackals and yelps of hyenas. He put both of them on a single tape."

"A mix of the cries of both?" asked Zarina.

"Dr. Torrence recommended use of the cassette if there was need of dispersing vultures. Both scavengers are in India.

"I was equipped with what in America -- so my daughter at Barnard College tells me -- is called a `boom box' from Sony that could greatly amplify the sound on the tapes. My daughter gave me the device a long time ago, for I had many audio cassettes of music.

"My father, when ambassador to the Court of St. James, had come to know Dr. Torrence."

"At dog shows I've been amused by the owners who look like their dogs," said Paul, out of left field. "Does Dr. Torrence look like a jackal -- a hyena?"

"I can assure you he does not look like either." But Josie laughed at the thought. "With the cassette, the good Dr. Torrence sent an article with a half page color photo of himself. Here was the exception that proved the rule."

The inspector interjected, "Torrence-san *utskushi desu-ne?*"

Josie translated, "Torrence is the very model of a striking, handsome, young man. Personally, I think beards detract," she added, "but there are women, even wives, who like hirsute men.

"If my daughter Yoriko goes to London, I'll have her call on him -- to thank him and tell him the use to which we put his splendid tapes."

"What happened to the young men who were guilty of the abductions, as well as the corpse bearers at the Towers of Silence?" Jack asked.

Zarina spoke up, "They were all arrested and are to be tried.

"Two days after Alina had been cremated, all four youths were brought to the Police Commissioner's office. He had asked the inspector, Josie and Bert, to be present when he interrogated them. The *nasesalars* were kept waiting in cells.

"Josie, you were there. I have been trying to remember what you told me."

"Nusswan, Varun and Arun remained silent," said Josie, "We suspected that the one named Rustom had influence and had coached them."

"Rustom! *Shujin* had never encountered anyone like the seething youth who sat before us. His performance -- all an act -- lasted from midnight to sunrise. At first -- like the others -- that Rustom had been mute, but then he exploded, demanding in Hindi that the Parsi community send an interpreter for them. The commissioner told us that he was shouting that their arrest had been stupid -- all a mistake."

"`The Bombay police were not buying that', I quote Bert," said Josie.

"`I think, young man, that you speak English as well as I do,' was what Police  Commissioner Varla said.  `Admit that you understand and speak English. My colleagues -- he pointed to the three of us -- don't speak Hindi,'" Josie took a deep breath. "No one spoke."

"An hour passed," added Josie. "`Yes, I speak English,' came forth from Rustom. `I insist on a lawyer.' We were all tired, and that brought relief."

"`All in good time', replied the commissioner. Food was sent for. The four youths were taken to other offices, isolated from each other."

"The police of the Crime Branch gave them no rest," said Josie. "The commissioner and I were with Rustom. As yet no confession. Finally, *Shujin* joined us; he placed his arm around Rustom's shoulders, as if he were his son. I held my breath. Rustom began to weep. My husband had become the boy's own father. He had missed his dead father."

The inspector spoke in Japanese to his wife. She translated, "He started to confess. The Police Commissioner asked him to wait until he had a tape recorder brought in. Then we learned of Peter Findley's role -- recruiting them. This added to my conviction that Alina had masterminded the abductions and what followed."

"Then what happened?" asked Jack of Zarina.

"The tradition of a jury trial was thrown out here in India when the British left in 1948," Zarina explained. "The framers of the new legal code, I've learned from my father, decided that it would be impossible to bribe a judge! My father and I had a good hearty laugh.

"It may be months, even a year, before all eight are brought into a court room for their trial before a judge." That was greeted with dismay.

"The Parsis can be very forgiving -- because of their youth. The community also hired for them a famous lawyer, Dr. Kishen Rau," concluded Zarina.

"With a track record of successful cases -- for defendants!" threw in Paul, smiling at his wife.

"True. And very costly, as lawyers go," said Zarina.

"What do you think will be the outcome?" asked Jack.

Zarina felt ashamed to say it, "They'll get off. Something that never would happen in the States, Paul?"

"Hah!" was Paul's response. He was thinking of two sons who had killed their parents.

"My father suspected that it was more than *paan* or *betel* that they had been addicted to -- the *nasesalars* of the Towers of Silence. Ordinarily they are loyal and devoted Parsis."

"If it was more than what many Indians use, *paan* and *betel*," I asked, "where did the other drugs come from?"

Zarina replied, "From Goa. Hard drugs like

heroin, morphine, have been coming into Bombay from Goa."

Mrinalini was curious about Alina Crezmar. "What kind of a person did they say this Polish actress was?"

"Alina was beautiful -- in an unconventional way, they told me.   At first she seemed to the Paranjotis to be a sympathetic woman. Her unceasing work to combat the spread of AIDS in Bombay had impressed them.

"`But she rarely smiled,' had said Zarina. `Then it was gone in a flicker,' added Paul."'

The great dancer, Mrinalini, shuddered. "That she took her own life fills me with horror."

"The inspector said to me that her Parsi husband was truly in love with his wife.

"Josie had countered that with, `Alina wished her husband dead. And he had done everything for her. He had bought her a Porsche, a great expense in India. She could never forgive him her burden of obligation. Japanese understand that only too well.'"

"You told me Alina didn't wish to be indebted to any male," said Mrinal, "There is misogyny; the word I am told for Alina is misandry: the hating of men. You've heard that too, Jack?"

"Zarina said that Alina transferred her disaffection for her husband Kursi to all Parsis. She hoped to be their nemesis."

"She was psychopathic," I said to Mrinal. "Some would correct me of that; it's now sociopathic. I guess I don't care about being politically correct."

Mrinalini interposed, "Might not communism in her homeland of Poland have driven her mad -- and the loss of her first husband?"

I told Mrinal I had asked Josie that very question...

"Tell me something, Josie," I said over desert. "Do you think it's possible that the combination of communism in her homeland and the loss of her first husband drove her mad?"

Josie said, "No, she was destructive. She sought to do ill to the Parsi community -- her husband's people."

"Alina's husband found a recent issue of the journal *Science* among her papers and books," said Paul. "An Australian woman scientist -- a researcher named Maydiane C. B. Andrade, of the University of Toronto -- wrote that the red-back spider sacrifices itself to his mate during copulation. Sexual suicide. That this odd spider will prance and hop and tap dance and somersault...all for the chance to be devoured alive by the female. Thus, a courting mate, the male, purposely courts death. I think that proves the case: misandry characterized Alina."

Zarina's comment was, "How awful!"

"And revealing," said Paul.

"There was good in Alina," said Josie. "She had cultivated the young American Damon, and he did respond to her efforts to get him to circulate posters around Bombay, dealing with AIDS awareness. One day, quite by accident, he had come upon her disguised as a monk. He had followed her, and in the marketplace he saw her meeting with four young Indian men.

"It puzzled him, and when he and Bert Appleton at last connected, he told Bert about having seen Alina, disguised as a monk, with four young men. With everything else, this convinced Bert that she was involved in these serial abductions and murders. So, when Bert conferred with the inspector and Josie and with the mayor and police commissioner, the pieces began to come together little by little."

"I was astonished that you, Josie," said Paul, "detected in Alina's behavior an acting out of an Ibsen heroine, Hedda Gabler."

Mrinalini nodded her head as she said, "Mrs. Utsumi must have spent a good deal of time translating the lines of the play."

"Indeed," I said. "That's how Josie knew the play as if it were her own."

"But most actors don't confuse their roles on the stage with their daily life," said Mrinal.

"Alina Crezmar, actress, did.

"Josie -- I was told -- had said, `I differ with that judge of Ibsen's play, *Hedda Gabler*...His last line.'

"`Which is?' had asked Paul Drake.

"`People don't do such things.'"

Mrinal was silent, caught up in her own thoughts about the tale just told.

I broke the silence with, "Once the four young men and the *nasesalars* had been arrested, order was re-established at the Towers of Silence. The Parsi community had been absolved of any blame."

Mrinal heard this and sighed, "Knowing that brings great relief. India is proud of its Parsi community. Their contribution has been great."

It was now quite dark. "Good night," I said to Mrinal, for I was tired.

As Mrinal rose to go inside, she waved a kiss to me, and said -- half to herself -- "It can be a strange and tragic world. Murder. Suicide. And people do *do* such things. But this is an interesting tale, Jack. Do you plan to write it down?"

<u>GLOSSARY</u>
Hindi words

acha	Yes
Vedya zala aheska	Calling someone a madman
Halkat melya	Calling someone a madman and a scoundrel
Bidis	Something which *kulis* smoke
Kimam	Tobacco paste
Paan	Tobacco paste in a leaf that is chewed; it is a mild narcotic.
Kya khabar, Pandit	What's up, fellow?
Are Bapre	My god!
Melya	A rascal
Tula aya bahini nahit ka?	Don't you have a mother and a sister? (A phrase used to shame somebody who is molesting a woman.)
Ba zarvat gelas	Go fuck your father!
Namaste	A greeting with hands clasped close to one's face or chest
Sahib	A polite address recognizing a man
Memsahib	A polite reference of recognition of a woman

Rani	Queen
Paiwand	A piece of white cloth used in some sort of ritual at the Towers of Silence; has something to do with pro-tecting the Parsi from pollution emanating from the victim. Exact use or translation of word is unclear.
Palu	The end of a woman's sari
Pavrita	Holy
Zoroastrian New Year	March 21st
sagdid	A ritual
Ramayana	Hindu classic
Thikka	A red mark on the forehead
Bo Tree	Under which Gautama Buddha achieved enlightenment.
Hanuman	Monkey God
Vishnu & Shiva	Divinities
Thugs	Devotees in 19th century of the goddess Kali
Hijdas	Trans-sexuals of India

Polish Words

O moj Boze	Oh my God!

O *cholera* — Used as a curse word

O *lanjo* — Shit!

Japanese Words

Shujin — Husband

Okusan — Wife

Seppaku — Harakiri -- death by disembowelment

So desu-ne — It's right, yes?

Ha-chan — Affectionate address to spouse

Honto desu — It's true

Hanashite — You speak.

Zamamiro — Kiss my ass!

Indian Terms

Sahar Airport — International part of Santa Cruz (domestic) Bombay airport.

Car: a black Contessa — A luxury sedan made by the Hindustan Motor Company

Kali — Goddess of death and destruction.

Joint Commissioner & Deputy Chief Minister — Government officials

EATON STREET PRESS
Other Mysteries from Jack Royce

The Train Stopped at Domodossola............6.95

Murder at the Kabuki................................6.95

Dressed for Murder.................................7.95

Coming Spring '97:

Bewitched by the Stage 7.95

Other Titles by New Authors
Coming This Spring

Breaking the Memory Barrier
by Patricia Trowbridge, D.C.H., R.N.

Eighth Row Center
by Roger Lobb, former Manager of the Royal
National Theatre of England

*The Depth of the Ducks: Stories of Fathers,
Sons, and Other Strangers*
a short story collection by Mitch Grabois

Finding Monju   by Earle Ernst

Eaton Street Press
524 Eaton Street #130, Key West, FL 33040
Fax: (305)295-0041 Phone Orders: (305) 293-3050